Escape to the Biltmore

Escape to the Biltmore

PATRICIA RIDDLE-GADDIS

to
my son, Shawn, for his historical expertise,
and to
Vincent, for his constant encouragement,
last but not least, to
my literary agent, Diana Flegal, for helping to make this happen

"*Escape to the Biltmore* is an enchanting novel. The story is swoon worthy and will satisfy any reader of historical romance."

- Tina Radcliffe, best-selling author of
Claiming her Cowboy and the Paradise Series.

"*Escape to the Biltmore* is a delightful love story, beautifully written and filled with hope. The heartwarming conclusion will have readers eagerly awaiting this debut author's next book."

- J. M. Hochstetler, author of the American Patriot Series
and coauthor of the Northkill Amish Series

"For those who love historical romances that cross the divide between the privileged classes and the impoverished, *Escape to the Biltmore* is for you. The author succeeds in bringing her readers a world reminiscent of Christy, and the Gilded Age of Henry James and Edith Wharton.

- Ruth Axtell, author of *She Shall Be Praised*

She considers a field and buys it;
Out of her earnings she plants a vineyard.
She sets about her work vigorously;
Her arms are strong for her tasks.
She sees that her trading is profitable
and her lamp does not go out at night . . .

Proverbs 31:16–19 (NIV)

Chapter One

Grand Central Train Station, New York
December 1895

A scream pierced the chill December air, freezing Dr. Richard Wellington's descent from a hansom cab. Yards away, a woman stood in the path of runaway horses, her white scarf fluttering behind her like the wings of a frightened bird before a predator.

Dropping his bags, Richard dove for the woman, catching her up into his arms. With a bone-jarring thud, they landed in a snow bank at the edge of the busy street.

A roar of silence filled his ears. Then, with the immediacy of danger alleviated, the city noises returned—the rumble of a nearby train, the jog trot of a horse, and exclamations of the crowd surrounding them.

"Is she alive, sir?" A man with sharp eyes bent over her.

"She was that close to those horse's hooves!" Another onlooker's pudgy fingers and thumb were held a fraction apart to illustrate the averted tragedy.

Ignoring the anxious questions around him, Richard placed a practiced finger on the woman's wrist and breathed a prayer of thanks. Her pulse was almost normal.

The crowd had thickened. A low murmur of expectancy crackling through the onlookers.

"She'll be fine," he announced to the mob. Pulling a handkerchief from his pocket he began to wipe the snow from her cheeks.

Wavy strands of red-gold hair had escaped from beneath her pert little hat, and now cascaded against the snow, their color reminding him of autumn leaves spilling from a basket. The gentle action seemed to revive her. The woman's eyelids fluttered and opened to reveal stunning turquoise eyes.

"I'm Dr. Richard Wellington," he said. "You've taken a hard fall. Can you hear me?"

A slight frown formed on her smooth pale forehead. "Yes, I can hear you." The next second, panic filled her eyes and she breathed out, "The horses!"

He glanced over his shoulder. The runaway team that had been pulling a mail coach was now halfway down the block where the driver had brought them to a standstill. Richard turned back to the young woman whom he judged to be not more than twenty-two or three. "It's all right. You're safe now."

He remembered how she had stood motionless. "You appeared glued to the street. What happened?"

She rubbed a gloved finger against her temple, her frown deepening as she struggled to remember. "I—I looked both ways before stepping off the sidewalk and all was clear. But then those horses appeared as if from nowhere and I couldn't move my legs." She gave a rueful shake of her head. "I've read about such instances in medical journals, but I never thought temporary paralysis could happen to me."

His eyes narrowed at her remark. "You read medical journals?"

She drew a long breath, as though frustrated with his questions. "Yes. I read medical journals because I'm a doctor."

A doctor? Had he heard her correctly? His fingers probed the soft kid leather of her boots. "Any numbness or pain?"

"No."

"Good. Any loss of movement in your arms?" He reached over and gently bent her elbow.

She raised both arms and wiggled her fingers. "All seems well. I don't think anything is broken." She attempted to sit up and he placed an arm around her shoulders to assist.

"I believe you have suffered a mild concussion." He continued in the unhurried manner he used when examining a patient. "Sometimes a hard fall will bring about confusion. I want you to sit quietly for a moment while I arrange for an ambulance to take you to hospital for complete bed rest."

She drew her brows together. "What makes you believe I have a concussion?"

Her question startled him. Unaccustomed to patients expressing skepticism in his ability to identify the nature of their illness, he drew in a long breath. "Because you seem a bit confused. Nothing to worry about though. In fact, it is quite normal for someone who has taken a hard fall."

She shook her head. "I'm not at all confused. A bit stunned perhaps, but certainly nothing that would indicate a concussion. I believe I should stand up now and get adjusted to my surroundings."

How could he convince her she needed additional medical supervision? Her upturned chin admitted no compromise. He had a train to catch but couldn't just leave her unattended. And where on earth was her chaperone? "Well, I suppose it would do no harm to get you out of this snow bank and allow you to walk around and test your strength." He stood, motioning to the onlookers around them. "Stand back, everyone, please." Then he stooped down, placing an arm once more around her shoulders, reaching for her gloved hand, and helped her to her feet. The bystanders sent up a cheer as the lady gained her footing.

A murmur passed among the spectators as a burly policeman arrived at the scene to survey the gathering. His horse snorted and pounded the cobbled street.

"Back away, all of ye now," he shouted in a thick Irish accent to the remaining crowd. "Up on the walkway, or you'll be standing before a judge this very day!" He blew a shrill whistle and many of the spectators scurried away like frightened mice. The officer reined his mount to a halt, his mouth below the dark mustache set in a hard line.

"Will ye be needin' an ambulance sir?" His dark eyes swept them over, head to toe, as though memorizing their disheveled appearance for future reference.

Richard paused. His patient seemed steady on her feet and was far too stubborn to be coaxed into a hospital. "We had a close call, but everything now seems to be in good order."

"Very well, sir." The copper studied them a moment before the clanging bells of a fire engine caused his horse to rear. "Hyah, get up there!" He hauled hard on the reins while directing his mount toward the new disturbance, farther down the lane.

"My purse!" She looked around as though seized by panic. "It must have fallen in the street. It contains my money and train ticket!" She stepped off the sidewalk in pursuit of her belongings.

Richard placed a hand on her shoulder. "Stay here and get your bearings. I'll search."

Before he had a chance to move, a young boy ran up and thrust the handbag at her. "Is this yours, ma'am?"

She clutched it with obvious relief. "Oh, yes. Thank you, my dear."

"You're welcome, ma'am." The child's engaging smile revealed two missing front teeth. She opened the beaded reticule and offered him a shiny coin. His eyes grew round. "Ah, you don't have to pay me nothin'." He pointed toward the sidewalk. "I saw it fly off your arm when the gentleman grabbed hold of you. Knew it couldn't a gone too far." He shook his head. "I didn't do nothing much."

"Oh, but you did," she insisted with a smile. When he looked puzzled, she continued, "For how can a lady travel without her purse?" She placed the coin in his hand and gave an affectionate ruffle to his matted hair before turning her attention toward the station door.

"Are you sure you're all right?" Richard asked. "No dizziness or nausea?"

"I'm fine," she interjected with haste. "How lucky for me that I left my medical bag there on the bench before crossing the street. Otherwise it would have been trampled by the horses." She brushed some dust off its handles before picking it up.

"So, you really are a doctor? Forgive me, I misunderstood."

Her eyes widened. "Is that why you thought I had a concussion?" Her little gloved hand waved away his chance to answer. "Don't worry, you aren't the first person to be shocked by my title. I'm Dr. Anna St. James, forever in your debt."

Another long blast from the train whistle assaulted their ears.

She flinched. "No wonder the horses were frightened."

He chuckled. "I'm inclined to agree. More than likely that's my boarding call. I'm not comfortable leaving you alone after such a disturbing experience." He glanced toward the imposing depot. "May I assist you back to the station before I rush off? Surely your traveling companion has missed you by now."

She smiled, and he noticed a cute little dimple in her left cheek.

"Actually, I'm traveling alone. These are modern times, you know."

A stray curl covered one eye, and he resisted the urge to brush it back. As though reading his thoughts, she gave it a quick shove beneath the brim of her hat. "Now that I have survived death, I shall make haste to the pharmacy. My medical bag simply must be replenished."

Mesmerized by this fascinating woman, he watched her walk away, stuffing more wayward strands of hair beneath her hat. *A woman doctor?* His head swam with this information. Why else would she be reading medical journals and carrying a medical bag?

He had been certain she was suffering from a concussion. Now he felt like a fool.

Remembering how little time was left, he turned on his heels and threaded his way back through the throng of people to pay his cab fare and gather the luggage he had left on the sidewalk.

Thanking the hansom driver for overseeing his things, he paused to inhale the scent of spiced apples and roasted chestnuts peddled by street vendors nearby. New York was an exciting place during the Christmas season. For a moment, he was disappointed that he'd spent most of his visit indoors at the medical convention. There had been time for sight-seeing, but he had chosen to study.

He stepped aside as a smiling couple with a small child, carrying stacks of colorful bundles rushed to board a waiting carriage. For a second, the loneliness of bachelorhood assailed him. How delightful it would be to stay over in the great city for a few days—if only he had a companion to share it with.

He brushed the thought away while reentering Grand Central. What was he thinking? He had no room in his life for any attachments. One romantic mistake was enough. Besides, his many patients depended on him. He had little time for self-indulgence.

His broken engagement two years earlier had taught him it was easier to stick with Bible study and the practice of medicine, rather than have his heart tied to a woman who might break it. No indeed, he would not place himself in a position of revisiting *that* kind of pain again. A shattered limb he could repair, but a broken heart was inoperable.

Looping his way through the stream of holiday travelers, he stopped to purchase a newspaper before taking his place in the ticket line behind a gentleman with a bulging portmanteau demanding a parlor car. While the railway agent explained to the irate traveler that all first-class cars had been booked many weeks in advance, Richard's mind wandered back to the lovely lady he had rescued. Recalling the unusual shade of her eyes beneath the sweep of dark golden lashes, her radiant smile was bright as the sun coming out from behind a cloud. His breath hitched at the memory of her beauty. It seemed like a benediction in comparison to his present surroundings.

But heaven forbid, the woman was a doctor. Probably a suffragette too. What on earth was the world coming to? The American Medical Association's various studies had proven that women could suffer immense damage to their mental and physical health by practicing medicine. Why would any female of good breeding take *that* kind of risk?

At last, the angry passenger stepped aside to speak with a railway supervisor, enabling Richard to purchase his fare home. After checking his luggage and medical bag, he hurried through the station, ticket in hand, hoping it wasn't too late to board.

While quick-stepping his way across the wide room, he noticed a young mother holding her crying baby, pacing back and forth beneath the enormous Palladian windows flanking the entrance hall. Had he one extra moment to spare, he would have stopped to make sure the baby's fussing was not related to some ailment. So many children died of influenza and other lung conditions during this time of year. *But this one seems fine*, he assured himself, as the infant's cries echoed throughout the terminal; such hearty wailing indicated a healthy set of lungs.

Relieved, he concluded the child was likely fighting against an afternoon nap. With a sympathetic glance in the weary mother's direction, he made his way around her and through the knot of travelers, heading for the station platforms.

As Richard set his boot out the door, the locomotive was sputtering past the terminal, its large wheels grinding against the tracks. Determined not to spend another night in New York, he jumped off the platform and broke into a run alongside the engine as it picked up speed.

Just missing the dining car, he managed to grab a handrail and swing himself onto the lowest step of the first Pullman. Wisps of steam curled up from the rails, dampening his face while reaching for the carriage door. Out of breath, Richard entered a parlor car, almost stepping on the toes of a lady wearing a preposterous hat with long red peacock feathers cascading over its brim.

The newspaper slid from beneath his arm and dropped directly at her feet. With a heave of her massive bosom, she placed a gloved hand over her heart. "Good heavens, sir! Do watch where you're going!"

Murmuring an apology, he scooped up the runaway paper and rushed through the Pullman and into a smoker, happy to feel the jolting floor beneath his feet. Finally, he was safe on board and heading home to the mountains and clean air of Asheville—back to the place he loved.

"Excuse me. Thank you. Pardon me," he murmured, avoiding elbows, assorted handbags, and portmanteaus until he reached the back of the coach. Feeling as if he had endured an obstacle course, he settled in beside the window. Stretching out his legs and dropping the newspaper to his chest, he pulled his hat down just enough to shield his eyes from the glare that was coming through the window.

He was thankful his visit to New York was drawing to a close. The medical convention had been informative, but he'd learned of no earth-shattering developments and had left the conference somewhat dissatisfied.

Ironically, the high point of his entire trip had been the Dwight L. Moody crusade he'd managed to attend. The evangelist's evening sermons did not fail to uplift his spirit, giving him a sense of inner peace.

As a physician, he knew that life could end in an instant, the body succumbing to the attack of any one of dozens of diseases. But Moody's words of encouragement gave him a quiet sort of hope in the face of this harsh reality. People were more than just physical bodies; they were also spirits and souls. Through a personal relationship with Christ, everyone might have both the promise of eternity in heaven, and a hope-filled life on earth—regardless of how much suffering was evident within the fallen world.

That thought, along with the movement of the train, relaxed him enough to straighten up in his seat and read his newspaper. He really wanted to catch up on events in the outside world. The medical conference had left him with little time to think about anything other than treating patients with tuberculosis.

He was about to unfold the New York Daily News when his gaze met the turquoise-eyed beauty he had rescued only a scant half-hour earlier!

Anna entered the Pullman from the parlor car, the door sliding closed behind her with a heavy thud. As the clacking of the wheels gained speed, she struggled to retain her balance; her hands now full with not only the medical bag and purse, but also a small portmanteau she kept in front of her to avoid bumping into other travelers. When she spotted her rescuer sitting near the back, their eyes met, and he rose to greet her, his expression kind and inviting.

Anna felt a tingle of excitement go through her as she remembered his strong arms sweeping her away from danger. "What luck to see you again," she said. "When you mentioned buying your ticket, I wondered whether we might share the same train."

He relieved her of the soft brown leather satchel, but she decided to hold on to her medical bag. "I had barely enough time to do my shopping, and then I ran all the way back to the station to board." She caught her breath. "Thank goodness I'd already purchased my ticket, or I might have found myself having to jump aboard." It was silly, this fluttering of nerves that caused her voice to catch. What would he think of her uneasy chatter?

A grin tugged at his mouth. "I know what you mean. I had to wait in line for my ticket and actually did jump on the train as it was pulling out of the station." He placed her portmanteau into an overhead compartment and resettled himself across from her.

"Did you really jump the train?"

He gave a solemn nod. "I did, indeed."

"You *are* serious. Now I am laden with guilt and quite certain that my earlier mishap caused your tardiness."

The sound of his rich throaty laughter lifted her spirits.

"Not at all," he said. "A grumpy passenger held up the ticket line by insisting on a parlor car, and that caused me to be late. Can you believe that someone would demand such a luxury at the very last minute?"

She grimaced. "Goodness no, not at this time of year. But I'm delighted you made it on board. And I want to thank you again for saving my life. I hate to think what might have happened if not for you." She placed a gloved hand on her chest, hoping to calm her racing heart.

"How are you feeling now? Taking a hard fall can create all sorts of problems, you know."

"Don't worry. I'm fine. But it's a miracle we're both still alive. And isn't it a coincidence for two doctors to be traveling on the same train?" She wanted to test his reaction, hoping she had misunderstood the disapproving look he had given her earlier.

A careless lock of raven hair fell across his forehead and he pushed it back with a sweep of one hand, his movement unhurried and smooth. "It is quite the coincidence for two physicians to be traveling on the same train—in the same car. Unless, of course, you happened to be attending the medical convention in Manhattan, as I was."

"Are you referring to the one sponsored by the American Medical Association?" She heard the note of disdain in her own voice.

"Yes, that was the one."

"We most likely would have met there if I had been allowed to attend. The AMA doesn't admit women doctors into their membership, you know. Perhaps someday they will realize women have a place in medicine."

Silence crackled between them like a direct challenge. The firm set of his jaw indicated he did not approve of her remark.

"Tickets, please, tickets!" The conductor cut into their exchange.

She handed over her ticket to the conductor who directed his gaze toward Dr. Wellington. "There's plenty of room in the storage compartment for that medical bag, sir. I'll be glad to tag it."

He waved his hand in a dismissive gesture. "The bag belongs to the lady doctor. You should ask her."

The conductor's salt and pepper brows formed into an arch above his spectacles. "Lady doctor, eh?" He harrumphed. "Next thing you know, women will be voting and driving trains, while the men stay home and tend the babies." He gave the tickets a sharp punch as though to emphasize his point, handing both to Dr. Wellington before moving on to the next passenger. His head wagged in disbelief as he continued his way down the aisle.

Anna shook her head. "Did you see his attitude? We're almost in the twentieth century, yet he dares treat me as some brainless ninny. He wouldn't return my own ticket to me—he gave it to you instead. I should file a complaint."

He stared for a moment at the tickets he was still holding, as though wondering why she was upset. "I'm sorry if you were offended." He handed the ticket back to her. "The train is packed, you know. Perhaps the old chap was just trying to help."

"Old chap indeed." She tucked it away in her handbag. "He addressed only you, as though I didn't exist."

When seeing the confused look in his eyes, she recomposed herself. This man had saved her life. There was no need to harp on the issues of gender inequity with a stranger. She softened her voice. "Oh, never mind. I still have my bag with me. That's all that matters, really. I should forget the entire encounter. It seldom does any good for a lady to complain."

Richard inclined his head. "I'm at your disposal, should you need anything further."

She gave him a brief nod before turning to gaze out the window. As he unfurled his newspaper, her thoughts turned in synchronization with each mile rushing beneath the train's wheels.

Rubbing her temple, she felt the stirrings of a headache. Perhaps if she ate something, the pain would subside, but dinner was hours away. Remembering her recent purchase at the pharmacy, she opened her purse to retrieve a candy and discreetly popped it into her mouth.

The peppermint taste took her back to childhood, back to Saturday afternoon trips to Coney Island where she had loved riding the carousel's hand-carved horses, with Papa standing at her side, making sure she didn't fall. She could almost hear the drummer and flute player that had provided the enchanting background music.

Removing a handkerchief from her handbag, she dabbed her eyes, glad the handsome doctor was still immersed in his newspaper. Returning the hankie to her purse, Anna's eyes fell on the creamy-white envelope embossed with the burgundy initials, D.V. on the seal. She turned it over to study the decorative script, and a faint scent of lilac drifted out from the linen paper as she opened it a second time.

Dear Anna,

I am ever so excited you have applied for a position at one of the many tuberculosis clinics in Asheville. Your interview for the post is in perfect timing for a visit to Biltmore. It will allow you an interval to relax beforehand and attend Uncle George's party on Christmas Eve.

You mentioned a desperate need to get out of New York. I am so sorry for all the grief you have suffered! Be assured, you are welcome as my guest at Biltmore House for as long as you like. I have sworn off Europe this season and plan to stay put, right here in Asheville, for a very long time, but I'll tell you more about that when you arrive.

Asheville is acclaimed as "The Paris of the South," and I know you shall love it! There is an opera house, a ballet company, and they even have streetcars. Also, I recently discovered that Elizabeth Blackwell, the first woman doctor, actually studied here and worked under Dr. John Dickens while teaching at a boarding school for girls, owned by the Dickens family. Perhaps we can visit the establishment while you are at Biltmore.

Let me know the exact date of your arrival so that I may personally greet you at the train station. I am looking forward to spending the holidays with my very best friend!

Sincerely yours,
Daphne Vanderbilt

Anna refolded the correspondence with careful deliberation, holding on to it while observing the lampposts and villages racing by in the receding twilight. Thank goodness for her friend's assurance of shelter until she could get back on her feet.

She was surprised to hear of Dr. Blackwell's affiliation with the Asheville boarding school for girls. What an oddity Blackwell must have been as a medical student in 1845! The first female doctor had waged many battles to become a physician, paving the way for other women to follow. Yet even now, fifty years later, women physicians were still regarded with disdain.

The rattle of the newspaper drew her attention back to her rescuer who scanned the pages. Long dark lashes shaded his rich brown eyes that were filled with a deep and settled peace. How disappointing it was to have seen those same eyes take on a look of surprise, and then disapproval when discovering she was a doctor. She was thankful that, despite his bias, he had gone out of his way to be kind to her, which was far more than most of her male colleagues had ever dared to do.

She drew a sharp breath and placed the letter back in her purse. Would her world ever unsnarl itself so that things could go right again?

Almost everything she held dear had been taken by her deceased father's business partner, Douglas Van Demark, who had promised to reinstate her former lifestyle through marriage. Anna knew that most women in her position would have accepted his offer, but she could not bear the thought of being tied to such a greedy man. Her refusal of Van Demark's proposal had hastened his quick foreclosure on all bank accounts, as well as her ancestral home. Suddenly, her world of bejeweled gowns, balls, and concerts had been transformed into one of abject poverty.

She pressed her lips together. After an entire year of grieving and struggling, her plans were falling into place. If her interview in Asheville was successful, she could save enough money to travel to Denver, where she hoped to practice medicine alongside her former classmate, Dr. Katherine Higgins.

The Western frontier was in dire need of doctors, and a woman physician had a much better chance of being hired. Moreover, in Colorado, women could vote in national elections and she could actually have a say in what went on in the world.

Anna returned her gaze to the scenery gliding past the window. The snowflakes, large and spirited, seemed to have no intention of settling down, nor did her restless mind.

She released a weary breath. If only Papa hadn't borrowed so much money. He'd had some difficulties with his business, but it wasn't like him to borrow more than he could repay. Something about Van Demark's story didn't add up. Had he cheated Papa out of more currency than what he owed? If that were the case, how could she ever prove it?

Disappointment rippled through her. There was no money for a private investigator or attorney. No way to prove her suspicion that something was terribly amiss. There was nothing to be gained from looking back. Somehow, she would find her way through this maze and begin a new life.

Chapter Two

Richard ran his eyes across the pages of the newspaper. *"President Cleveland and Family Decorate White House Christmas Tree with Electric Lights,"* blazoned the headlines.

He stifled a chuckle. The current was unaffordable for most Americans. How illogical of the President to predict that electricity might someday replace gas lamps and candles. The very idea was pure nonsense.

His eyes scanned down to the next caption: *"New Weather Bureau Chief Predicts Holiday Blizzard for East Coast."* Now that seemed far more likely than the president's expectation about Edison's electricity.

Richard glanced out at the fat snowflakes splashing against the window, threatening to block his view of the outside world. If only the storm might hold off, at least until he arrived home. He had patients to see before the holidays, and the party at Biltmore was on Christmas Eve, only a few days away. He received the invitation two years ago, while Biltmore was still under construction and had planned to attend with his new bride. That was before Julia had broken their engagement, along with his heart.

He inwardly recoiled at the idea of attending the party alone but had no choice. George Vanderbilt was his best friend. Although he loathed the empty chatter that passed for polite conversation at these social gatherings partie, he would be present. If the situation were reversed, George would do the same.

He turned his attention back to the newspaper. *"Gibson Girl depicts 'New Woman.'"* Charles Gibson's art represented the fashionable upper-middle-class society woman of 1895. His sketches portrayed the Gibson Girl as a pretty and feminine young woman who worked outside the home while seeking the right to vote.

Richard stifled a groan. This was suffrage propaganda. Only a small percentage of women were in favor of the vote, and even fewer were pursuing a career. Women were meant to be cherished and protected, while men handled the distasteful matters such as finances and politics. It was a simple and Godly way of life that had worked for many generations. Why would anyone want to change it?

Partially hidden by the paper, he stole another glance at the beautiful lady as she gazed out the window. The small number of women students he'd known while in medical school wore drab clothing and were always fuming about something. There was nothing plain about this one. She was gorgeous clear down to the shapely turned ankle peeking out from the hem of her skirt.

While admiring her profile, he noticed another wayward curl had escaped from beneath her hat and curved alongside her cheek. She gripped a folded letter in her small hand. Was the correspondence from a sweetheart? Was she married? Probably not. No gentleman would allow his wife to travel without a companion.

Richard's thoughts were interrupted when the conductor returned through the Pullman door at their end of the train. "Ladies and gentlemen," he announced, with a loud clearing of his throat. "A window has been broken in the dining car and you will be served dinner in your seats this evening."

"What are we supposed to do?" A female voice wailed near the front. "My children need to stretch their legs."

"Hold on a minute, lady, there's no need to panic." The conductor walked down the swaying aisle toward the frustrated passenger. "The porter will be along shortly to take your order, and everyone will have dinner on schedule—in their seats."

He pulled a gold watch from his pocket to examine the time. "Our first layover is in three hours, at Pittsburg Station. We'll be there for at least an hour—plenty of time to let your children move about and have a late meal in the restaurant, if you don't want to eat on the train."

"Three hours? That's a long while to wait," the woman said, as one of her children began to cry.

Murmurs of discontent filled the coach. Children whimpered in distress while their mothers tried to soothe them.

The conductor's lips compressed into a tight line. "The choice is yours, madam. You can either dine in your seat or wait it out until we reach Pittsburgh. And please quiet your children. Youngsters need a firm hand." He glared down the aisle at the woman doctor who faced him without flinching. "Sometimes women do, too." His remark dripped with sarcasm.

Richard managed to suppress an intense longing to wipe the sneer off the conductor's face. Perhaps he should file a grievance with the railway and alert the proper authorities about this employee who seemed to enjoy intimidating female travelers. Richard loathed the lowborn remark he'd made earlier about women voting and driving trains. A true gentleman might reflect upon such things in private, but expressing them aloud, and in mixed company, was unthinkable.

Dismissive of the unhappy stir he'd caused, the conductor closed his watch with a snap and disappeared through the other end of the car. A long beat of silence filled the coach, but eventually the murmur of voices rose again.

Richard glanced over at the beautiful lady, surprised she remained so calm after yet another show of the conductor's unseemly behavior. As if reading his mind, she spoke in a low voice. "I wish there was something I could do to help." She gestured toward the woman and her children. "It's difficult for little ones to sit for extended periods of time." Her voice trailed off when the train hissed and slowed to a crawl.

"Look, Mommy!" A child's high-pitched voice chirped as the train stopped at a small station that had a window display of St. Nicholas.

Richard chuckled. "This may be all the little tykes needed to distract them for a while." The children squealed with delight as the train started up again, chugging slowly through the ornate little village that was all dressed up for Christmas.

She leaned closer to the window. "Look at those lovely lampposts decorated with holly! Aren't they a delight?"

Richard cupped his hands to the glass pane for a better look. A lamplighter walked unhurried to his wagon, ladder in hand, while leaving behind him a row of flickering lights that burnished the dusk. "The town looks like a Christmas card," he said, giving one last admiring glance at the village before settling back into his seat. "I just hope this weather doesn't present any serious delays."

Her delicate brow creased with concern. "Yes, it really would be a shame to miss our destination because of a snowstorm." Then, as though thinking it through, her worried expression was replaced by a soft smile. "We shouldn't concern ourselves, really. I feel almost certain the railway men are laboring to clear the tracks ahead of us. Lots of workers are most likely receiving extra pay for their efforts. Perhaps it will make their Christmas brighter."

He felt his lips curving into a smile. This unique lady was assuring *him* the train would make it through the storm. *How very charming.* Most of the women he knew would lament the weather's toll on their latest Paris fashions. Her caring spirit for the workers, along with a calm intellectual approach to the situation, fascinated him.

Soon, an attendant arrived to take their dinner orders. They both decided on tea and sandwiches. A few minutes later, the porter set up a table between them, while a waiter followed behind, rolling a cart laden with a tea service and multiple trays of sandwiches, along with a platter of elegant deserts.

"On such a cold evening I might have liked hot soup," she remarked, as though to herself.

The porter smiled, producing a white linen cloth from beneath the trolley to cover the table. "The lady may have soup if she so desires." The man addressed Richard while adding a small vase of flowers to the center of the tabletop. "I can inform the cook."

"Oh, no, please don't do that." She gave a flutter of her hand. "This looks delicious. No need adding anything to such a lovely meal."

"Very well, then." The man agreed with some uncertainty, glancing at Richard for guidance. "If you are sure the lady is pleased?"

For the first time in his life, Richard was embarrassed by the expectation that he reply on behalf of his dinner companion. When traveling with his mother and sister, he always spoke for them without a second thought, and heretofore their lives ran in smooth and conventional grooves. Meeting this woman made him feel as though he had fallen into the rabbit hole from *Alice in Wonderland*.

"The lady has expressed her preference." Richard waved the porter away. "Shall I ask the blessing?"

She gave a brief nod before bowing her head.

"Father, we thank you for this food. We also express our gratitude for your protection today. Remain with us on our journey, helping us to be ever mindful of your presence. Surround us with your angels and see us safely to our destination. We ask this in Jesus' name, Amen."

After the prayer, he watched with admiration while she poured the tea, handling the sturdy railroad cups as if they were fine china, accomplishing the task as gracefully as though they were in the comfort of her own parlor, and not on a swaying train. Richard was grateful she didn't expect him to perform the tea service, and that she seemed to accept tea pouring as a customary female responsibility.

Taking a sip of the fragrant draught, he leaned forward. "I was thinking about how discourteous the conductor was to the other lady passenger just now. And of course, there was that earlier incident of his rudeness toward you." He deliberately kept his voice low. "I've decided to file a grievance on behalf of you both."

~

Anna studied him for a moment, trying to decide if he was serious. No one had ever taken the time to advocate for her. Could this man truly be different? "You would actually go to that much trouble for me—I mean us?"

"It would be no problem at all. The man's behavior was deplorable. Believe me, I am more than happy to be your defender in this matter, unless, of course, you would prefer another to act on your behalf."

She placed the teapot back on its matching tray and spread the starched napkin across her lap. It was true she had no one to support her, especially now that her father was gone. The thought of having a male advocate was in its own way somewhat reassuring.

"I believe if a gentleman such as yourself were to approach the railroad authorities concerning the incident, it could make a positive difference in the way women travelers are treated."

He unfolded his napkin. "I shall make a full report as soon as I can speak with the proper authority." There seemed a glad little ring to his voice and he appeared buoyed by her approval. "Might I ask your destination?"

She reached for a sandwich. "I'm spending the holidays with friends at Biltmore Estate in Asheville. Have you heard of it?"

He seemed surprised. "Indeed! I make my home in Asheville, and George Vanderbilt is a very good friend. In fact, it was he who encouraged me to leave Great Britain and practice medicine at one of the many tuberculosis sanatoriums in Asheville."

Anna could hardly contain her curiosity. Could it be that she might see more of him in the future? "I'm familiar with medical studies surrounding the mountain air and hot springs in Asheville. Isn't the town a magnet for patients with respiratory diseases?" She almost told him about the post for which she had applied but decided it would be premature to mention it to anyone just yet.

He nodded. "It most certainly is. There are at least fifty TB sanatoriums in and around the area. Lots of people are settling in the Southern Mountains to escape the bad air of the industrial North, and many visit Asheville from all over the world for respiratory treatments. George Vanderbilt's elaborate new estate has made it even more visible."

Anna took a tiny sip of the scalding tea, and with haste, placed the cup back in its saucer to cool. "The opening of his home has been in all the newspapers. There was an article this morning in the *New York Daily* about his forthcoming Christmas Eve party. I received an invitation to the event from his niece, Daphne, who is a life-long friend."

A grin tugged at the corners of his mouth. "I have met Miss Vanderbilt. Didn't she inspire her uncle to have this particular celebration?"

Anna couldn't help but smile. Even when they were in school, it was Daphne who had made certain all their classmates received a birthday gift, or some tribute for an accomplishment. "I'm sure it was Daphne." She took a bite of the petite sandwich. "I understand Biltmore House is quite the show place. I'm looking forward to my visit."

Richard nodded as though pondering the information she had given him. "*The London Times* recently reported that Biltmore rivals the grand palaces of Europe."

"Does it really contend with those majestic castles abroad?" She stirred more cream into her tea, hoping to cool it. "I should think that you, as a European, would have a better perspective on that sort of thing than most."

"I suppose," he said with a faint smile. "George has always been enthralled by the many chateaus in Europe. He has given me the grand tour of Biltmore, and there's no doubt it's magnificent. It even has Edison lamps." He gave a slight shrug. "But when one looks at the larger canvas, such sumptuous material trappings lessen in their importance."

She took another sip of tea that was now of moderate temperature. At one time, she might have vehemently disagreed with his stance on material trappings, but after living in poverty for over a year, she was better able to understand his point of view. "I know what you mean. There are more important things in life than material possessions."

Anna thought she saw a glimmer of admiration in his eyes.

"How remarkable that you share my feelings on this topic." He gave a little wave of his hand. "I enjoy luxuries as much as the next man, but surely there are more significant things than rivaling a palace that is halfway around the world. Especially when so many people are struggling."

He straightened a bit, as though to underscore the importance of his thoughts on the matter. "Ignorance and poverty often go hand in hand, which is why it is our responsibility to assist those who are less fortunate. Of course, George Vanderbilt has never shirked on his generosity to the poor."

Anna gave a slight nod. What would he think of her own impoverished living quarters? The cramped room in a tumble-down boarding house on the Lower East End was without so much as a writing desk on which to pen her correspondence. She was smack dab in the middle of the ignorance and destitution of which he spoke, yet he assumed that she was worlds away from such an environment.

For a moment, they were quiet amidst the chatter of those around them. The light from the lamp brought out gold flecks in his eyes. She glanced away, feeling self-conscious by the closeness that seemed to be developing between them.

As though sensing her uneasiness, he changed the subject. "Do you have a very busy practice in New York?"

"Most of my patients live on the Lower East Side, packed into dark apartments. They struggle to make ends meet."

A slight frown creased the space between his eyebrows. "I've heard about the dangers of disease and crime in that part of the city." He hesitated, as though weighing his words with care. "Forgive me if I seem impertinent, but do you go alone on your rounds?"

"Oh, yes." She almost laughed at the expression on his face, a cross between horror and chagrin. "It's not so frightening, really. Besides, my patients would never harm me. They welcome my help."

He held his cup in both hands, staring into its depths as though attempting to divine a way to admonish her for taking such a risk. "It's important to have a good rapport with one's patients. I must say, I admire your courage."

Anna swallowed the last bite of her sandwich. "I've never thought of myself as courageous. I'm quite fond of my patients. It took a while to find my way around in that section of the city, but now I know it like the back of my hand, including some interesting shortcuts." She laughed to herself. *Through my backyard and around the fence. Or across the hall where Mrs. Jones and her three children all resided in one cramped room.*

He turned the teacup in his hands. "You know, it has just occurred to me that I have a colleague in Manhattan who needs an assistant. I'd be happy to give you a reference, if you happen to be interested. It might lift your spirits to be removed from the ruffians and filth in that scruffy part of town."

Anna bit back her anger. But how could she blame him for lumping all the Lower East End residents into one big mass of unwholesome crime and filth when she had once done the same? "Would that be the post offered by Dr. Patrick MacMullen?"

"It would." His answer was guarded. "Do you know him?"

She took a sip of tea. "Oh yes, we've met. I interviewed for that position weeks ago, and he refuses to hire a female physician. He offered me a post as his office nurse, but I told him I hadn't earned my medical degree to roll bandages for the rest of my life." The words slipped out without warning. It wasn't a habit of hers to undermine nurses, but she was weary of male doctors hiring women physicians to serve in that capacity.

"A well-trained nurse is hard to find." His voice softened almost to a whisper in the ensuing silence.

"So is a well-trained physician," she countered.

The two stared at each other for a moment before his eyes twinkled once again, and she felt her own lips curve upwards into a smile. Within seconds, they were both laughing.

"I don't dispute your defense of nurses, Dr. Wellington. In fact, I've found them to be an invaluable aid in my work. The Henry Street Visiting Nurse Service, for example, has assisted several of my patients and I consider them to be outstanding."

"Are you referring to Lillian Wald's establishment?"

"You've heard of her?" She almost choked on her tea.

"I have. In London, they refer to Miss Wald as America's Florence Nightingale. I understand it is her wish to provide nursing services in all public schools—a worthy goal."

Anna helped herself to a small slice of chocolate cake, surprised that he was current on the social issues of New York. "It really is a praiseworthy objective."

He raised a brow. "Then you would agree she is accomplishing far more than just rolling bandages?"

"Yes, of course." She held a forkful of cake in abeyance. "But did you know Miss Wald's earlier intention was to become a doctor? She actually attended medical school for a while."

Richard shook his head. "No, I didn't know that. I wonder why she didn't finish her training."

"I believe she decided to meet the needs of an immediate crisis—one that could not wait for several years while she completed a long jaunt in medical school, especially since she had already earned her nursing degree."

He took a long drink of tea before speaking. "Well, I think it was astute of her to realize she could help her patients without becoming an MD."

Anna felt her cheeks grow warm. How typical of a male doctor to believe a woman could function best as a nurse. She took a sharp breath. "What raises my dander is how the AMA promotes nursing to deter women from finishing medical school. I agree that skilled nurses are greatly needed, but if I accepted a nursing job, I'd feel as though I were supporting the AMA's efforts to discourage the advancement of female physicians."

Before he could respond, the porter appeared.

"Is everything to your satisfaction, sir?"

"Delicious."

"Very well, sir." He gave a polite nod and moved on to the other passengers.

Suddenly, she felt embarrassed by her harangue about the American Medical Association's edict against women doctors. It was in bad taste for her to carry on so, especially since he had saved her life.

Richard's face grew thoughtful. "I must say I did not realize the AMA promoted nursing to discourage the advancement of women doctors."

Anna shook her head. "Forgive me for being so outspoken."

"Not at all. You communicate in a most refreshing style. I must say that I am enjoying our discourse."

Her cheeks heated anew by the warmth of his words, and she dropped her eyes in unanticipated shyness. What was it about this man that made her heart flutter like a hummingbird? She felt excited and annoyed at the same time. Excited because he made her feel like a desirable woman. Annoyed because she didn't have time to drop all her dreams to be flattered by a handsome doctor.

"More tea?" he lifted the pot, but she waved away his offer.

"Now, about filing that grievance with the railway officials," he said, refilling his own cup. "I believe the authorities will listen to me. Perhaps my concerns will prompt them to make necessary changes."

"It's most honorable of you to consider doing such a thing. Not many men would take the time to defend the cause of strangers."

His lips curved into a slow smile. "Nonsense! Any gentleman would do the same. I'm quite sure of it."

"Well, I'm not so sure. In fact, I believe most men would let the incident go without a second thought."

"How might you know that?" he asked, in a banter tone.

Amid the click of glasses and clatter of silverware, she leaned back into the seat and folded her arms. "Oh, I just know."

Chapter Three

When the train arrived in Pittsburg, Anna was already in her nightgown, brushing out her hair. After turning down the wick of the bedside lamp, she raised the window shade to view the great station that was still ablaze with life.

Her thoughts traveled back to Dr. Wellington, and how he had prayed over their meal as though God were his very best friend. She smiled, remembering her beloved late grandmother who had shared a similar confidence that God always listened to his children.

Gram's strength was capable of withstanding life's harshest blows. How she wished her own faith might measure up to her grandmother's. It wasn't that she didn't believe in God. It was just that her heart was wounded, and she was too tired to ask for anything, especially after so much had been taken away.

Would Dr. Wellington follow through on filing a grievance with the railway? She knew the answer almost before completing the thought. *Yes, he was the kind of man who stood by his word.*

A trolley car caught her attention as it sped along, just beyond the rail terminal and buzzed to a stop before a procession of nighttime revelers, waiting its arrival. The merry laughter of men in evening dress and women in dainty opera cloaks echoed through the night as they boarded. Anna wondered if she would ever feel free to enjoy similar pursuits again.

Another train thundered by, rattling the window and shaking her cabin. When she leaned forward to draw the shade, her hand stilled as her gaze caught the shadowy silhouettes of a man and woman standing in the far corner of the platform. Blissfully unaware of their audience, the two were locked in a passionate embrace.

She closed her eyes, somewhat embarrassed for intruding upon their intimacy. A shiver rippled down her spine while recalling her dinner with the handsome doctor. Throughout the meal, an almost tangible mutual awareness, both intoxicating and terrifying, drew them together.

Her tummy had never done so many somersaults. She, who'd always thought her school girlfriends to be so silly in their talk of getting butterflies over a boy, had now, and within the space of only a few hours, understood exactly what they meant.

Was he married? She hadn't noticed a wedding ring. Most married men would have mentioned a wife, or children. She chided herself for thinking such things. Her plans didn't allow for emotional entanglements.

A dagger of fear pierced her. What if she did not obtain the position at the clinic? How would she ever save enough money to accomplish her dream to begin a new life?

She shuddered, drawing her robe closer while remembering Van Demark's proposal. He had sent a note by courier, inviting her to his office shortly after Papa's death, with the promise of working something out regarding her late father's estate.

Her hands trembled with fear as he gazed at her from across his desk. A sparkling diamond cluster ring competed with his gaudy tie pin. "Miss St. James," he began, "I won't beat around the bush. I have asked you here to propose matrimony."

Had she heard him correctly? "Matrimony?"

He nodded. "I'll remove the lien from your home and erase your father's numerous debts as soon as we are wed."

The cool strength of his presentation restrained her from lashing out in anger. How dare he suggest such a thing! She clasped her hands together to calm herself before answering. "There must be some misunderstanding, Mr. Van Demark. I agreed to meet with you because I thought you meant to offer a solution, a temporary forbearance, perhaps."

His glittering eyes swept over her like a serpent. "My dear, I am prepared to lavish my wealth upon you and erase all this bad business threatening to mark your family's good name." He puffed his lower lip out speculatively. "In return, you shall elevate me into society. You see, Miss St. James, a man in my position requires a certain amount of esteem that someone of your social class can garner. Ultimately, the arrangement I offer would be of great benefit to us both."

Anna sat speechless until his next words, "Of course, as my wife you will put aside your little hobby of practicing medicine."

A wave of disgust settled in the pit of her stomach. "I'm afraid I must decline your offer, Mr. Van Demark. I could never marry someone I didn't love."

His eyes glinted. "Love?" He gave a cruel little laugh. "My offer is a business arrangement, fair and square. I helped your father in his time of need, and I am now extending my generosity to his daughter. Your beauty and refinement will be an asset." His eyes swept over her again, like a broker assessing a prospective purchase.

Anna stood, gathering her cloak and purse. "A true business arrangement does not require promises at the altar, sir."

A flush climbed from his stubbly upper lip and mounted to his forehead. "Consider wisely," he said, following her out the door. "When Mrs. Astor discovers you are destitute, she will pity you, but not one of her Four Hundred will offer their help." His heavy under lip curled down into a sneer. "I'm richer than any of Mrs. Astor's crowd and she'll have to accept me eventually. But your good name would speed up the process." He flicked a cigar ash onto the sidewalk as she boarded the carriage.

What he said about Mrs. Astor was true. But Anna had never cared about her own role in society. Instead of responding to his taunt, she slammed the door, barely missing his hand. When the hansom pulled away from the curb, she felt as though all the blood had drained from her body.

Her reverie was broken with a jolt and the screech of metal against the track, the train's whistle piercing the night. The romantic couple jumped apart with one last kiss. The young man boarded as the locomotive moved out of the station, steam rising like silver gauze into the darkness.

She snapped the shade down and knelt beside her bed to pray. It had been a long time since she'd had a talk with God. Dr. Wellington's petition had been so comforting. Should she try something similar? "Dear Father," she spoke aloud. She tried again but could only utter "Please help me" before climbing into bed. Finally, she drifted off into a fitful sleep, the peaceful brown eyes of her new friend appearing in her dreams throughout the night.

While reclining in his berth, Richard's thoughts returned to the conversation he'd shared with Anna St. James. Closing his eyes, he remembered the delicate tint of her complexion and fine-boned features. His blood raced while allowing himself to imagine how her rosebud lips might feel pressed against his own, and he marveled at how in one evening she had managed to quietly challenge his entire outlook on women doctors.

He drew a ragged breath. Though he remained firm in his belief that women should not have careers or vote, he had to admit their conversation had been most enjoyable—more so, in fact, than any exchange he'd ever had with a woman.

Yes, Dr. St. James was interesting. Funny, how her valiant stance had left him feeling that she was stronger in many ways than himself. Her obvious concern for the poor reflected a depth and breadth of character that went far beyond the ordinary 'society ladies' who took a social interest in the lower classes. It was puzzling because she carried no trace of gaudiness that might betray humble origins, and her clothing was haute couture.

Richard shook his head. His little sister, Emily, had also fallen for the "New Woman" propaganda and had recently been expulsed from one of Europe's finest finishing schools. She had been caught smoking cigarettes and sneaking away from the conservatory grounds with several other girls to play golf with the boys at St. Simon's School.

As exasperating as it was, he couldn't restrain a grin in the dark. According to his mother's recent letter, Emily and the other girls had beaten the boys at both tennis and golf, creating quite a stir.

His mind wandered back to the beautiful woman doctor. There was such a vulnerability in her eyes that changed almost magically, from turquoise to aqua, like light and shadows on the sea. Still, women were created to care for family and home. Why would she, or any woman, chafe at the notion? He wondered how it might feel to guide this gorgeous woman, pampering her until she could place all career and suffrage nonsense behind.

Richard chided himself for having such ideas. He wasn't interested in becoming romantically involved right now. But that didn't mean he was dead, did it? He could still admire that lovely heart-shaped face and those alluring eyes that surpassed the definition of beauty.

After kneeling to pray, he noticed his cloak had fallen from its hook behind the door. Scooping it up, he saw several strands of long gold flecked hair, caught on the button of his collar. Without thinking, he laid his cheek against the wispy threads and a faint scent of roses stole over his senses, recalling the soft pressure of her head against his shoulder when he'd whisked her out of danger.

He placed the garment on the back of a chair with quiet reverence, and climbed into bed, hoping the rhythmical chugging of its wheels would lull him to sleep. But a new song was singing in his heart, and the memory of Anna St. James kept him awake until dawn.

⌒

Anna awoke early to a persistent knocking. Struggling out of bed, she put on her robe and opened the door a crack. A porter in starched white jacket stood holding a silver tray.

"Your breakfast, Miss," he announced.

She stood aside, taking care to wait behind the door while he placed the laden tray on the window table. "Where are we now?" She stifled a yawn.

"We're in the hills of Western Pennsylvania," he said, pouring her tea. "This storm is slowing us down, so we can expect a long layover at the Cumberland Mountain Station this afternoon."

"Cumberland Mountain?"

"Yes-that's in Maryland, Miss."

She reached into her purse for a coin.

"Thank you, Miss," he inclined his head, still managing not to look in her direction. "The morning newspaper is beside your tray."

Anna closed the door behind him and raised the shade, using a lace-trimmed hanky to wipe away the window frost. The train rattled against the wind, coughing up swirls of acrid smoke as it crawled through the stark scenery, reminding her of an infirmed patient gasping for life.

Seating herself at the table under the window, she nibbled on a slice of toast and drank most of her orange juice. Glancing over the headlines, she saw nothing of interest other than news of the blizzard still raging along the East Coast.

Would the handsome doctor sit with her again today? The idea made her want to look her very best. Putting the paper aside, she searched through her trunk for something to wear, thankful for the few nice garments she'd been able to bring along on her journey.

Finally, she decided on the emerald green suit. She especially liked the softly ruffled skirt, and jacket with leg o' mutton sleeves. It was one of the few elegant and practical outfits she kept after her move.

While fastening the tiny buttons on her bodice, she giggled, recalling a recent, colorful letter from her colleague, Dr. Katherine Higgins. When making house calls, Katherine wore trousers, riding her horse astride and carrying a .38 revolver for protection. While sitting before the small dressing table mirror, Anna pinned her hair into a coil at her nape and tried to imagine what it might be like to ride a horse astride while wearing pants.

Anna admired her friend's pluck, but she was hesitant about going that far. Who knew whether she might need to don a similar outfit in the mountains around Asheville? Perhaps the stopover would be a good rehearsal for her new life in Colorado.

Adjusting her hat, she took a closer look into the mirror and grimaced at the signs of exhaustion that had settled over her features. To conceal the dark circles, she took a silver compact from her purse and tapped the powder puff under her eyes. Then, almost as an afterthought, she pinched both cheeks until spots of color bloomed against her pale complexion. With a final straightening of her jacket, she picked up her medical bag and purse before leaving the compartment.

Anna paused at the door when nearing the coach. Was the doctor already there? Peering through the murky glass, she spotted him a few seats down the aisle, reading a magazine. Her heart did a little drum roll, noting the finely sculpted outline of his face and the masculine width of his shoulders.

"Excuse me, Miss." A porter came up behind her, rolling a trolley laden with coffee and Danish pastries.

"Oh certainly, pardon me." She felt her face redden at having been caught staring through the window, gawking like a school girl. Standing aside, she allowed him room to push open the heavy door and followed him through the entrance, she made her way down the length of the swaying car.

Just as yesterday, the sound of lively conversation competed with the clattering wheels of the train, and clink of cutlery against china. She neared Dr. Wellington's seat and was pleased when he looked up from his reading, his face breaking into an immediate smile. Buoyed by his response, she paused beside him.

He immediately stood, indicating the empty window seat facing him. "Won't you join me?"

Anna nodded her assent and he remained standing until she seated herself.

"I hope you are feeling refreshed this morning." His eyes held hers for a moment and she grew warm beneath his gaze.

"Yes, thank you." Feeling it necessary to fill in the awkward pause, she continued. "After the train left Pittsburgh, I could hardly stay awake." She was glad he couldn't read her mind. If that were possible, he would know she had dreamt of him for most of the night.

He settled back in his seat. "I understand we haven't traveled very far from there because of the storm." He glanced out the window. "I suspect our new weather bureau's prediction of a blizzard hitting the coast is coming to pass."

She nodded, placing her medical bag and purse beneath the window. "Yes, but isn't everything lovely? The snow has transformed the world into a stunning white wonderland."

He smiled, as though recollecting. "I've always loved this kind of weather. When I was a child, my brothers and I spent hours sledding and building forts in the drifts. By the time Nanny called us into the house for tea, we were almost frozen."

Anna visualized this handsome doctor as a mischievous, light-hearted boy, playing with his siblings. "What fun you must have had with your brothers."

He folded both arms over his chest. "We did have lots of good times together. And we couldn't seem to get enough. After having our fill of tea and biscuits, we were ready to go back out and start all over again." A slow smile worked its way across his features. "Of course, Nanny seldom allowed us to repeat our morning adventures because it would have interfered with the demands of our strict governess. She gave poor Nanny a tough time if we weren't ready to give our studies full attention after lunch."

"How many siblings do you have?

"Two brothers and one little sister—and you?"

"I was an only child. My stepmother wouldn't allow me to play in the snow for fear I might contract pneumonia. I was always climbing out the bedroom window though, building snowmen on my balcony."

Richard threw his head back and laughed. "What a clever child you must have been. How on earth did you explain the snowmen to your stepmother?"

She laughed along with him. "I didn't need to. I had a most wonderful nanny who always knew exactly when to draw the drapes."

"You were fortunate. My nanny adored her brood, but she would never have gone that far." He paused to look out the window at a horse-drawn sleigh occupied by a joyful looking young couple. "My younger sister Emily gave poor old Nanny far more heartache than did any of us boys." He shook his head, a ghost of a smile touching his lips. "She was always climbing trees and getting into trouble."

Anna chuckled, remembering her own tree climbing adventures and the many hours she had spent playing with her dolls, bandaging their imaginary wounds and nursing them through various episodes of illness. Fearing he might disapprove, she gave herself a mental shake, deciding not to share the information. "My nanny was a rather young woman. In retrospect, I do believe she had as much fun as I did."

"Were you awfully lonely without siblings?"

She gave a little shrug. "Not too much. I had my books and dolls to keep me company."

He offered her a crooked grin. "You know, as much as I adored having siblings, I sometimes craved the luxury of my own company. From the way you tell it, being an only child carries an appeal all its own."

She sighed. "In many ways it does. And really, how can one miss what they never had?"

Richard nodded, and for a few minutes they sat in companionable silence while the train rolled along at a leisurely pace. Anna realized her remark about not missing siblings wasn't entirely true. She now wished with all her heart for a brother or sister to share her innermost thoughts.

Soon they came to a village filled with little white houses crowded together. About that time, and as if from nowhere, a group of young boys ran up to the railroad tracks and began sprinting alongside the train, throwing snowballs. Dr. Wellington stuck out his tongue at the rowdy group and the boys burst out laughing, tossing another ball of snow that narrowly missed the window.

Their merriment came to an abrupt halt as the door at the far end of the coach banged open and a tall man with red hair entered the car. "Is there a doctor on the train?" His eyes darted about in fear. "My wife is having a baby!"

Chapter Four

Richard rose to his feet, almost colliding with Dr. St. James, who had done the same. In a few strides, he reached the distraught man.

"I'm Dr. Wellington. Where is she?"

"Frederick Watson," he said, clutching Richard's hand like a lifeline. "She's in our private car, near the back of the train." He gave a polite nod to Dr. St. James before turning back to Richard. "I'm glad your wife is with you. Elizabeth will appreciate the company of a woman right now."

Richard turned. "She's not—"

"He's not—" They both began at once.

Before Richard could finish his explanation, she continued in an even voice. "I'm Dr. St. James. Dr. Wellington and I are not married. We just happen to be traveling on the same train."

"A woman doctor?" Confusion filled the man's eyes. "Well, I believe my wife might like that as well." He turned back to Richard. "But I want you to oversee things. No offense, ma'am—er—doctor." The man stuttered between the two words while giving her a stern frown.

"None taken," she said, with a slight smile. "The important thing is getting your wife the medical attention she needs."

His facial muscles softened. "Oh—you're right, of course. Just come this way."

Richard allowed his friend to precede him, noting that she carried her medical case.

"You were right to keep it with you," he said, gesturing toward the bag. He felt embarrassed that a lady physician was better equipped for the emergency than he was.

"How far along is your wife?" Richard asked, while hurrying down the aisle of the next rail car.

Mr. Watson's face reddened. "Slightly over eight months. We've been in Philadelphia since early November, visiting my parents. The baby wasn't due until mid-January, and I thought there would be ample time before her confinement." He stopped to take a handkerchief from his trouser pocket and mopped the perspiration from his forehead. "If only she could have waited two more days!"

Richard chuckled. "Babies don't always follow our time table."

"Apparently not," Watson murmured, opening the door to his private Pullman. They entered an elegant parlor with mahogany paneling and plush furnishings. A hallway of gilded mirrors led to the master bedroom where the wife, whom Richard judged to be in her early twenties, was in bed and propped against several pillows. Her small face was flushed and damp with perspiration.

Mr. Watson rushed over to kiss her on the forehead. "Elizabeth my dear, we're in luck. Can you believe it? I found not just one physician for you, but two. And one of 'em's a lady doc!"

Anna paused at the foot of the wide bed, attempting to gauge whether the woman's open mouth of surprise would lead to acceptance or disapproval. She was relieved when the young woman's face broke into a pained smile. "How nice it is to meet a woman doctor." She spoke with a soft Southern accent.

Dr. Wellington stood near the patient's bedside. "How frequent are your labor pains, Mrs. Watson?"

The young woman's clear blue eyes revealed fear. "I-I don't know exactly. They're coming about every fifteen or twenty minutes, I think. It's our first baby, and I'm scared to death." Tears spilled down her cheeks. "Oh, I just don't know if I can do this. It's much more painful than I ever imagined." She began to sob in earnest.

Dr. Wellington handed her a folded handkerchief from his pocket. "It's only natural to fret, especially since this is your first child. Have you been in labor for very long?"

She closed her teary eyes for a moment, as though straining to remember. "I think I must have been in labor all night. The pains stopped just before dawn, and I thought it was a false alarm." She opened her eyes. "I'm not due until mid-January, but my labor resumed around seven o'clock this morning."

"That sometimes occurs, especially with the first baby," he acknowledged. "But rest assured, you are in good hands." A small grin turned into a full smile as he glanced over at Anna. "In fact, I am almost certain Dr. St. James and I together have delivered more babies than there are passengers on this train."

Anna took a step forward, relieved and pleasantly surprised by his words. "That's a goodly amount, but the doctor is probably correct."

Mr. Watson patted his wife's hand, and Anna's heart was warmed by the flash of devotion that passed between them.

The room became silent while Dr. Wellington did a cursory examination, listening to her heartbeat and measuring blood pressure. After a few minutes, he met Mr. Watson's eyes. "Your wife's blood pressure is a bit high."

Anna took a small writing tablet and pen from her purse, handing them both to Dr. Wellington.

The father-to-be knotted his hands together. "Is that—is that cause for concern?" His lower lip trembled.

Dr. Wellington jotted a few more notes on the tablet before answering. "Not necessarily. Many women have a higher-than-normal blood pressure during labor. Still, we'll need to keep a close watch."

Anna wondered how Mrs. Watson could possibly focus on the task of giving birth with her nervous husband pacing the room. The poor man looked as if he might pass out at any moment, and when he grabbed hold of the bedpost to prevent himself from falling, she decided it might be a blessing to them all if he did.

Dr. Wellington's eyes met hers, and a flash of understanding passed between them. The faint suggestion that he recognized her concerns without one word being spoken was a form of intimacy she'd never experienced.

Feeling the heat creep up her neck and into her cheeks, she picked up a silver-mounted hairbrush from the dresser and turned to their patient. "Would you like for me to arrange your hair?"

"Oh, would you?" Mrs. Watson said with a bit of a sigh.

Dr. Wellington turned his attention back to the father-to-be. "Why don't we go to the dining car for coffee, while Dr. St. James examines your wife more thoroughly? These things take time you know, and you need to gather your composure for later, when the baby arrives."

Watson raked a shaky hand through his hair, causing the short carroty locks to stick up like bristles. "Well—perhaps. What do you think I should do, dear?" He glanced at his wife for guidance.

She gave him a loving smile while reaching up to smooth away the cowlicks from his hair. "Frederick, you're as jittery as a long-tailed cat in a room full of rocking chairs! Go on over to the dining car and get some breakfast. The lady doctor and I will be just fine."

Still seeming unsure, he shifted from one foot to the other before turning back to Dr. Wellington. "You will return to oversee the birth of my child, won't you?" He gave Anna a sidelong glance. "No offense intended, Miss. I don't mind your assisting as a nurse, but I prefer the gentleman doctor to be in charge of the—er—event."

Over the years, Anna had developed a thick skin toward middle-class men who voiced their disapproval of her profession. "None taken." She forced a smile while continuing to pin her patient's lemon-colored tresses into a chignon on top of her head.

Dr. Wellington turned to her with an apologetic look in his eyes. "I'll be back in an hour or so. Might I bring you anything?"

She paused to glance around the room. "We'll need plenty of hot water and towels."

"Of course." He raised his brows. "Anything else?"

Anna glanced at Mrs. Watson. "Would you like some chipped ice?"

The woman's eyes lit up. "Oh, that would be wonderful."

He rubbed his jaw, as though to mentally question whether such a treat would be accessible on a train.

Anna placed Mrs. Watson's brush back on the dresser. "They were serving sorbet last night."

He slapped a palm to his forehead. "Thank you for setting me straight on that one."

Mr. Watson stooped down to place a reverent kiss on his wife's brow. "I'll get that ice for you, darling—even if we have to stop the train and gather it from a frozen lake." Anything you want. Just say the word and it's yours."

Mrs. Watson gave her husband a beseeching look. "What I really want, Frederick dear, is for the lady doctor to deliver my baby." She glanced at Dr. Wellington. "No offense, but I'd really much prefer a woman to help me through this." Her face flamed as she dropped her eyes and toyed with the lace border on her sleeve.

Dr. Wellington cleared his throat. "I am not in the least offended, Mrs. Watson. I have no objection to your request."

A smile appeared on her cherubic face. "There now, Frederick, it's all settled. Dr. St. James will see to me and the baby. You can go now and find some chipped ice. I declare, my mouth is so dry I feel like I've been eating cotton."

Her husband looked a bit abashed that she had overridden his will. "As you wish, my dear, but I still want Dr. Wellington to supervise the birth of our child. You know my job is to take care of you."

She drew a sigh of resignation as her husband walked toward the door and stumbled over a table bearing a vase of roses. The scene was comical, but no one laughed when the man immediately dropped to his knees to gather the wounded blossoms before placing them back into the container. "I'll order more roses for you, dear."

Dr. Wellington had an amused look on his face when he turned to Anna. "I'll request those things of the porter straightaway."

"If you have no objection I would like to dispense Valerian Root tincture to Mrs. Watson to help lower her blood pressure."

"Good idea." He lowered his voice to match her own. "That will also ease her pain until it's time to administer chloroform. Do you have any with you?"

She nodded, and his face broke into an easy grin. "I thought you might. It will certainly come in handy later."

Anna was reassured by his statement. Some doctors still believed the pain of childbirth should be endured, refusing to interfere with what they considered to be God's curse on all women since Eve. How good it was to know that he shared her views on at least one thing!

⌒

Upon entering the dining car, the men were greeted by the pleasant aroma of gingerbread. After seating themselves at a window, both ordered strong hot coffee, with generous helpings of the moist and spicy cake.

"Are you quite certain my wife will be all right with your friend?" Mr. Watson's well-manicured fingers worked around the hem of his napkin before finally placing it on his lap.

Richard's hands closed around the warm coffee cup. He had dealt with many nervous fathers-to-be, but this one took the prize. The arrival of babies was an everyday occurrence, and he was convinced Dr. St. James could do no harm. If anything, her presence seemed to have a calming effect on Mrs. Watson. "Women have been delivering babies for centuries, and mankind is no worse for the wear." He placed the coffee cup back on the table and took a big bite of the gingerbread, hoping Watson did not know about the American Medical Association's ban on female physicians.

The man's eyes brightened. "As a matter of fact, I was delivered by a midwife. Funny how we forget such things." He shook his head as though to somehow make up for his lack of recollection.

Richard stifled a chuckle. *As if he would remember his own birth. The poor man was a bundle of nerves.*

Mr. Watson speared the gingerbread with his fork. "Do you have children, doctor?"

Richard took a long drink of coffee, remembering all too well that his hopes of becoming a husband and father were connected to Julia. "I'm afraid I haven't found the right girl yet." He said, deciding the best way to avoid a painful walk down memory lane was to keep the man talking about his own life. "Are you hoping for a boy or a girl?"

"Oh, a boy, of course." He paused. "I'd love a daughter too, someday, but a son is necessary for carrying on the family name and business. Don't you agree?"

Richard nodded, and then thought of Dr. St. James, wondering what she would think of his reply to the question of gender. Shaking the thought of her aside, he cleared his throat. "Ahem, what—er—what is your line of work, sir?"

Watson added more sugar to his coffee. "My father is president of this railway and I act in an official capacity, traveling up and down the East Coast, settling all sorts of disputes and customer complaints. He hired me right after I graduated from college with the hope I'd settle down. Truth is, he wanted me to do something constructive with my life, but that didn't happen until I met my beautiful bride." Watson scooped a forkful of gingerbread into his mouth and a cluster of crumbs fell onto the front of his jacket. He gave a nervous laugh while brushing away the tiny morsels.

"Oh? How did the two of you meet?"

"Elizabeth was visiting her cousins in Philadelphia, and we were introduced at a dinner party. She wore a lovely blue gown that matched her eyes. It was love at first sight."

Richard listened, his coffee forgotten. "I've often wondered if there really is such a thing as love at first sight." He shook his head. "It seems a far-fetched notion, and as a man of science who has never personally experienced it, well, I suppose I am somewhat skeptical."

The man chortled with what seemed to be an air of superior knowledge. "You can stop wondering," he said. "The first time I laid eyes on my Elizabeth, I was smitten and couldn't think about anyone or anything else but her. Take my word for it, doctor, when you find a woman you cannot stop thinking about, you'll know she's the one for you." His voice deepened with conviction. "Of course, Elizabeth is very headstrong. She wouldn't consent to marrying me unless I promised her father we'd make our home in the South."

Watson leaned back in his chair, smiling with recollection. "So, I gave him my word that we'd reside in Asheville, and in return he gave us his blessing. Best decision I ever made." He thumped his hand on the table for emphasis. "If she had wanted us to move all the way to Africa, I would have agreed."

As Watson continued his nervous chatter, Richard's mind wandered back to his first meeting with Dr. St. James. He'd hardly thought of anyone else since pulling her from the jaws of death. Her beautiful eyes and gold-flecked auburn hair reminded him of some sweet princess in an old storybook. She had taken a most unusual hold upon his thoughts.

The man's prattle about love was getting to Richard. Besides, something he said earlier had caught his attention. "It just occurred to me you might be the man I should talk to. You mentioned settling customer complaints for this railroad?"

Mr. Watson made an apologetic wave of his arm, as if sure of the direction Richard planned to take. "We've had some grievances lately about the uncomfortable seats on this particular train. I can assure you we plan to replace all of them after the New Year. It's a shame we couldn't get them installed before the holidays."

Richard shook his head. "Oh no, it's nothing like that. In fact, I haven't felt the least bit of discomfort on my journey. Actually, my concern has to do with an incident that occurred last evening."

Suddenly, looking very official, Mr. Watson removed a small notebook and fountain pen from his coat pocket. "By all means, share whatever is on your mind, doctor. I should like to take notation if you don't object."

Richard nodded his approval, amazed at how the man now appeared calm, and not at all like the jittery person of a few minutes earlier. "Actually, my concern has to do with the conductor." He lowered his voice. "He was quite rude to Dr. St. James and another lady passenger last evening. I think he should, at the very least, receive some sort of reprimand for his behavior."

Watson's pen poised in midair. "Tell me all about it."

Richard gave a quick nod. "Well, first, the man insisted Dr. St. James check her medical bag, even though she made it quite plain she didn't wish to do so. His manner was most disrespectful. Then, after punching her ticket, he handed it to me, as though she were invisible!"

Mr. Watson did not look up from his scribbling as Richard continued. "There was also another lady passenger, a young mother traveling alone with her children. She expressed concern about dinner not being served in the dining car—her little ones were restless, you see, and needed to stretch their legs. The conductor was most impolite, telling her she would just have to make do."

Mr. Watson put down his pen, the tips of his long tapered fingers touching one another while considering the situation. "Is that it? He told her to make do?"

Richard was annoyed. "Well, no, actually there was quite a bit more to it." He rubbed his neck, trying to focus on the incident as it had occurred. "The conductor informed the other lady passenger that she and her brood could wait and eat at the Pittsburg Station which was three hours away. He was most discourteous."

Watson glanced down, writing a few more notes before looking back up. "Anything else?"

"Yes, as a matter of fact there was." Richard took another sip of coffee. "He made an embarrassing affront about children *and* women needing a firm hand, looking directly at Dr. St. James, as though speaking to her."

Mr. Watson leaned forward. "Did the conductor threaten your friend or the other lady passenger?"

"Certainly not." Richard felt a twinge of irritation toward the man, but realized the conductor's remarks were subtle, especially when repeated in past tense.

Their conversation was interrupted when the conductor himself entered the dining car. For a few minutes they sat in silence while the man under discussion barked orders at a porter and then slammed out the exit door with force, causing the gold-plated clock on the wall to quiver.

Mr. Watson let out a long breath. "I'm beginning to see what you mean. The man is belligerent, to say the least."

Richard gathered his composure, thankful that Watson had been able to witness the conductor's behavior for himself. "It was the man's domineering attitude that raised my hackles. If he had shown the same insolence toward my mother or sister I would have considered filing a lawsuit against the railway. Frankly, I feel sure you would have been appalled had he used the same tone with your wife."

Watson gave a vigorous nod. "Oh, why yes, I'm sure I would." He tapped his pen on the table. "Still, I presume your mother or sister would not travel unaccompanied, would they? I know Elizabeth wouldn't. I'd never allow it." He picked up his fork and finished off the gingerbread as though the subject had been closed.

Richard bristled. "I beg to differ. My younger sister sometimes travels alone, back and forth from school during holidays. I might add that my mother occasionally takes the train into London." He drained the last of his coffee. "Respectable ladies do sometimes travel alone, sir."

Mr. Watson straightened. "Certainly, they do." He gave a slight wave of his hand. "School girls, widows, or spinsters like Dr. St. James."

Richard could not help but take offense at the man's use of the word *spinster* in relation to his friend. Memories of her luminous eyes and dainty hands hovered about his consciousness like a butterfly. Absolutely nothing about her reflected the plain image associated with spinsterhood. But it would have taken several years to complete her medical training and she was likely a bit older than he'd originally thought which would probably place her in that category.

Richard gave a reluctant nod. "Yes, spinsters and widows do sometimes travel alone, as do schoolgirls on holiday."

Watson placed the napkin on his plate and leaned back into his seat. "Our railway offers a first-class ladies' car on every train. These accommodations shelter female travelers from the less genteel population."

Richard crossed his arms. "I believe you miss my point, sir. The problem on this train has not been a lack of civility among the travelers. Besides, women are growing increasingly independent and they deserve to be treated with respect, regardless of the class in which they travel."

Watson gave him an indulgent smile while putting away his notebook and pen. "I see you are a far-sighted man, Dr. Wellington. I want you to know I'll consider this matter." He paused. "And you're right. I would be outraged if anyone spoke in that manner to my wife or mother."

Richard could hardly believe he'd just made a rallying discourse for the rights of women in a changing era. The man likely thought he was allied with the suffrage movement. Well, let him think whatever he wanted. It made little difference so long as future women travelers were protected from intimidation.

"Sir, I shall rest assured, knowing you'll handle this situation with good judgment."

Watson inclined his head. "I promise to look into the matter straightaway and make certain nothing like this happens again."

The clock above the door chimed a soft tune, as though in agreement with the result of their conversation. "Time has gotten away from me," Richard said, rising from the table. "I should make haste to look in on your wife."

Watson fumbled with his hat, twirling it between his hands like a top, before finally putting it on. The nervous father-to-be had returned, but Richard was glad to know he could be business-like when necessary.

"Some of the men are putting together a card game, and they've invited me to play." He furrowed his brow. "That is, unless you feel I should stay close to Elizabeth. I'll do whatever you believe is best." He rose from the table and stumbled, barely catching himself by grasping the back of a chair. He drew in a quick breath, letting it out with obvious relief. "I'm quite all right. Just concerned about my wife."

Richard felt a sudden pang of sympathy for him. Who knew how *he* might react if the situation were reversed? "Joining the other men is an excellent idea." He placed a steadying arm on the man's shoulder. "We must keep your wife as calm as possible and having your mind occupied will help. I recommend that you distract yourself."

Watson appeared relieved. "Then I shall wait it out in the smoking car."

"That's a good idea," Richard said, shaking his hand. "As soon as your child is born I will bring you word."

Chapter Five

After the men left, Anna turned all attention to her patient. "Mrs. Watson, I need to examine you to see if everything is as it should be. But first, let's get you into a fresh nightgown. Do you have any bed pads and clean sheets on hand? If not, I can ring the porter."

The young woman pushed herself upright, pointing to a trunk stationed in the corner of the room. "There are some items in there. I left it unlocked because I was afraid Frederick might lose the key."

"That was wise of you." Anna laughed, peering into the big wooden chest that contained several thick bed pads, crisp folded sheets and an infant basket filled with clothing for a newborn. "I must say you came well prepared. Most first-time mothers have little idea of what they'll need."

"I tried to bring along everything, just in case something like this happened before we arrived home. I really wanted to return to Asheville much earlier, but Frederick was convinced it wouldn't be necessary. He also sent my maid home three days ago, to oversee the final preparation of the nursery. I really didn't want him to do that, but he thought it was the right decision. The poor dear. I know he means well." She let out a half-sigh, half laugh.

Anna listened while helping her patient out of bed and into a fresh nightgown. "Well, I think it was most insightful of you to bring all of this along. When did your water break?"

The young woman's face pinked. "That happened when Frederick went out to search for a doctor. I'm so sorry." Her lower lip quivered. "I wanted to get out of this soiled gown, but y'all came back sooner than I expected." She glanced down at her hands that cradled her stomach.

Anna patted her shoulder. "No need for apologies." She replaced the sheets with quick precision, and as she finished getting her patient back into bed, Mrs. Watson drew in a sharp breath at the arrival of another contraction. "I'm so scared," she confessed through clenched teeth.

"Don't be afraid." Anna used her most soothing voice. "Having a baby is the most natural thing in the world. Breathe as deeply as you can—like this." She demonstrated by drawing a long breath and then slowly exhaling. "It will help you bear the pain."

Mrs. Watson took in a breath, releasing the air out slowly until the discomfort subsided. "That seemed to help. Is it something new?"

Anna fluffed the pillows and straightened the blankets. "No, I learned the method while visiting Russia a few years ago. For many generations, the midwives and doctors there have used relaxation and deep breathing to calm women in labor. I've incorporated some of those methods into my practice."

She smiled and smoothed a ruffle on the sleeve of her gown. "How wonderful, to travel the world and learn so many things. Dr. St. James, I feel that I am in very good hands."

"Oh, you may call me Anna," she said, while locking the bedroom door to dissuade anyone from entering during the examination. Ordinarily, a moving train was not an ideal setup for a doctor's office, but the luxurious railcar, with its tufted velvet furnishings, was far better than the humble dwellings of her patients in New York.

Mrs. Watson leaned back into the comfort of her pillows. "No, I would prefer to call you doctor. You must have studied a very long time to get your degree in medicine, and I think it would be disrespectful to address you otherwise." She expelled a deep gasp. "My cousin wanted to attend medical college, but her father wouldn't allow it. I don't think she's ever quite forgiven him. She says that he ruined her life."

"That's too bad." Anna walked over to the lavatory to scrub her hands. "I was fortunate my own father supported me. Without his encouragement, I might not have made it through medical school."

Mrs. Watson shook her head. "Men rule the world. At least that's what my stubborn uncle said when he refused to pay his daughter's tuition. She now owns a millinery shop in downtown Asheville."

Anna withdrew her hands from the soapy water and reached for a fresh towel. "Does she enjoy selling hats?"

The young woman pursed her lips. "I don't think so. She's saving up money to pay her tuition. Bless her heart, I just hope she's able to fulfill her dream. It's very important to her."

"I hope so too." Anna nodded while drying her hands. It seemed ridiculous that a husband or father would *allow or disallow* a grown woman to do anything. Why couldn't men and women simply live as equal partners?

When examining Mrs. Watson, Anna bit her lip to keep from expressing her disappointment aloud. The unborn child was in a transverse-breech posture. Unless the baby repositioned itself during labor, a Cesarean procedure would be required and that was something she didn't want to do. Far too many mothers died from post op infections after surgical childbirth.

"How is everything?" Mrs. Watson's voice rose, as though sensing something was wrong.

Anna released the breath she had been holding, wanting to tell her what was going on. But Dr. Wellington was in charge and it was not her place to interfere. "You have several more hours before your child arrives." She said with an enthusiasm that sought to dispel the surrounding gloom.

After washing her hands again, she mixed the correct dosage of Valerian root tincture. Supporting Mrs. Watson's head Anna held the glass to her lips.

"That tastes horrible." The young woman made a dreadful face, pushing it away.

Anna was unyielding. "I know it's bitter, but please drink it all up for the sake of your baby." She hoped those last words would inspire her to cooperate.

Through clenched teeth, Mrs. Watson allowed her to hold the glass back up to her lips, swallowing every drop before her head fell back on the pillows. "How I wish my mother were here. She would know exactly how to make me feel better."

Anna's heart went out to her. "You could send her a telegram when we arrive at Cumberland Station."

Her eyes glazed. "Mamma died two years ago, just after Frederick and I were married." The tears brimmed over. "There's no one like your mother in a situation like this, is there?"

Anna handed her patient a clean hankie. "I lost my mother when I was very young. Perhaps both our mothers are watching over us now."

The young woman's eyes brightened. "Do you think so? Sometimes, when I pray, I feel like Mamma is right beside me. It gives me a sense of peace to think heaven might not be so far away—that maybe our loved ones can somehow see the happenings in our lives."

Anna had a vague recollection of her own mother's gentle arms around her when she was still very young. She could not, however, remember any maternal love expressed by her stepmother. A picture of her stepmother, Claudette, flashed into her mind, elaborately gowned and bejeweled as she sat among the New York society matrons at teatime.

"I like your thoughts." Anna sponged her patient's face with a wet cloth. "How beautiful to consider heaven as a place filled with people who care and watch over us."

Mrs. Watson's voice grew stronger. "The Bible says that a great cloud of witnesses from heaven surround us. I've always imagined our deceased loved ones among those, and I do believe they are aware of us. Perhaps they even speak to God on our behalf."

A banging on the door interrupted them. Anna straightened the bed covers before answering. In the doorway stood a porter holding a large pail of chipped ice. She stepped aside, while with carefully averted eyes, he placed a steel bucket on the dresser. Another attendant followed close behind, pushing a cart filled with towels and two large pots of boiling water. Anna reached for her purse, but the porter waved away the silver coin she offered.

"It's all been taken care of by the doctor." He bumped into his helper as they both attempted to exit the compartment at the same time. If you need anything else, just ring." Glancing back over his shoulder, his face was a bright shade of red.

After thanking the men with a straight face, Anna closed the door and broke out into laughter. "Those poor fellows were in such a nervous rush that I thought one of them might jump out a window to escape."

Mrs. Watson gave a faint smile. "I declare, I don't think I have ever seen a funnier sight. They acted like they might get trapped in here with us."

Anna scooped a small amount of ice into a glass, offering a teaspoonful to her patient who savored the frozen mixture. Then, a moment later her smiling eyes were filled with agony when another contraction seized her body.

"Remember, take slow, deep breaths." Anna instructed, while adjusting the pillows.

When the pain subsided, Mrs. Watson's teeth began to chatter. Anna did a quick search through the closet and found extra blankets, adding them to the other covers. "Try to get some rest," she whispered. "The medication will make you drowsy."

After tucking her in, Anna noticed a gilded-framed picture on the dresser. Picking it up, she observed a woman with graying blonde hair, upswept in a pompadour. Her twinkling eyes bore a striking resemblance to Mrs. Watson, leaving Anna no doubt about the woman being her patient's mother. Placing it back on the dresser, she glanced around the room once more, this time noting there was only one armchair. They would need another one for the long vigil ahead.

Tiptoeing into the parlor, she located a wing-backed chair in front of the window that would serve the needed purpose. Running her hand along its fine velvet, Anna suddenly felt the need to gaze upon the outside world for a moment. When opening the drapes, she could see it was snowing harder than it had earlier. The train rattled against the wind as if trying its best to race alongside the battering storm.

A group of children—likely brothers and sisters, frolicked on the snow-covered lawn of a big farm house. The brood waved at the train and the engineer answered by giving a long blast on the whistle. Anna smiled and half-lifted her hand to the little ones as they were lost to view.

For a moment, she allowed herself to ponder how nice it might be to have children of her own. The thought of rosy baby fingers grasping her hand caused Anna to experience an exquisite kind of joy, making her wonder what life would have been like as a mother instead of a physician.

During her years in medical school, while her friends married and had children, she had taken each day with her chin up and an eye to conquer her studies. Now, in her heart, she felt a deep loss, greater perhaps than the need to prove her worth as a doctor.

Get a hold of your feelings, her inner voice warned. *Having a husband and children would force you to give up all you have been called to do. Besides, is anyone except the insufferable Mr. Van Demark waiting in line to propose marriage?*

She reminded herself that being a good mother required far more than kisses and lullabies. All her medical experience had taught her that babies required endless care. Diapers must be changed, noses needed to be wiped, and an entire assortment of obligations. Perhaps someday she might adopt a child, but until then, she would have to be content and enjoy her time with the babies she delivered.

Pressing her knuckles together, she glanced at the clock, wondering what could be keeping Dr. Wellington. He needed to know about the baby's breach position, and she hoped he would not insist upon a caesarian delivery.

Mrs. Watson's moans brought her back to reality and she pushed the additional chair into the bedroom. There was serious work ahead and she prayed it would all end well.

Richard quietly slipped into the Pullman, not wanting to disturb Dr. St. James while she measured their patient's blood pressure. The fancy hat she had worn earlier now rested on the dresser, like a crown, with its exquisite plumes standing upright. His heartbeat quickened when the owner of the elegant bonnet turned to greet him with a smile.

"Blood pressure is almost normal, and her contractions are coming every six minutes." She placed the stethoscope back on the table. "Could I consult with you in private, doctor?"

The somber look on her face made him wonder what she wanted to discuss. Could it be that Mrs. Watson did not want him there? If so, then how would he be able to convince Mr. Watson that Dr. St. James was competent enough to handle the birth all by herself, especially when he had no idea how skilled she was?

Richard gave a brief nod and followed her through the luxurious rooms all the way to the vestibule outside the Pullman door.

The frozen rain and snow pounded so hard against the roof that he feared it might cave in at any moment. As she started to speak, the train's wheels gave a grinding sound and came to an abrupt stop, throwing them off balance and tossing her into his arms. It took him a moment to right her, as soft hair brushed against his face and a subtle bouquet of rose perfume stole over his senses. "My dear, are you all right?" He spoke in a whisper, fearing his voice might betray how much he liked holding this beautiful woman in his arms.

She pulled away from him as a brakeman shuffled down the corridor, his small, dark eyes lighting up with interest when seeing their quick parting. "Nothin' to be alarmed about," he said. "We stopped here for a few minutes cause of all that ice and snow. Men are out there now, shoveling it off the tracks so we can get her into Cumberland Station."

Richard cleared his throat. "How far is it to the terminal?"

"Bout a mile or so." The brakeman touched his hat before moving farther down the narrow passage.

Richard turned back to her. "My apologies. What did you wish to speak with me about?" Hoping to diffuse her embarrassment, he used his most professional tone.

She folded her hands in front of her, appearing composed, except for the lingering color along her cheekbones.

"The baby is in a transverse-breech position, but I'm hoping as Mrs. Watson's labor progresses, the child's head will engage for a normal delivery. If not, I would like to perform an internal cephalic version, delivering with forceps."

He pondered her words, uneasy with the prognosis. Had she perhaps misdiagnosed the breech position? "Turning the baby with forceps could be fatal," he said. "A caesarean is the only sure way we can save the child, and hopefully the mother. Do you think she would mind if I examined her?"

She drew back in obvious alarm. "With all due respect, doctor, I believe Mrs. Watson has made it clear that she wants me to care for her. Besides, I am confident she could give birth normally if the baby's head were properly engaged. Her measurements certainly indicate it."

Richard folded both arms across his chest. "You did measurements?" Pelvic measurements were the most up to date maternity technique. He'd never performed the procedure himself because the training wasn't yet available while he was in medical school.

She inhaled a deep breath, as if drawing in strength. "Yes," she said. "It's a routine procedure at Women's Charity Hospital. I've successfully delivered over a hundred babies using this method."

Richard smiled in spite of himself. "Are you serious? Over a hundred babies?"

Her chin notched higher. "That is correct, sir. And none of the mothers suffered from postpartum infection.

His initial aversion dimmed in the light of her experience. "I don't like the idea of performing surgery on a moving train." He rubbed his chin. "I suppose we'll do things your way and hope for the best."

The look of relief lightened her features.

Richard ran a hand through his hair. "I should inform Mr. Watson of the complications his wife is facing."

The relief that had previously shone in her eyes was replaced by worry. "Oh my, you don't think he'll come back before the baby is born, do you? I mean—well I'm concerned that his nervous condition could make things more difficult for everyone." She glanced behind her, as though the topic of their conversation might appear at any moment.

He stifled a grin. One minute this lovely lady was looking him straight in the eye, talking to him like a male colleague and within the next instant she was blushing and looking behind her for a nervous father-to-be who was nowhere in sight.

"I think Mr. Watson has thrown himself into a card game and would prefer to stay put until his little heir is born. I'll go back and speak with him before things become too hectic. It appears we have a long day ahead."

As Richard made his way through the numerous cars, he realized he was gaining more respect for this woman doctor. Perhaps the AMA should allow women into its membership, but only in the field of obstetrics.

〜

When Dr. Wellington returned, Anna had her sterilized instruments laid out on a table that she had scrubbed with disinfectant. She looked up in surprise at the sound of a rattling trolley. The appealing doctor was pushing a tray laden with coffee and sandwiches.

She chuckled. "What's all this?"

He gave a boyish grin. "In order to protect our patient's privacy, I decided to play the role of porter." He parked the cart behind the door. "Coffee?"

At her grateful nod, he poured two cups of the steaming liquid, adding cream to both. "The men are still shoveling snow from the tracks." He handed her one of the cups. "According to the porter, we will stay at Cumberland Station overnight and continue our journey tomorrow, after the storm moves on," he shrugged. "At least we'll be at a terminal during the worst of this weather. Maybe we can send a telegram if we need to."

Anna nodded and peeked in at Mrs. Watson who was sleeping, albeit fitfully. The medication had worked. "I wonder if there's a hospital nearby."

A troubled look came into his eyes. "Afraid not. According to the engineer the nearest hospital is fifty miles away."

"Did you speak with Mr. Watson?" Anna took a sip of the hot coffee.

"Yes, and he accepted the news much better than I expected, by giving us his blessing to do all within our power to save both mother and child."

Anna considered his words. "We will," she said, with more confidence than she felt. Would she be able to pull this off without a hitch, as she had done so many times at the Women's Charity Hospital? Or would this turn out to be the one case in over a hundred that didn't survive?

Mrs. Watson moaned, and Anna was immediately at her side, Dr. Wellington following close behind.

"If a choice must be made, then let my baby live," she said in an agitated whisper. "I will happily go on to be with God, knowing my child is all right."

Anna reached over and smoothed the golden tendrils of hair away from her forehead. Had she overheard their whispered conversation from the next room? "There's no need to fret, Mrs. Watson. Your baby will soon be coming into the world." She placed a fresh damp washcloth on her forehead. "Would you like some more ice?"

"Yes, please, but is my baby all right?" She paused, a frown on her face. "I dreamed he was in trouble and I couldn't help him."

"It was only a dream." Anna offered her another teaspoon of chipped ice and tucked the blankets around her. "There now, go back to sleep, dear. You'll need your strength for later, you know."

"But my baby?" she persisted. "I can't help feeling you aren't telling me everything."

Anna glanced at Dr. Wellington, hoping he would explain the circumstance they were facing.

He cleared his throat. "We do have a slight problem, Mrs. Watson. Your baby is breech. Do you know what that means?"

Mrs. Watson stared at the doctor's face, as if willing him to tell her it was nothing to be alarmed about. Like a puppet, she nodded her head.

He continued in a low voice, as if he were talking to a child. "A breech position is when ..."

"Will my baby be all right?" A whimper escaped her lips.

Anna almost answered for him, but he replied before she could muster the right words.

"Dr. St. James is going to turn him into the right position, so that you can have a normal delivery."

Anna breathed a sigh of relief. Thank goodness he was telling her the truth. It had never been her policy to hide things from a patient, and she was tired of tiptoeing around the reality of what they were up against.

"What if that doesn't work?" Mrs. Watson whispered.

He paused, as though somewhat surprised by her question.

"If properly done, there's no reason for the procedure not to work. Dr. St. James has delivered countless babies this way. I am confident there is nothing for you to fear." He reached out to give the patient a reassuring pat on the shoulder.

The calmness of his demeanor made Anna's heart rise with the hope that somehow all would be well.

Mrs. Watson's teeth suddenly clenched, and her body stiffened with pain. "My ch—child deserves to live," she gasped.

"Take a deep breath," both Dr. Wellington and Anna advised at the same moment. The concern in his brown eyes softened into a twinkle as his glance met hers.

When the discomfort finally subsided, Mrs. Watson bit the inside of her lip, and reached for Anna's hand. "Promise me you'll save my child even if you cannot spare me."

This was a request she had heard many times under similar circumstances. So far, she'd never had to make such a choice, and hoped this situation would not be the exception. "I do promise." Anna lightly squeezed her hand. "Now, I'm going to give you another dose of medication."

Mrs. Watson gulped down the bitter concoction before making a horrible face.

Anna chuckled, "That's the spirit. You don't have to like it, so long as you take it."

The patient gave her a faint smile as Dr. Wellington spoke up. "Mrs. Watson, would you like for me to read to you from the Psalms? I find they often bring comfort during times like these."

"Oh, please do." Her head fell back on the pillows with exhaustion. "I love the Psalms, especially the twenty-third."

Dr. Wellington began to read aloud, and Anna sat down in a chair beside Mrs. Watson's bed, listening to the comforting words.

The Lord is my shepherd, I shall not want.
He maketh me to lie down in green pastures:
He leadeth me beside the still waters.
He restoreth my soul ..."

Chapter Six

Richard walked in long strides toward Cumberland Station. The snow, now over a foot deep, sifted its way over the tops of his boots, and a cold north wind howled, blowing the stinging flakes into his face.

When he finally reached the sheltered platform, he stopped to catch his breath and check the time—half past four. Mrs. Watson was in the final stages of labor. Still, he'd delivered enough babies to know there was plenty of time to send a telegram to his staff in Asheville, letting them know his train had been delayed by the storm.

Placing a gloved hand in his coat pocket, he checked to see if he had the note Dr. St. James wanted telegraphed to Daphne Vanderbilt. Yes, the folded paper was there. Richard gazed back at the long line of trains that were waiting out the blizzard. The snow was falling so hard he could no longer see the sleek black rail car belonging to the Watsons. *What a storm. Would they really be able to resume their trip at sunrise?*

With head bent into the gale, he pulled down the brim of his hat and resumed his journey until, through squinted eyes, he could make out the long flight of steps leading up to the station. As he'd supposed, several people thronged the entrance.

Just as he reached the stairway, another burst of wind almost tore the breath from him, but he continued to push forward until at last he made it to the top step and flung open both doors to the entrance, allowing himself, and those behind him to proceed into the building at a faster pace. The bitter wind accompanied them inside the terminal and raced through the foyer, billowing the heavy draperies on the windows and causing the chandelier prisms to tinkle a haunting melody.

A startled railway agent appeared and drew the remainder of weary passengers into the vestibule before slamming the doors closed behind them. "Ghastly weather!" He grunted. "Never saw anything like it."

Despite the blizzard, Richard's heart was lifted by the cozy warmth of the train station. A Christmas tree, decorated with bright-red candy canes, stood beside a stone fireplace where several people were warming their hands. He took in the welcoming blaze and scanned the room until his eyes came to rest on a noble looking staircase. At the foot of the steps was a sign with the words: *Telegraph Office,* and an arrow pointing upwards. He raced up the stairs to find a hive of activity, with a long line of passengers waiting to send notes to their loved ones.

As he took his place behind the others, a shadow of uncertainty hovered around the margins of his judgment. Would they be able to safely deliver the baby? He had allowed a woman doctor to talk him out of performing a caesarean. He could still carry out the surgical procedure if necessary, but the required sterilization of the entire room might not be enough to prevent an infection. The Pullman's heavy drapes and carpets, though beautiful, could be a breeding ground for germs.

As he gazed out the station windows, the snow pelted down with renewed vigor, keeping time with the telegraph sounder that clicked in the background. It was perfect weather for the festivity of Christmas, but would they be able to continue their holiday journey anytime soon? The engineer had informed everyone that by tomorrow morning the train would be moving again, but now, with the weather so harsh, he found it difficult to believe anything might budge in less than twenty-four hours.

After sending the telegrams he descended the staircase. A big clock on the wall made a loud preliminary whirring sound as it began to strike five, causing him to pick up his pace with renewed purpose.

God be with us, he prayed, while plodding back through the huge drifts of snow. *Guide us in bringing this new life safely into the world and protect both mother and child.*

⁓

Anna was washing her hands when Dr. Wellington entered the Pullman.

"Telegrams are on their way." He joined her at the lavatory.

She caught the faint scent of his shaving soap and her pulse quickened. Withdrawing her hands from the water, she was annoyed with herself for having romantic thoughts in so serious a situation.

He gave her a slight smile. "How's our patient doing?"

Mrs. Watson moaned in the background.

"She's ready." Anna gave him a clean towel. When her hand brushed against his, the contact sent a shiver through her arm, fleeting as the wings of a butterfly, but powerful in its effect. The enchantment was broken by a sudden burst of wind thundering around the rail car and knocking an ornamental vase off the dresser. She shivered as a cold draft snaked around her ankles. "The storm seems to be gathering energy. I hope we aren't wrenched off the tracks."

"We'll be fine." His voice remained calm as he dried his hands. "The engineer assured me his train had withstood greater storms than this one."

Anna appreciated his tranquil demeanor. It had been a long time since she had felt that kind of assurance.

Mrs. Watson's face contorted into a grim mask of pain. "I can't take any more of this suffering." Her words were broken in a cry of agony, and great beads of sweat rolled down her forehead.

Dr. Wellington spoke to her in a soothing voice. "My dear, it will all be over soon, and you'll have something wonderful to show for your efforts today."

"I hope so." Her voice quivered while turning her head from side to side as another contraction caused her body to stiffen with pain.

Dr. Wellington nodded toward the bottle of chloroform that waited on the bed stand. "I'll prepare the anesthesia. Check again to see if the baby's head is engaged. We may need for her to push."

Anna did a brief exam while he gave soothing reassurance to Mrs. Watson. "Scream if you want to," he said. "No one will hear you over all the noise that's going on outside. And even if they do, it doesn't matter."

Anna was touched by his sensitivity. It was nice for a male doctor not to dismiss the agony of childbirth.

"I'm giving you just enough of this to take the edge off your pain." He placed the handkerchief over Mrs. Watson's nose and drew it away before she completely passed out. "Tell me, Mrs. Watson, are you wishing for a boy or a girl?"

"A boy—for Frederick," she replied groggily, then closed her eyes.

"Any changes in the baby's position?" He placed the handkerchief back on the bed stand.

Anna shook her head. "The baby is still transverse, but the patient has dilated a full ten centimeters."

He handed her the sterile instruments and resumed his place beside their patient who opened her eyes at the onslaught of another contraction. "Hold on to my arm," he said. "You won't hurt me."

While Mrs. Watson gripped the doctor's arm with all her might, Anna gently slid the forceps into the birth canal and around the sides of the baby's head, turning the infant into the correct position. "When you have another contraction, I want you to push as hard as you can," she instructed.

Within seconds, Mrs. Watson cried out in anguish while compelling her body to force the child out. "I feel like I'm being ripped in half." Her voice was shrill with pain.

When Anna saw the baby's head crown, she breathed a sigh of relief. "You're doing great."

As another deep pain engulfed her, she pressed both hands against Dr. Wellington's arm, causing a cufflink to pop out of his sleeve. From Anna's peripheral vision she saw the golden ornament flash through the air and crash to the floor, spinning a strange duet with the howling wind.

"Push again!" Anna raised her voice above the bizarre symphony of noise surrounding them.

Another hard push released the baby from its mother's womb, and Mrs. Watson fell back against the pillows in exhaustion.

"It's a boy!" Dr. St. James held up the red-faced baby who demonstrated the power of his brand-new lungs.

Mrs. Watson raised her head. "Is he all right?"

"He appears to be perfect." Anna cut the cord and applied antiseptic to the incision.

"His lungs are healthy." Richard said.

"Thank God." Mrs. Watson's head dropped back on the pillow. "Someone needs to let Frederick know he has a son."

"I'll see to that in a moment." Richard took Mrs. Watson's wrist to check her pulse, while Dr. St. James dipped a washcloth into a basin of warm water and bathed the infant's wiggling body, patting him dry, as he mouthed the air and wailed.

"Her pulse is normal." Richard picked up a tiny bottle of silver nitrate from the instrument table and gestured toward the bright lamp beside the lavatory. "If you'll hold the little stranger under the light over there, I'll administer these drops."

She wrapped the baby in a snug blanket before carrying him over to the well-lighted corner of the room. When the drops fell into the infant's eyes, he started to cry in exasperation.

"There, there, you poor little darling." She wiped the dribble off his eyelashes and cheeks and began singing a lullaby. Almost immediately, the child stopped crying, as though sensing her kindness.

> *Lullaby, and good night, with pink roses bedight,*
> *With lilies o'er spread, is my baby's sweet head.*
> *Lay thee down now, and rest, may thy slumber be blessed!*
> *Lay thee down now, and rest may thy slumber be blessed!*

Her voice stirred something tender in Richard's heart, and he found himself staring at her Madonna-like beauty. The Brahm's tune she sang sounded more like a prayer than a lullaby. Her voice was pitch perfect. Mesmerized, he watched and listened while she finished the song and carried the baby back to his mother's waiting arms.

While handing over the infant, a wisp of hair escaped from her chignon, and he felt a sudden longing to kiss the feathery little curls on her nape. From there, his imagination took flight, causing him to wonder how it might feel to loosen the pins from her tresses and allow the long silken locks to tumble unrestricted into his hands.

The baby fussed, interrupting the direction of his thoughts to regain his composure.

Mrs. Watson loosened the blanket to take a closer look at her newborn. "He has his father's hair." She stroked the baby's carrot-colored locks with a fingertip. "And just look at those perfect little fingers and toes!"

Richard couldn't help but smile while watching the new mother croon over her infant. "I agree, he really is in fine form. See how alert he is? I believe the little stranger knows we're admiring him."

Mrs. Watson's eyes widened. "Do you think he really knows we're talking about him, doctor?" She gazed at her son with pride, as though viewing an invisible gift of insight.

He tucked the blanket back around the baby. "I'm certain on an instinctual level he is aware of the love surrounding him. Love is very powerful, you know."

Dr. St. James glanced up with a smile as she placed the soiled laundry into a hamper. "He really is a beautiful baby."

"And no injuries from the use of forceps," Richard noted with satisfaction. "I must say you did a fine job, Dr. St. James."

"Thank you, doctor, and please call me Anna."

"Only if you call me Richard."

Their eyes met. She brushed back a wisp of hair from her forehead, giving him a small smile. "Thank you, Richard. I'm sure your prayers helped."

His name softly wrapped in her cultured voice caused Richard's spirit to soar. He was glad, however, when the baby began to cry again, because it engulfed the sound of his pounding heart.

As Richard made his way through the train in search of Mr. Watson, his thoughts remained focused on Anna. Watching her cuddle and sing to the newborn had caused him to desire things he didn't dare express.

Nearing the dining car, he caught a whiff of rosemary chicken mingling with the aroma of roasted potatoes and strong coffee. What little amount he'd managed to consume for lunch was long gone and the culinary bouquet made his mouth water. He was tempted to stop and gulp something down, but kept walking, knowing he must fulfill his mission.

Just as he was about to enter the smoking car, Mr. Watson burst out the door, almost knocking him down. "There you are!"

He stopped short at seeing Richard. "I was just on my way to find you." He chewed on the end of a cold cigar, his face pale. "Is everything alright? It seems ages since you went to Elizabeth. I've been so worried."

Richard had never been more thankful to be the bearer of good news. "No need for worry, sir. Congratulations, Mr. Watson, you have a handsome baby boy."

The man's jaw dropped open. "A boy? Y—you mean I have a son?"

"Yes indeed, sir!" Richard put out his hand. A second later, Mr. Watson took it and began pumping it up and down.

"Well, I'll be da—I mean—goodness! A boy, you said?"

Richard nodded, his smile expanding.

Watson tugged at one earlobe. "And Elizabeth?" His tone hitched to a higher note. "What about her blood pressure? Were you able to get that under control? Is she all right?"

"Both mother and baby are fine." Richard used his most reassuring tone. "Dr. St. James has a few more details to take care of, but soon you'll be able to see your wife and son. Come, let us go celebrate the good news with your friends."

Visibly calmed, he led Richard into the smoking car. "Listen, everyone," Watson raised his voice to a shout. "I have a boy."

The room erupted with excitement. The men heartily clapped Mr. Watson's back and then burst into a spontaneous chorus of "For He's a Jolly Good Fellow." One barrel-chested man with a bushy mustache lifted the new father right off his feet and placed him on the piano, as cigars and brandy were passed around with applause.

Richard accepted the brandy but declined a cigar. While singing along with the others, he was thankful everything had turned out in favor of the young couple. *Thank you, God,* he silently prayed while the men continued their joviality. The day could have ended in disaster, but thanks to Anna's remarkable skill, it had turned out well.

⌒

Anna placed the baby in the bassinet and gave her patient a sponge bath before helping her into a powder-blue nursing gown.

"Thank you so much for everything." Mrs. Watson spoke in a whisper. "Having you here made all the difference in the world."

"My pleasure." Anna had found a bottle of chilled milk in the small kitchen's icebox and added a sandwich from the tray that Dr. Wellington had produced earlier in the day. "You need to eat and regain your strength."

Mrs. Watson consumed the entire sandwich and drained the milk glass without stopping for air. Then Anna lifted the newborn out of the bassinet, placing him in his mother's arms. With a little coaching, the baby began to nurse with contentment.

Anna took a long breath, relieved the day had not ended in disaster. She knew the victory was not entirely due to her skills, but also to Richard's help and prayers. Her face grew warm with the remembrance of their agreement to be on a first name basis. What an interesting trip this was turning out to be.

Chapter Seven

Richard scanned the coach until his eyes found Anna. How regal she looked in the wide brimmed hat that matched her navy-blue dress. He strode past the other passengers, determined not to miss a chance to sit with her. She glanced up from her reading and they exchanged a smile.

"Our journey has certainly been an interesting one." He took the seat directly across from her. "When I left New York on Monday, I never dreamed we'd be caught up in a snowstorm."

There was a sparkle in her eyes. "I know. Here it is, Christmas Eve, and I expected to arrive at Biltmore yesterday."

He chuckled. "We were lucky to get out of Cumberland Station yesterday afternoon. It really appeared as though we'd be stuck there for quite a while. I suppose we should be thankful the storm moved faster than the new weather bureau chief predicted."

She smiled, and a lovely dimple appeared on one rosy cheek. "Maybe the excitement of getting home in time for Christmas pushed the men along to get the tracks cleared."

"I'm sure you are correct," he said. "By the way, I checked in with our patient a few minutes ago. Mother and baby are doing quite well, and the new father seems like a different man."

She nodded. "When I checked on them last night he was on cloud nine. I'm glad he finally calmed down. For a while I thought he might require psychiatric care before it was all over."

He grimaced. "The poor man had the worst jitters I've ever seen. I was tempted to sedate him if he didn't get hold of himself."

Her lips curled and soon their laughter filled the coach. "Oh, the poor dear." She removed a lace trimmed hankie from her sleeve, wiping away tears of merriment. "I'm glad he is doing so much better. His wife and child will certainly need his strength in the days ahead. What is his occupation? I forgot to ask Mrs. Watson."

"Mr. Watson's father owns this railway." He lowered his voice in a conspiratorial tone, as the conductor entered their coach to deliver a tray. "While we were in the dining car, I had the opportunity to speak with him about the conductor's deplorable behavior toward you and the other lady traveler. He plans to look into it for me."

Anna glanced over at the man, now engaged in conversation with a passenger. "What wonderful news," she whispered, clasping her hands together. "I do hope he is able to implement a change in his behavior."

How Richard enjoyed seeing the twinkle in her eyes. It felt as though they were partners in a pleasant scheme, and he enjoyed the warmth of their companionship. "He promised to keep me apprised of all changes. I don't intend to let him off the hook, either."

The coach suddenly grew dark and several of the travelers gasped. "We're just moving through a high mountain pass," the conductor announced. "No need for alarm."

No sooner were the words out of his mouth than the train emerged from the inky shelter of the gap with a triumphant entry into a backdrop of snow-covered mountains. Their imposing structures folded one behind the other in greens and blues, each peak rising majestically into the sky.

She leaned closer to the window. "This is spectacular."

"Indeed, it is." He eyed the frozen lace glittering from every bush and tree in the valley below, and his heart soared with joy at his return home. The stresses of the medical conference and the general sense of grime he associated with the city fell away as he contemplated the pristine sight. He couldn't prevent himself from quoting aloud from a Psalm. "When I consider thy heavens, the work of thy fingers, the moon and the stars which thou hast ordained; what is man, that thou art mindful of him?"

"Is that the poetry of John Donne?"

"No, actually it is the writing of King David from Psalms 8. It's from the Bible—a book that inspired much of Donne's poetry. Every time I leave these mountains and return home, I am overwhelmed with the beauty of this place."

She studied him, a smile playing around her lips. "I've never known anyone quite like you."

"Indeed? How so?" He laughed, his mood lifting even higher at the sight of her beautiful face there among his beloved mountains. Did she find him as intriguing as he found her?

Anna brushed the folds of her skirt. "The way you speak of God and the Bible. I have never known anyone quite so . . . religious. It's almost as though you believe God is right here on the train, traveling along with us." She waved a gloved hand as though to underscore her point.

Richard's heart raced as she watched him with steady eyes. "God is traveling along with us."

She nodded. "Of course, I know God is everywhere. But you make it seem as though he is physically present."

He suppressed a smile. "I am not at all religious. A few years ago, I suppose I might have been considered so, because I regularly attended church and could recite all the prayers." He paused and gazed out the window at the blue haze shrouding the mountains. "But something was missing, and I couldn't quite name it. I loved my work. I followed all the rules that were taught to me since boyhood. But no matter how hard I worked at being good, no matter how much of my time was filled with charitable works, I just couldn't seem to feel God's presence in my life."

She seemed to drink in every word, yet her reply showed she analyzed what he said, as a good scientist would, not taking anything at face value. "You quote the Bible and speak of God as though he is a close and personal friend. How, then, can you not consider yourself religious?"

Once more his eyes swept over the stately mountains, striving to collect his thoughts well enough to convey them. Explaining his spiritual awakening had never been easy, perhaps because it was so unique and personal. But how could he refuse to answer, especially when he had brought up the subject in the first place?

He drew a careful breath while searching for the right words to express his deepest convictions. "Maybe I do appear religious, but I like to think of myself as *spiritual*. Before my awakening of faith, there was an empty space in my heart that was never quite satisfied."

Anna gave a slight frown. "How did you overcome that feeling of emptiness?"

Richard leaned closer to her, careful to keep a respectful space between them. "I didn't do it on my own." His voice regained its usual self-assurance. "One Sunday evening when I was on my way home from visiting a patient who lived far out in one of the mountain coves, I happened to come upon a little church. The people going inside were dressed poorly, but they all looked so happy—as if they were delighted by life itself. In that moment, I thought about how nice it might be to have whatever it was that made them appear so joyful. I decided to join them."

Her eyes sparkled. "What was it like inside the church?"

He rubbed his chin, trying to recreate that night for her. "It had a unique appeal. A plain little altar with a wooden cross behind it. No stained-glass windows or adornments. There was also a small choir, but they certainly didn't have the trained voices I was accustomed to hearing."

She gave a wry smile. "That must have been disappointing."

"No, actually it wasn't. The people of Southern Appalachia sing traditional folk songs and hymns, passed down by their Irish and Scottish ancestors. Most can't read a single note of music, but they can play a good number of instruments by ear, and often sing together in harmony. I was overwhelmed by the way they lifted their voices to God with such spontaneity and free-flowing emotion."

"Are they Baptists? Methodists?"

He paused. "There are Baptist and Methodist churches in Appalachia, but this one was non-denominational. You see, many of the early settlers escaped the restrictions of their established religions back home and adopted a less formal style of worship. Most mountaineers are independent thinkers and don't like to feel as though they are "owned" by any particular institution, religious or otherwise."

Appearing intrigued, she tipped her head to the side and a runaway curl cascaded over her shoulder. "I didn't realize there was such a thing as non-denominational worship."

"This was a new experience for me. The minister of the little church was a plain looking fellow who read straight from the Bible and spoke of God's unconditional love. There were no clergy robes or prayer books." Richard shook his head. "I must admit the lack of pomp made me a bit uncomfortable at first, but I was drawn to the words he spoke. He explained in very simple terms that Jesus Christ gave Himself on the cross for the sins of the entire world, and we could experience God's Grace by being born again."

Her expression sobered. "I've heard that expression used by the Salvation Army missionaries who preach on the Lower East Side. I never knew quite what it meant." She pushed the stray curl back beneath the brim of her hat. "I thought it was shibboleth."

"I thought so too at first. But in simple terms it means to see God in a new light. Anyway, I was captivated by the pastor's sincerity, and stayed until the end of the sermon. The minister closed the service with an altar call. I went forward to publicly accept Christ into my heart, and that one act of faith changed my life."

He couldn't help but smile in recollection. "I went away with the realization that I was covered in God's grace and there was nothing I could ever do to earn or lose His unconditional love."

Anna was silent some moments while the hum of conversation filled the train around them. When he thought she would say nothing else she looked at him intently. "What happened after you went forward?"

Richard suppressed a chuckle. Had she expected the heavens to open, or an angelic choir to break out in song? "Nothing outwardly changed. I went home and had my tea." At her upraised brows, he smiled. "But everything within me was different. It was as if I'd had ..." He paused, searching for the right word.

"An epiphany?" she provided.

"Exactly! The next day, as I went about my medical rounds, I discovered differences in myself that I can only attribute to my experience at that little church. My patients became more precious to me. I had a new level of compassion and found myself truly interested in their lives and families. I also began to read the Bible. Verses that had never made sense to me before brought answers for which I had long searched."

Anna drew her brows together. "A lot of modern-day people don't believe the Bible is anything more than a historical book." She raised her gloved hand as though to fend off his response. "I don't believe that, of course."

"I used to feel the same way," he said. "Now I know better."

For several minutes they sat in reflective silence. The winter sun poured its soft yellow light onto ice coated foliage, and a bird soared down from one of the high mountain peaks, landing with grace on a clearing below.

Anna was glad her new friend had shared his spiritual journey, but did he believe everyone should have the exact same experience? Wasn't God much bigger than that?

She returned his gaze. "I've always been a believer. I joined the church with several other children when I was twelve. In fact, it was on that special day when I felt a divine calling upon my life to become a doctor."

Anna paused, remembering the white dress and corsage of pink roses she wore on that Sunday morning so long ago. "The term *born again* wasn't used, but I remember our minister reciting John 3:16 during our preparation." She paused, trying to remember the exact words.

His lips crooked upward into a smile. "For God so loved the world that he gave his only begotten son?"

"Yes. That's it. That whosoever believeth in him, should not perish but have everlasting life. If only—" She glanced down at her hands.

"What?" He raised a brow.

Would he think less of her if he knew she had doubts? She shook her head. "If only I had more faith. Sometimes I don't feel God's presence at all. Many of my patients are born into poverty, and they struggle all their lives just to feed their children. It doesn't seem fair!" She paused. "Oh, I still believe in God. It's just that I've never understood why He doesn't do something to alleviate all the suffering in this world."

He regarded her with kind eyes that seemed to look right into her soul. "I understand how you feel, Anna. In fact, I cannot tell you the number of times I have had similar thoughts. But we live in a fallen world and God uses us to do His work on earth."

"You make it all sound so simple—"

He gave a little half shrug. "When everything seems to be crumbling all around me, or if a patient isn't responding to treatment, I take a moment to tell God that I trust him, no matter how the situation appears. Sometimes, after doing this, an idea will pop into my head regarding what my patient needs, and the remedy will work. At other times, the person I am concerned for walks away from his deathbed without any help from me at all." A sad look filled his eyes. "And then there are those times when nothing changes, at least not from my own limited perspective. But even then, God gives me his peace when I ask for it."

"I'm not so certain I could ever do that. I have to see things for myself in order to grasp them fully."

He laughed. "You may be a doubting Thomasina, but God loves you just as you are. And if you committed your life to him then you are indeed born again. Accepting Christ doesn't mean that we have to receive him in a designated place."

"Are you saying that God loves me no matter what I think or feel? I thought one had to be good to receive his love."

"No one is ever good enough. That's why God's grace is sufficient. Lean into it when you have doubts. He will give you his peace, and you might even have a different outcome than what you expected."

They sat in reverent silence as the train puffed its way around the winding bluffs.

Anna pointed out a log cabin that was perched like a bird on the spur of the mountain; a great nest of tall plumy pines surrounded it. "How lovely it would be to live in such a place."

Richard gave a dismissive wave of his hand. "As picturesque as it may appear, I'm sure it is without indoor plumbing or running water. Can you imagine hauling wood and other supplies up that steep trail?" He pointed to the winding mountain road that climbed upward with shadowed curves toward the cabin.

Her smile wilted as the rustic cottage lost its appeal. "I'm certain that at least half of the water would slosh out of my bucket by the time I reached the top."

He tried to imagine her climbing the mountain with a pail of water in her hand. The picture that formed in his mind did not fit with her cultured appearance.

Anna pointed to another high footpath leading straight up to another log cabin similar to the first. "Could a carriage possibly make it up there?"

"Goodness, no," Richard chuckled. "One might be able to lead a horse, or better yet, a mule, up that precipitous path, but never a carriage. In fact, I often begin my house calls on horseback before being forced to continue on foot."

Her eyes narrowed. "It sounds as though the people in Appalachia are no better off than my patients on the Lower East Side."

He nodded. "In many ways that's true. But the mountaineers have fresh air and grow their own food, giving them an advantage over the East End residents of New York."

"Asheville, North Carolina!" the conductor shouted, balancing himself down the swaying aisle of the coach. "Asheville Station in ten minutes." The train lurched and slowed down to a crawl.

Richard gestured at a large structure near the tracks. "That's the Asheville Textile Mill. Many of the locals work there."

She audibly shuddered at the looming brick building belching black smoke from its chimneys. "What a dark looking place. It reminds me of factories in New York." Shifting in her seat, she accidentally revealed a shapely ankle. He averted his eyes as she smoothed her skirts to cover the exposed skin.

"The employees slave through fourteen-hour shifts for very little pay." He pointed out a row of small white bungalows nearby. "But the housing for mill workers is generally better than the typical log cabins dotting the hillsides."

She leaned toward the window, looking back at the tiny cottages. "But they're all crowded together."

"That's true, but they're equipped with indoor plumbing and bathrooms. Inside the mill, things aren't so pleasant because the place is filled with numerous hazards. A constant mist descends upon the workers in the weave room, creating a perfect environment for tuberculosis, as well as other respiratory infections. Still, many of the laborers prefer the mill over the hardscrabble farms they left behind."

A slight frown appeared on her smooth forehead. "Why would they choose darkness and certain illness over the freedom of sunlight and fresh air?"

"Because carving out a garden on the side of a mountain is backbreaking work. The mill pays a steady wage, allowing them housing and a small backyard garden with a chicken coop—not to mention an open line of credit at the company store."

"You have certainly given me much to think about." She clasped her hands together, as though trying to make sense of it all. "It seems there are looming social problems wherever one goes. I wish I could make things better."

He glanced back out the window and smiled at the sight of two children, wrapping a red scarf around their snowman's neck. "I'd love to make the world a better place too, Anna. I like to think I can do that by helping one person at a time. Besides ... our guardian angels surely saved us from being trampled by those horses, suggesting that our work on earth isn't finished yet."

She grew quiet, as though to reflect on how quickly their lives could have been snuffed out. As the train descended a hill, she remarked upon the winding waterway below, the silver ribbon shivering against the rocks as it hurried toward its destination.

"That's the French Broad River, and until the railway came through Asheville, it was the main channel for goods to arrive in the mountains." He gestured toward a few scattered picnic tables along the shore. "It's quite beautiful during summer when everything is in bloom. A lovely place for picnics and boating. Lots of people gather there on summer days for recreation." For a moment, he imagined the two of them sharing a romantic lunch on the shores, walking hand-in-hand alongside the river afterwards. He shook aside the thought as the train's wheels gave a shrill grind and the coach quivered to a standstill. Suddenly, the sound of chatter and excitement filled the car as passengers gathered their belongings to disembark.

He rose to his feet. "This is my stop. You should arrive at Biltmore Village in about twenty minutes."

Her eyes widened. "You mean there are two train stations in Asheville?"

He smiled, pulling on his gloves. "There are indeed. George Vanderbilt had a small depot constructed near Biltmore so that his guests wouldn't have far to travel after their arrival. It's quite convenient. Will I see you tonight at the party?" He paused, meeting her eyes while moving aside for an impatient passenger.

"Why, yes, of course." Her smile returned, as though pleased they would meet again.

"It will be a wonderful opportunity to unwind from our busy trip. But for now, I must make haste and visit my patients. I've been too long absent." He inclined his head. "Although it's Christmas Eve, sickness and disease know no holidays."

After Richard disembarked, Anna peered out the window, straining her eyes to see through the steamy mist of the train, until at last she saw him hurrying through the crowd. Her heart drummed with deafening force into her ears as he stopped and spun around, his eyes going straight to her window. She lifted her hand, making a small wave. He smiled and doffed his hat before disappearing into the crowd.

She closed her eyes for a moment, recalling the feel of his powerful arms as he'd lifted her away from danger, and imagined those same arms encircling her in a more intimate manner. What would it be like to have such a man protect her from the many troubles she now faced?

She attempted to curb the direction of her thoughts. There could be no dreams of gallant lovers. Her mind must remain focused on beginning a new life. As she settled back into her seat, great puffs of steam hung low in the winter air, swirling around the bustling attendants as they loaded the last trunks into the luggage car.

The conductor waved his arms and mounted the steps from the platform shouting, "All aboard!" After a final flurry of activity outside, a few stragglers scrambled on the train just in time before the great locomotive lurched forward, sputtering and chuffing past the station, building momentum for the last leg of her journey. A moaning wind rose like a sob and whipped around the train before settling into steady harmony with the steam whistle.

The early afternoon light cast a rainbow of colors around the trees, and she scooted closer to the window, bending her head low to view a hillside cabin where a woman tossed feed to a bevy of chickens. Farther down the tracks, a man paused from stacking wood beside his front porch. As the engineer blew the whistle in salutation, the man lifted his hat.

Only a few minutes passed before they entered an exquisite neighborhood of stately homes with exaggerated sloping roofs and big open porches. All of them boasted expansive front yards and neatly trimmed hemlock hedges. A little girl in a red dress stood alongside her nurse at the entry of her home, smiling as two workmen carried a huge Christmas tree through the imposing front door.

Shoppers rushed along the sidewalks, and snowflakes the size of goose feathers drifted through the air. Men turned their coat collars up, while women, wearing the latest fashion, braced themselves against the winter wind as they hurried out of stores, carrying stacks of packages tied with red twine.

A few of her fellow travelers began singing carols.

> *"Hark! The herald angels sing,*
> *Glory to the newborn king!*
> *Peace on earth and mercy mild,*
> *God and sinners reconciled."*

Her heart lifted with a new kind of gladness and she settled peacefully back into her seat. Soon the train entered a deep forest of thick pines, and a few seconds later, it slowed and came to a stop before a lovely bit of stone architecture, a perfect artistic match for its surroundings.

"Biltmore Station!" The conductor shouted.

Anna gathered her things and headed for the door. As soon as she stepped down, she saw her friend, Daphne Vanderbilt, waving from the platform, her golden curls rippling out from beneath a blue bonnet.

"There you are, dear." Daphne's chipper voice and bright eyes made her appear much younger than her actual age of 26 years. "You must be exhausted from your trip," she said, kissing her airily on both cheeks. "I can't believe you were delayed so long by the weather."

"I'm fine, really," Anna laughed. "I actually delivered a baby while waiting out the storm in Cumberland, Maryland."

Daphne's blue eyes widened with surprise. "Oh my, you—what? She lowered her voice to a whisper as a brakeman walked past them. "You delivered a *baby*?"

The sound of the station agent slamming trunks and luggage into the baggage room momentarily interrupted their conversation.

Anna smiled. "You'd be surprised at the number of babies born in the most unexpected places."

Daphne raised a questioning brow. "But—on a train? Is the mother alright?"

"Mother and son are doing fine, but I must admit it was a bit harrowing for a while, because the baby was breech." For a second, she relived those tense moments as her hands manipulated the baby into the right position while Richard kept a close watch on their patient's vital signs.

The pink came softly into Daphne's cheeks. Anna realized her friend was embarrassed and didn't know the meaning of a breech birth. It never failed to amaze her that most women seemed to have little knowledge about childbirth, other than the murmured conversations between married women.

An older couple shuffled toward them to board the train that was now puffing up for its journey. Anna waited until they passed before taking time to explain. "The baby was lying crosswise in his mother's womb," she whispered, as they continued down the platform.

Daphne blinked in surprise. "Was it because the mother was careless?"

Anna gave her friend a questioning look.

"For traveling so close to her confinement?"

"That wouldn't have caused the problem. They were not expecting the baby's arrival until mid-January and they had their own private rail car. The situation wasn't as bad as it sounds."

"So then—the baby came early?" Daphne still had a puzzled expression in her eyes.

Anna shook her head. "No, I don't think so. You see, sometimes it's easy to miscalculate one's due date. Anyway, both mother and baby are fine, but it could have been much worse," she said, remembering those tense moments.

"Oh, my, yes, I can imagine." Daphne's tone was solemn. The two women walked arm in arm around a stack of trunks that were tagged and waiting to be loaded on the train.

As they descended a flight of stairs leading to the street, Anna's heart jumped with excitement at the sight of a bright red sleigh awaiting them. A regal black stallion raised his head high, snorting great clouds of frost from his flared nostrils, his harness and bells jingling in the wind. "Is that—for us?"

A slow smile formed on Daphne's bow-like lips.

Anna laughed. "It's been years since I've ridden in a sleigh and this one looks as though it might have arrived directly from the North Pole!"

Daphne chuckled. "A few days ago, when the snow began to accumulate, I mentioned to Uncle George that it would seem more like Christmas if we could transport our guests to Biltmore in sleighs. The next thing I knew, he had it all arranged." She paused to take a breath. "Of course, most of our visitors arrived days ago, so you missed the big procession from the train station. It was quite enchanting, with all the bells jingling at once! Uncle George and I led the procession."

"You really do have a marvelous uncle!"

"Oh, he's extraordinary." Daphne's blue eyes sparkled. "He's so free-spirited, much more than the rest of my family" She lowered her voice as the coachman assisted them into the sleigh. "They all thought Uncle George was out of his mind for building a home so far away from New York." Daphne's curls bobbed from beneath the bonnet as she shook her head. "But he doesn't require the approval of others. I admire him for that."

Anna remembered her stepmother's words about George Vanderbilt, and how he lacked interest in the family business, preferring instead to spend his inheritance on a lavish lifestyle filled with artistic endeavors. "I can't blame him for wanting to get away from New York." She settled into the crimson velvet seat beside Daphne.

The liveried coachman covered them with an enormous bear-skin before climbing aboard to take the reins. Anna pulled a pair of warm gloves from her purse, removing the lighter ones she'd worn on the train. "I really want to hear all about what's been going on in your life," she said, turning to give her friend a smile. "Is it very far to the house?"

"At least thirty minutes. Just enough time to chat before the other guests overwhelm us. Oh my, are you engaged?" Daphne leaned closer to look at the pearl and diamond ring on Anna's ungloved hand.

"Heavens no. This belonged to my grandmother and I wear it for sentimental reasons." Anna gave a sharp laugh. "Of course, Claudette thinks I should be wed by now. She wanted to marry me off to my father's business partner."

Daphne rolled her eyes. "Why would your stepmother want you to marry that old flirt?"

Anna adjusted her cloak closer against the chill. "Papa died owing him a great deal of money and he foreclosed on our home. He froze all our bank accounts, and then proposed matrimony in exchange for all he had confiscated." She paused, swallowing back the painful memory. "Claudette thought I should do as he asked, to save us from embarrassment. He wanted a place in Society and knew he would be accepted married to someone of my pedigree, but I couldn't marry a man I didn't love."

Daphne reached for her hand. "I'm glad you didn't. It's always better to marry for love."

Anna brushed a strand of hair away from her forehead. "I've given up on love. I need to make my own way in this world without depending on anyone else."

Daphne narrowed her eyes. "Oh, you can't mean that Anna. You simply mustn't give up on love. But about Van Demark foreclosing on your home ... where are you staying?"

Anna swallowed another lump in her throat, stunned that she still became emotional when discussing her situation. "I'm staying at a boarding house near the hospital." She couldn't bring herself to mention that her new living quarters were in the most destitute part of the city.

Daphne frowned. "A boarding house? Oh, how brave you are. I would have gone straight to a hotel and checked into the most comfortable suite available."

Anna smiled, amused by her friend's naïveté. "There wasn't enough money for a hotel. Besides, the rooming house is walking distance to my patients."

Daphne's face was a puzzle of confusion. "Did Claudette move with you?"

Anna heard her own laughter echo throughout the surrounding woods. The idea of Claudette sharing the threadbare room was ludicrous. "Heavens no, she's been in Europe for the last year, her own trust fund still intact. Fortunately for her, Papa's business mistakes did not leave her destitute. But that's really a blessing. I don't know how I could have supported both of us."

Daphne's eyes flared with anger. "You mean she's frolicking across Europe while you struggle? Why didn't she share some of her money with you, I'd like to know?"

Anna took a deep breath, invigorated by the slight sting of cold air that filtered through her lungs. "She offered to give me an allowance as her companion, with the caveat that I give up my medical career. Claudette thinks my work as a doctor is unladylike."

Daphne sighed. "How I wish ladies didn't have to hide their brains behind manners and good breeding. But rest assured, you are welcome as my guest at Biltmore for as long as you like, and I will help you financially."

Anna squeezed Daphne's hand. "I couldn't take your money, dear. But I'm hoping to secure the post I applied for. That would help me get back on my feet again."

Daphne straightened in her seat. "Whether you get the situation or not, I still intend to help you. What are friends for?"

Anna opened her mouth to protest, but Daphne held up a warning hand. "We can discuss the particulars later. For now, let's enjoy this beautiful season of miracles and good will."

The ride to Biltmore was enchanting. Their breath rose in cloudy puffs against the frigid winter air, and sleigh bells announced their approach through a fairy-tale forest that glistened with appeal. As they traveled deeper into the wood, there came a soft murmur of gentle music from birds calling to one another from the tree tops. The threads of their song spun itself into a lovely harmony that seemed to shut the vaulted woodland away from the rest of the world.

Lost in the lure of her surroundings, Anna couldn't keep from thinking how romantic it would be to share this ride with Richard, and she imagined them enjoying the beautiful forest with all its allure.

Pressing her lips together, she squelched the daydream and focused on her friend. "Tell me all about this new love of yours, Daphne."

"Oh, how did you know?" Her face bloomed.

"Because you're sparkling!"

Her friend's eyes took on a dreamy look. "His name is Edward." Her tone became almost reverent. "We met last year, when Mumsie and I sailed to Europe. He'd just graduated from seminary and was on his way to preach at one of the great cathedrals there." The girl's eyes filled with sorrow. "Mumsie says he is beneath my station. But how can that matter? I love him and don't give a fig about whether or not he has money."

"Were you able to spend much time with him while abroad?"

"Oh yes, and we have corresponded faithfully ever since."

Daphne paused to wave at a couple who were skating without effort on a smooth, round pond bordering the drive. The skaters

waved in acknowledgment without missing a beat of the graceful
waltz, their joyful laughter mingling with the tinkling sleigh bells.

"Newlyweds." Daphne's tone was playful. "Uncle George was
best man at their wedding last summer. He invited them here for
Christmas, thinking their bliss might enhance our holidays."

Anna turned to look back at them, mesmerized by the way they
moved with such grace. An unexplained yearning made her wonder
if she might ever find this type of love. "Do tell me more about the
situation with Edward and your mother," she said, settling back
into her seat.

Daphne gave a short, unhappy laugh. "Mumsie has her heart
set on my marrying some British aristocrat. She wants me to have a
title, and I suppose she would love for all of society to revere her in
the same manner as they did Aunt Alva, when she married off poor
Consuelo to the Duke of Marlborough."

"Oh no," Anna cried out in dismay. She recalled the marriage
of Daphne's cousin, Consuelo Vanderbilt, only a few weeks earlier.
It had been hailed by the *New York Times* as the most beautiful wedding ever to take place in America, even though the bride had stood
at the altar, weeping behind her veil.

"Oh yes." Daphne's voice became testy. "Mother was recently
befriended by an impoverished duchess, and rumor has it that she's
on the hunt to find her eldest son a rich American." Her cupid lips
quivered. "Mumsie has invited them for a visit with us in Newport
next summer, but I have no intention of being there. Uncle George
has given me permission to remain here for as long as I want, but
Mumsie doesn't know this."

A sigh escaped Anna's lips. "Do you think your Aunt Alva is
playing a role in all this?"

Daphne nodded. "I believe so. Lately, Mumsie has been spending a lot of time with her. But I won't allow myself to be bound by
a miserable marriage like Consuelo. Oh, Anna, I have no desire to
become a Duchess." She released an agonizing sob and Anna handed

her a hankie. After dabbing away the tears, she gave a long sigh. "I'm sorry to be like this. It's no way to welcome my best friend, and I hope you'll forgive me."

"Nonsense," Anna said, patting her on the shoulder. "But whatever on earth are you going to do?"

The light returned to Daphne's eyes. "Edward has proposed marriage and I accepted. If I have it my way, we'll be wed when the Duke and his mother arrive in America.

Anna gave a little cry of joy. "Oh, my goodness, that's wonderful!"

Daphne inhaled a deep breath, as though drawing in strength. "Mumsie doesn't know it yet, but Uncle George is planning to talk with her after the holidays. He wants to try and make her understand how much Edward and I love each other. If that doesn't work, we plan to elope next summer. George has agreed to help us run away if necessary. He says he will never forget poor Consuelo's tears while standing at the altar and will not allow that same misfortune to happen in my life."

Daphne wiped away another tear, while the north wind sympathetically wailed up and down its own unique scale, rustling the brim on her bonnet and stirring up ice and snow sparkles around them.

"Is the wind always so forlorn here?" Anna pulled the bearskin rug tighter around her knees.

"I'm afraid so," Daphne giggled, her usual humor returning. "That's one thing Asheville has in common with Chicago. Both are windy cities."

Anna ran her hand back and forth along the fringe of the fur blanket. "I feel certain everything will work out for you and Edward, especially if George is willing to help. Do you want a big wedding?"

Daphne brightened. "Oh, goodness no. I want to be married right here at Biltmore, with only a few close friends present. Will you be my maid of honor?"

She blinked with surprise at her friend's sudden question. "Will I? It would be my privilege. I can't wait to meet Edward. I know he must be delightful."

Daphne's lips trembled through a smile. "Oh, Anna, he is truly the love of my life."

Considering her friend's words, Anna wondered what it might feel like to experience this kind of joy. "I'm very happy for you, dear friend, and I pray your uncle will get through to your mother. If she doesn't come over to your side, you should definitely shun tradition and follow your heart."

"Oh, thank you," Daphne said, through shining eyes. "I knew I could count on your support."

"Always." Anna nodded. "What are friends for?"

The horse slowed as the road wound into a dark ridge surrounded by tall pines. Rounding the next curve, nothing could have prepared Anna for her first glimpse of Biltmore House. It was every bit as splendid as the newspapers had claimed.

The majestic castle stood in the distance, its turrets and towers cradled by mountain ranges folding one behind the other in a wide spectrum of blues. Despite its imposing nature, it didn't dominate the surroundings, but seemed to emerge from the landscape as though it had always been there and completely belonged. The horse seemed to know his journey was almost finished and picked up speed, galloping right up to the big front door.

Daphne arose from her seat. "Isn't it magnificent?"

Anna nodded. "It really is. Especially with those beautiful mountains in the background."

They disembarked and climbed the limestone steps, guarded by two huge marble lions with their necks draped in holiday greenery. A gust of wind whipped through the valley and Anna shivered as the butler greeted them at the door.

⌐

Daphne made a quick introduction. "Bosworth, this is my friend, Dr. Anna St. James."

"So nice to meet you, doctor." He took their wraps. "Please excuse our temporary disarray. We're in somewhat of a fluster getting ready for the party."

A footman carried an arm full of holly, while behind him scurried a maid clutching the handles of a tray bearing a huge gingerbread house. The soaring marble arches in the entrance hall were centered by a circular solarium, filled with bright red poinsettias and holiday greenery. One of the servants balanced himself on a ladder while placing an ornament on a Christmas tree that swept all the way up to the second-floor balcony, and the surrounding arches opened to various rooms with swags of pine and cedar draped over the doorways.

Daphne touched her elbow while they walked toward the staircase. "I promised Grandmother I would accompany her into town today for some last-minute shopping. You're welcome to join us if you like."

Anna stifled a yawn. "No thank you, dear. I believe I shall take a rest. May I borrow one of your gowns for this evening? I'm afraid my wardrobe is down to its lowest terms," she whispered, not wanting to be overheard by the butler who was following a few steps behind.

"My room at the boarding house doesn't have a closet. Just a few hooks driven into the wall where I hang the dresses that I wear for work."

Daphne's eyes rounded. 'How horrible for you!"

Anna laughed. "It's not so bad, really. I managed to retain a few of my nicer things by stashing them into a steamer trunk that now doubles as a nightstand. But I didn't save any of my fancy gowns because I felt certain that *that* part of my life was over."

Daphne gave her a quick smile of reassurance. "You have more courage than anyone I know. And of course, you may borrow from me. Mumsie and I purchased a number of Worth gowns while in Paris earlier this year." She rolled her eyes. "I'm sure she must be preparing my royal wardrobe for the impoverished Duke."

Anna couldn't help but smile. Daphne had always been very light hearted and could see the humor in most situations.

A young woman wearing a pink uniform with white collar and cuffs walked hesitantly up to them and Daphne placed an arm around her shoulder. "Ellen, this is my best friend, Anna St. James. You will make certain she has everything she needs, won't you?"

"Yes, Miss Vanderbilt. Sure nough, I'll be glad to look after her." The girl had a soft Southern accent.

"Anna, you're in good hands." Daphne hurried up the stairs ahead of them, taking two steps at a time until disappearing from their sight.

The maid led Anna down a hallway, passing a collection of bedrooms with plaque holders on each door, indicating the name of the visitor residing within. Most were Vanderbilt family members from New York, but there were a few other names she recognized, including Edith Wharton, the novelist.

At last, they reached a more secluded wing where she was ushered into a luxurious suite, furnished in soft blue oriental carpets with similar shades of blue and green repeated throughout. The windows were endowed with silk draperies, pulled back to reveal a spectacular mountain view. A Christmas tree stood in the corner beside the fireplace and she took the time to examine the curious decorations of hand-painted ornaments.

The maid cleared her throat. "Miss, would ye' like for me to draw your bath? Nothin' better than a good soak to help a body relax."

Anna had grown accustomed to caring for herself. "No thank you my dear. If I need anything I'll ring for you."

The girl appeared puzzled for an instant, then bobbed a curtsy before leaving the room. Anna wandered into the luxurious bathroom, turned on the tap and sprinkled lavender salts from one of the decorative jars beside the tub. She gave an audible sigh of pleasure when sinking into the deep water, grateful to be enveloped by the steam.

For over a year, she had taken only sponge baths, unable to endure using the one grimy tub shared by all the residents in the boarding house. Even after a good scrubbing with bleach, it still appeared filthy, so she avoided it altogether. She had almost forgotten what a luxury it was to be covered by hot soapy water.

After a long soaking, she changed into her dressing gown and sat down on the plush sofa. Gazing into the crackling logs of the fireplace, her eyes moved upward to a huge portrait of Consuelo Vanderbilt above the mantle. The girl's hair was piled high on top of her head, making her appear much taller than she really was. Her body was straight and thin as a taper, a consequence no doubt, of all the hours she had spent strapped into a steel posture rod by her mother's mandate. The delicate girl looked elegant in her flowing coronation robes, but her sparkling tiara failed to draw attention away from the profound sorrow in her eyes. The thought of Daphne being condemned to a similar fate was heart-rending.

Trading money for the titles of cash-strapped British aristocrats was all the rage these days, a tactic of the newly rich to pretend superiority over The Four Hundred who would not admit them into their society. While Anna did not relish her own impoverished state, it was far better than being married to a man she didn't love. "All the more reason for women to become as independent as possible," she whispered up to the portrait.

The crackling fire hissed, as if in agreement, but the young girl's grieving eyes remained frozen in time, like a fairytale princess under some dark spell.

Chapter Eight

The horses squealed in protest as a gust of wind sent a mist of snow throughout the forest. The driver's quiet voice calmed the stallions, while Richard stared out at the sparkling white powder that glistened around the lanterns of his coach. Although the weather remained frigid, it failed to cool his face that was still warmed by the memory of Anna.

She seemed so utterly unspoiled, lacking the artifice of other girls he had known. But as much as he had enjoyed her company on the train from New York, he knew that after tonight's party he would most likely never see her again, a realization that caused his chest to tighten with unexplained melancholy. *Get her out of your mind*, his inner voice urged. *She's a woman doctor, probably a suffragette, and would never trade her way of life for a husband and family.*

The inner argument continued, until at last the soft grinding of stones beneath the carriage wheels ceased, and he saw the dark mustached George Vanderbilt welcoming guests from beneath the arched porte cochère of Biltmore.

"Glad to see you, old friend." Vanderbilt shook his hand. "How was your trip?"

Richard shoved a hand through his hair as they walked a few feet away from the arriving guests. "I was stranded in one blast of the blizzard that hit the East coast, but I can't complain, especially since I made it home before Christmas."

George laughed. "Ah yes, so I heard. Daphne's best friend was held up by that same snowstorm. It's likely you shared a train. She's a doctor, you know."

He felt his face grow warm but managed to remain nonchalant. "Yes, that would be Dr. St. James."

George paused for a moment to light his pipe. "I understand she graduated first in her class at medical school."

"Did she?" Richard visualized her walking across the stage to receive her degree and wondered how she might appear in the drab dark cap and gown. He decided the flush of her cheeks and stunning eyes would light up the darkest room.

An impudent smile played beneath Vanderbilt's dark mustache. "Nothing to say to that, old friend? Surely you would agree she is unique."

It took Richard an extra moment to find the right answer. "Yes." He kept his voice steady. "Especially compared to some of the other female physicians I have known."

George smiled like a man who had just discovered a secret.

"Don't get any ideas." Richard raised a warning hand. "It's not like that."

"No?"

"No. I've absolutely no intention of getting involved with a woman anytime soon. Maybe never."

George took several puffs from his pipe and tactfully changed the subject. "I want you to take a look at my new stallion. I took him riding earlier today and he couldn't get enough."

The snow crunched beneath their feet as they walked toward the stable. At the entrance, they were met by a liveried attendant, and Richard's astonished eyes scanned the glazed brick walls with Edison lamps. "You have the current in your stable?"

George gave a short laugh at his friend's disbelieving tone. "Indoor plumbing too. My groomsmen and drivers have apartments in the back and I want to make it pleasant for them, as well as for my horses."

Richard nodded. George Vanderbilt was a fine employer. He provided the locals with New York wages, and it was well known throughout the mountains that Biltmore was a blessing to the region's economy.

A groom brought out the jittery stallion, and George pulled a shiny red apple from his pocket, offering it to the eager horse. "Daphne has known Dr. St. James for many years," he said, stroking the steed gently. "Talk about beauty and brains."

"The woman doctor or the stallion?"

George chuckled. "You know of whom I speak."

Richard shrugged. "Yes, of course she is beautiful, but I was shocked to discover her profession."

George continued to stroke the horse. "Maybe she wants to make a difference in the world. Isn't that why you became a doctor?"

Richard groped for an excuse. "Women aren't blessed with the temperament to practice medicine."

The horse finished eating the fruit, then snorted and pounded his hooves on the cobbled floor, causing them to chuckle.

"Oh, I don't know about that," George said, patting the horse's withers. "As a child, I always ran to my mother when I injured myself and found her to be far more consoling and helpful than my father." He paused for a moment as though thinking it through. "Maybe we just haven't given women a chance to show us what they are made of." He gave a little wave of his hand. "Lots of ladies are moving out West to start businesses, and Annie Oakley is making a name for herself as a professional sharpshooter. Times are changing, Wellington, and I for one do not wish to be left behind."

Richard was relieved for the opportunity to divert attention from his personal life, steering their conversation back to the woman sharpshooter. "I saw Annie Oakley perform in London when she was touring with Cody's Wild West troupe. My little sister was determined to go, so I accompanied her."

George's dark eyes widened. "Well, upon my soul, was that when the little beauty shot the tip off of Prince Wilhelm's cigar?"

Richard laughed. "It was indeed. The crown prince asked her to shoot the cigar from his *mouth,* but she refused, saying she would shoot the ash off the tip if he'd hold it in his hand. No one thought she could do it. The audience became silent as a tomb when she raised that big gun of hers and knocked the fire right off the end of his cigar *with one shot.* I tell you, the crowd went wild and gave her a standing ovation, led by none other than Queen Victoria."

Amazement shone from George's eyes. "My, that must have been a real sight to behold. I'd really love to see Annie Oakley perform. Do you think I could get her to do a show in Asheville?"

Richard shrugged. "You might. Perhaps you could invite her to Biltmore for a July Fourth celebration."

George stroked his mustache. "It might be worth a try. Of course, she's probably booked years in advance. Women today are so forward-thinking." A sudden sparkle appeared in his eyes. "During my last trip to Paris, I met a beautiful young American who believes women should have the right to vote." He paused. "At first it was a bit odd to hear her talk—and talk intelligently, mind you, about politics and suffrage." He gave Richard a mischievous grin. "I'm returning abroad after the holidays to visit her again."

"Is it serious?" The groomsman led the horse back to its stall and they walked back out into the brisk night.

"Could be," he said. "Edith loves the arts as much as I do." He lifted one hand in a casual gesture, his pipe's smoke curling upward. "She comes from a prominent family, and her great uncle was Peter Stuyvesant, the first governor of New York."

Richard noticed his friend seemed happier than usual. "Could your bachelor days be nearing an end?"

George laughed and clapped him on the back. "If that should be the case old chap, you'll be the first to know. But for now, let us put aside this talk of females. I've been considering planting a vineyard, and I'd like to discuss it before getting tied down to party matters."

⌒

Anna sat up on the sofa with a yawn and smoothed her hair. The clock told her she'd slept away the entire afternoon.

"I see you're awake now." The maid's Southern accent had a sing-song lilt. "I came in earlier, but you were sleeping like a rock, so I decided not to wake you. Miss Daphne sent up some dresses." The girl nodded toward the two footmen who carried a large trunk, placing it at the foot of the bed.

"What time is the party?"

"Oh, it's already started, Miss." Ellen nonchalantly turned up the Edison lamps and opened the trunk.

Anna arose from the sofa. "Then I should make haste."

Ellen removed the tissue paper from gowns that were in the trunk and began shaking them out. "Ah, you don't have to hurry none, Miss. They won't be dinin' til nine o'clock, and the guests are just now arriving—the local ones, that is."

The trotting of hooves lured Anna to the window. Sumptuously clothed ladies wearing glittering jewels were disembarking from carriages below her balcony. Other coaches were turning into the private entrance to drop off guests. She drew a deep breath, relieved she had plenty of time to get ready for the evening ahead.

Ellen pulled a long sigh. "Why, I'd be half-starved if I waited that long to eat my supper. Of course, nine o' clock is a far better time to eat than later. At some parties, they don't serve food until midnight. But Mr. Vanderbilt is a good Christian man, and bein' that it's Christmas Eve, he scheduled an earlier dinner. I guess he figured some of his guests might want to attend midnight services."

Anna went over to get a closer look at the soft green gown that Ellen was holding.

"All these gowns are real pretty," Ellen said matter-of-factly, "but I think this one here would suit your hair and complexion best." She smiled. "See, it has nice long sleeves to keep you warm, and it's not low-necked, so you won't catch your death wearing it."

Anna slipped into the evening dress and stood before the mirror, admiring the strands of Nile green and golden-brown beads that trimmed the long bishop sleeves and high neck. "This one is perfect. I agree with your choice, Ellen."

The girl's smile revealed a lovely dimple in her cheek. "Do you need me to arrange your hair, Miss? I just finished fixing Miss Daphne's a little while ago."

Anna stepped back into her robe. "Yes, that would be wonderful of you," she said.

Ellen folded the selected dress over her arm. "Let me go get this pressed. I'll be back in two shakes of a lamb's tail to get your hair gussied up for the party."

Anna had finished her tea when the girl returned with the gown. After getting dressed, she sat down at the mirror while Ellen swept her hair into a chignon on top of her head, taking care to leave a pleasing fullness that framed her face.

"Miss Daphne sent this to you," she said, fastening a necklace of diamonds around her neck.

"How dear of her," Anna said, viewing the back of her hair through a silver-handled mirror. "Ellen, you are a talented stylist!"

"Thank you, ma'am." Ellen stood back to study her handiwork. "I'd sure like to open my own salon someday, but for now I guess I'll stick to doing the hair of guests here at Biltmore."

"You'd do well in your own salon."

Ellen smiled. "I appreciate you saying that. And I don't think you need any other jewelry except the necklace. She sent matching earrings and a bracelet, but that might take away from the good lines of the gown. What do you think, doctor?"

Anna nodded. "I don't like wearing a lot of baubles, and the dress *is* elaborate enough on its own. You have excellent taste."

"Thank you, Miss. If you need anything else, just ring that little bell." She bobbed a curtsy before hurrying out of the room.

Not quite ready to go downstairs, Anna walked out on the balcony for a breath of fresh air. It had stopped snowing, and the sky was filled with clusters of stars that shone over the long line of carriages below.

While taking in a deep breath, she felt a new appreciation for her surroundings. It was wonderful to be away from the constant noises she heard each night from her lumpy bed in the rooming house. Drunken outcries, screaming babies, voices that were shrill and others that were thick, made Asheville feel like heaven.

Her thoughts traveled to Mrs. Astor, who would now be overseeing last minute preparations for her annual Christmas party. There would be murmurs about Claudette's trip abroad, and whispers of her own move into a boarding house. After an elaborate dinner, the men would retire to the library for cigars and brandy, talking about the dreaded "new people" who were proving to be the ruination of New York society. They would thrash out various ways of welcoming Claudette back into the fold, after an acceptable time had passed.

Anna shook these thoughts aside, returning to her room. Walking over to the oval gilt-framed mirror, she looked at the pleasant style of her gown, pleased by how the forest green color complemented her skin and hair. The full skirt, embellished by points of white silk all around the hem, flattered her small waist. It had been ages since she'd been to a party. Perhaps it would be fun to forget about everything for a few hours and enjoy the holiday spirit.

The first-person Anna spotted as she descended the grand staircase was George Vanderbilt, greeting his guests in the entrance hall. The flickering candlelight played against his slender build, making him appear almost ethereal. As she drew closer, his eyes lit up with recognition. "Good evening, Dr. St. James. What a pleasure to see you again. How long has it been?" He extended his hand.

Although society mandated that a lady never shake hands with a gentleman, offspring of the *nouveau riche* had dispensed with much of the "Old New York" protocol. She rather liked the informality and extended both gloved hands in a sisterly fashion. "It's been far too long, and I'm delighted to be here." She swept an arm toward the marble fountain encircled by poinsettias. "Biltmore is far more beautiful than I imagined."

Vanderbilt's eyes strayed over to the area she had implied, as though seeing the artistic arrangement for the first time. "Thank you. It's truly a pleasure to have you celebrate the holidays with us."

"The pleasure is all mine," she said. "The sleigh ride from the train depot put me right in the Christmas spirit. Daphne and I spent the entire interval recalling old times!"

His eyes held a glint of warmth. "I'm planning a coaching party for my guests next week and I hope you'll join us. It was Daphne's idea, so it's bound to be lots of fun."

Anna laughed. "I'm sure it will be. Daphne has a natural ability to create pleasurable recreation."

"Indeed. It seems my niece never runs out of plans, especially when it comes to merry-making." George lowered his voice. "Daphne really needs your support right now. I understand she shared some things with you earlier."

Anna nodded. "Yes, and she can always count on me for encouragement."

The look of relief came over his face. "Thank you."

A footman appeared and escorted her into the baronial banquet hall as imposing as a medieval castle. Crystal glasses and silver cutlery gleamed against a white table cloth, and an enormous chandelier, all decked out in holiday greenery, was suspended over the center. Electric lights of various colors illuminated a majestic tree that stood beside the fireplace, and the scent of pine filled the air.

Daphne wore an elegant blue gown of crepe de Chine that matched her eyes. Her neck and ears were decorated with diamonds.

"My, but you do look stunning." Anna touched her friend's arm.

Daphne smiled, an impish light in her eyes. "Mumsie insisted on this heavy jewelry. She wants me to practice wearing these burdensome trinkets, so I can show them off to the impoverished Duke when he visits next year." She shook her head, causing a blonde curl to bounce against a dangling earring.

"Did your mother really say that?"

The girl rolled her eyes. "Yes, but I'm trying to go along with whatever she wants so she'll stop breathing down my back." She lowered her voice to a whisper as they were seated at the table. "Consuela's biggest mistake was protesting her mother's wishes and threatening to run away with the man she really loved."

Anna gave her friend a sympathetic nod, remembering the stories of Consuelo's mother locking her daughter into her room a week before the wedding, to prevent her escape. Hopefully, George Vanderbilt would not allow Daphne to suffer the same fate.

Suddenly, Dr. Wellington entered the room and Daphne tugged on Anna's sleeve. "Isn't he dashing? I made certain Bosworth seated him across from us."

Anna had to admit that her friend was right. He did appear quite distinguished in his formal black tailcoat, superbly molded to his broad shoulders. He stopped for a moment to converse with one of the other guests before scanning the room. His dark hair sparkled with the residue of snowflakes, causing a few dampened locks to curl over the back of his collar. Their eyes met, and her heart became a flutter of butterflies when he walked toward her with a purposeful stride.

"Merry Christmas, Anna."

She smiled, hoping no one could hear her heart that beat like a kettle drum. "Merry Christmas, Richard. It's still cold, but at least we aren't trapped in a blizzard."

He gestured toward the triple fireplace where huge logs blazed high. "The fire makes this mammoth room feel almost cozy."

Daphne caught his dry humor and giggled. "I think Uncle George is burning an entire tree all at once. Earlier this afternoon, my young cousins were having great fun playing in that hearth and they certainly didn't like being hustled out of it for the logs to be stacked for tonight's event. All they could talk about was finding *another* one to play in."

The rich and throaty sound of his laughter lifted Anna's spirits. "That's because they're excited about Santa's arrival. After all, a cool and empty fireplace will be his most likely point of entry."

Before anyone could offer a comment, the renowned author and socialite, Edith Wharton, entered. As always, she was the epitome of understated good taste in her chic black gown with elegant rubies nestled at the base of her throat. She and her husband were seated next to Richard.

"How lovely to see you, dear," she addressed Anna. "I had tea with your Aunt Mildred last week, and she filled me in on all the wonderful things you're doing for women and children on the Lower East End."

"You are most kind." Anna was certain the woman knew all about her financial downfall, but Mrs. Wharton wasn't a snob. Born into the cradle of New York society, her pursuit as a writer had made her somewhat of an outcast among The Four Hundred, with many referring to her as a Bohemian.

Daphne gave a playful grin. "Her work stretches beyond the confines of New York, Mrs. Wharton. She now delivers babies on trains."

Daphne's mother, who was seated farther down the table, leaned forward to give her daughter a stern glare. It seemed to Anna that her friend shrank before her eyes.

Mrs. Wharton looked surprised, but tactfully did not comment, turning her attention back to Anna. "I'm writing an article for *The Ladies Journal,* about the poor working conditions inside that dreadful shirtwaist factory on the East End. It would be marvelous to hear your thoughts on the likely dangers therein, and how we might help."

Anna started to reply, but a sudden hush fell over the room as George Vanderbilt entered alongside his mother. Maria Louisa Vanderbilt was well past her sixtieth year, but her posture and fine bones reflected a still youthful beauty. After she was seated, George addressed his guests.

"Friends," he said, looking about on all his guests, "ten years ago, while visiting Asheville with my dear mother, I decided to make my home here in these lovely mountains and surround myself with art from all over the world." He paused, then with a flourish of his hand, ended, "I now give you Biltmore, my little mountain escape, finally finished, for the most part." Amidst the chuckles he continued, "I am honored to have all of you here during my favorite time of year. Mother will now ask the blessing; afterwards, we shall all stand for a Christmas toast."

Everyone bowed their heads as the Vanderbilt matriarch prayed in a sweet old voice that still had the vibrant quality of youth in its fringes. The prayer gave Anna a sense of peace, making her glad to have accepted Daphne's invitation, instead of spending the holidays alone in her room, or having Christmas dinner in some cheap dinette.

At the prayer's end, they all stood, and George raised his champagne glass for a toast. "In this season of good will, may all of you receive the blessings of joy, excellent health, and a prosperous New Year. Merry Christmas, and God bless you, everyone."

Everyone lifted their glasses in response. "Merry Christmas!"

The butler gave a subtle nod to the pianist stationed in the corner of the banquet hall and the young man's fingers touched the keys, producing the opening notes of *God Rest Ye Merry Gentlemen*. The tune lightened the atmosphere with an additional layer of festivity, while footmen served the first course of Consommé Royale.

It had been a long time since Anna had tasted anything so delicious. The rich broth served with a savory garnish of hard-boiled eggs and herbs had always been a holiday favorite. Nowadays, her diet consisted of simple foods, mostly bread and cheese, with black tea, and maybe an occasional piece of fruit when she could spare a few extra pennies.

Mrs. Wharton seemed to have forgotten about asking for her opinion about the shirtwaist factory, turning her attention to Dr. Wellington. "Where is that beautiful young woman I remember so well? I'd heard the two of you were engaged."

Anna's heart fell with disappointment. Of course, there would be someone special in his life. With his broad shoulders and handsome demeanor, why wouldn't there be? He was gorgeous.

"Julia and I are no longer betrothed." His answer was quiet, his words almost lost behind the pianist's lively tune.

Hope returned to her heart, while a powerful sense of guilt pervaded her conscience. How could she allow herself to feel joy over his loss? What on earth was wrong with her? She simply must snap out of it and think about someone other than this handsome doctor.

With a quick suffusion of color, Mrs. Wharton apologized. "I am so sorry—I—I didn't know, doctor. Forgive my blunder."

He waved aside her words. "You couldn't have known. Julia and her mother returned to Chicago over two years ago. We decided to say little about it. You know how the gossips love to focus on such things."

Mrs. Wharton nodded, quickly changing the subject by talking about her latest trip to Great Britain, but a palpable tension remained in the air, until the irrepressible Daphne broke in.

"Dr. Wellington, I hope you haven't forgotten about the children's party tomorrow afternoon. You'll be there, won't you?"

Chapter Nine

Richard glanced up from his consommé, relieved to move away from the topic of his ex-fiancé. "Certainly. How many children do you expect to attend, Miss Vanderbilt?"

"At least sixty, perhaps more." Her voice chirped with enthusiasm. Then, to several listening guests she explained, "Uncle George is having a party for the children of his staff tomorrow afternoon, and I'm overseeing it. Santa will be there, and we plan to have lots of games, refreshments, and gifts."

Richard chuckled in an attempt to lighten the atmosphere. "My function at the party will be to provide medical treatment for anyone who shows up sick." He shook his head. "It hardly seems fair. I'd much rather play the role of Santa, or at least have charge of games and refreshments."

Daphne feigned a pout. "Well, really, Dr. Wellington, I wish I'd known how you felt before I forced Uncle George into playing Santa. I'm sure he would love for you to take his place."

"Oh no." He held up a warning hand. "I wouldn't want to miss the opportunity of seeing George all decked out in a Santa costume. I shall, as always, play the role of healer while watching from the sidelines."

Daphne brushed a curl from her forehead. "The staff had *their* Christmas party this morning." Her voice trailed off as though she wanted to say more.

Anna gave her friend a faint smile. "And how was it? Did the staff enjoy themselves?"

"Oh yes, it was grand. Everyone had lots of fun, especially after Santa presented each of them with a nice bonus check."

"I've heard about the generous Christmas bonuses George gives his staff," Mrs. Wharton lamented. "If my own servants were to hear of his generosity they might revolt."

"Uncle George believes it's his duty to care for the servants." Daphne's tone became more serious as the pianist transitioned into a softer tune. "The staff at Biltmore are loyal and hard-working."

Richard nodded. "If everyone treated their employees as well as George, it would certainly be a better world."

George spoke up. "It seems I have a cheering section at the end of my table. Raise your voice, Daphne, so that everyone will hear all the good things you're saying about me."

Daphne giggled. "A good thing we were praising you, uncle. I'd forgotten about the perfect acoustics of this room."

George took a sip of champagne. "Daphne is correct about my staff being hard working and loyal. They deserve every penny of their pay and I consider myself blessed to have each one of them." Then, as an afterthought, he raised his glass. "To the staff at Biltmore!"

"To the staff at Biltmore." The dinner guests echoed his sentiments.

"Teddy and I spoil our servants too, don't we, dear?" Mrs. Wharton turned to her husband who gave a low harrumph while slurping down the last spoonful of Consommé.

"Most servants are paid far more than they're worth." He glanced up at the butler who was refilling his wine glass. "Give em an inch and they'll take a mile."

Mrs. Wharton cast the butler a honeyed smile. "Pay my husband no mind, Bosworth. He was speaking about our own staff back home, and not the fine employees at Biltmore."

"Certainly, Madam." Bosworth gave Mrs. Wharton a subdued smile, his bearing appeared more like royalty than subservience.

Mrs. Wharton resumed her conversation, while the second course of broiled Spanish mackerel and cucumber salad was served. "I've been interviewing women who work at the shirtwaist factory and those poor souls are locked into that dark sweatshop for the entire duration of their shift." Dabbing her lips with a napkin, she gave an audible sigh. "I'm certain none of them could escape, should the building catch fire. Something simply has to change for the better soon, or you'll see my picture in the papers, heading up a march on behalf of suffrage."

She raised her eyes heavenward, as though appealing to the Deity. "We simply must have the right to vote. How else can we convince the men in power to help those poor women who are working in factories without a labor union?"

Anna gestured her impatience. "I sometimes think we may never have the vote. At least not in the East. Perhaps we should move to Denver, where women can *already* cast their ballots in national elections."

Mrs. Wharton raised her glass again. "Well, bully for Colorado! At least they've given their female citizens a chance to participate in political decisions."

"Hear, hear!" Daphne rejoined.

Richard clenched his jaw, unable to hide his annoyance. "Ladies, I was in Denver four years ago, and I had to arm myself for protection. The streets were filled with mud and gunfire. Colorado is certainly no place for a lady."

Anna's turquoise irises flashed. "My colleague has a medical practice in Denver and she enjoys living there. She will be casting her ballot in the presidential election next year. So, you see, the mud and gunfire are insignificant compared to having the full privilege of American citizenship."

Richard was puzzled. How could something as simple as casting a ballot motivate a lady to trudge through mud and mire and all sorts of danger?

Clasping both hands together, Mrs. Wharton leaned forward. "Anna, my dear, you are tempting me to relocate. Let's do, Teddy," she said, turning to her husband. "We could move to Colorado next spring and I'd be able to vote in the presidential election, come autumn."

Mr. Wharton gave his wife a sharp glance, but she seemed undaunted by his obvious disapproval. "Journalists are predicting the presidential campaign between McKinley and Bryan will be the most dramatic in American history. How wonderful it would be to vote in this election. Perhaps all of us ladies should move to Denver!"

"I am actually considering it." Anna's voice rose.

"Are you really?" Mrs. Wharton almost knocked over her water glass.

Anna took a sip of Champagne. "Well, the western frontier needs doctors and it would be an excellent place to start a medical practice, not to mention the additional benefit of having my vote counted in local and national elections."

Mrs. Wharton nodded her approval. "If you decide to go, I hope you'll extend an invitation. After you're settled, of course."

Anna nodded while taking a dainty bite of mackerel.

Richard tried to curb his irritation. These women had no idea what it was like out West, yet they spoke of it with the same excitement as a shopping trip!

Taking a long swig of ice water, he allowed the crisp liquid to cool his throat before speaking. "Anna, practicing medicine in Denver would be even more dangerous than making house calls on the Lower East Side. In New York, you might at least get the attention of a policeman in a dangerous situation, but in Colorado you'd be lucky to find a lawman who wasn't paid off by some wealthy cattle rancher or saloon owner."

The color in Anna's cheeks deepened. "My colleague carries a .38 revolver for protection. Perhaps I'll learn to shoot and do the same."

"Good for you." Mrs. Wharton clasped her hands together with delight. "A lady should always be prepared to defend herself." Shifting her focus, "Now, Dr. Wellington, I do wish you'd tell us more about your experience on the western frontier." She waggled a delicate finger. "And don't hold back. Do tell us, how long were you there?"

Still reeling from the visual of Anna carrying a gun, Richard did a quick search through his memory for a story he could share in mixed company. "I was there for three months while my colleague convalesced from pneumonia. That was four years ago, but during my tenure, I removed bullets from the limbs of outlaws and set the bones of men who brawled all weekend while spending their entire pay envelopes at saloons."

Daphne's fork slipped from her fingers and clanked on the china plate, her face pale. "I suppose I shall have to wait until suffrage is passed here in the East. It would be dreadful to live in a place such as that."

Richard was sorry he had spoiled Daphne's appetite, but he hoped she would influence Anna to stay on the East Coast where she belonged. Otherwise, he might spend the rest of his life worrying about her safety.

Mrs. Wharton chuckled. "There, there, Daphne, let's not toss in the towel just yet. Tell us more, doctor." She gave him a coquettish grin.

He leaned back in his seat. "I stayed at a first-rate hotel, believing I'd be insulated from the constant ruckus of blaring music and gunfire. Unfortunately, my lodging was directly across the street from a saloon where liquor flowed like a river, and at sundown the roads and sidewalks became thick with drunks and brawlers. Forgive the crude picture I paint, but as I said, Colorado is no place for a lady."

Anna's chin shot up. "So, your visit to Colorado was four years ago?"

"Yes, shortly after my move to America." He watched, in amazement, at the transformation that came over her, reminding him of the cat that swallowed the canary. What was she thinking? No sooner than the question formed within his mind, he saw the answer coming as she squared her lovely shoulders.

"The women of Colorado have been voting in local elections for the last two years. Since that time, their stand on temperance has closed many saloons and forced others out of town. I'm sure you would now find Denver far more pleasant."

Mrs. Wharton added a pat of butter to her bread. "Come to think of it, I remember reading something about that in *The New York Times*. As I recall, the only major opposition to women's suffrage in Colorado was from the brewery industry. Apparently, they were concerned that closures might come if Colorado women were able to vote." She gave a light laugh. "As it turned out, their fears were justified."

"You're exactly right, Mrs. Wharton." Anna's voice was triumphant. "Their scheme backfired when the bar girls made known their sympathy for the suffrage cause. Many of them were—uh—working seven days a week and felt that women voters would impose stricter laws."

Daphne giggled. "I'm sure they deserved a day off."

Anna gave her friend a sidelong glance. "Women voters in Colorado helped close many of the saloons in Denver, and across the state. Even those on the borders can no longer open their doors on Sunday, and missionaries are now able to plant new churches for the families who live there. This has been a tremendous blessing to the entire area."

"I had no idea," Richard said. "To think that a group of ladies might be able to do such a thing is quite amazing."

A slight frown ridged Anna's brow. "Not *just* a group of ladies, Richard, but a huge number of women *voters*. Without suffrage they couldn't have closed down the saloons."

Richard chided himself for stirring her ire. He'd heard men talk about being in the doghouse for not saying the correct thing to their wives or sweethearts. Once again, he'd fallen back into the rabbit hole of Wonderland, into a new world that ran on different principles.

Oiling the conversational tension, Mrs. Wharton didn't miss a beat. "Speaking of churches, is anyone here familiar with the choir from Trinity Parish? Teddy and I heard them caroling this afternoon while shopping downtown. They were delightful."

Daphne smiled. "I have, and I just loved their rendition of *Jingle Bells.*"

Mrs. Wharton nodded. "That's exactly what they were singing today. It was so cheerful I wanted to dance a jig."

By the time their main course of roasted turkey was served, Anna's brow had smoothed out. The controversial discussion of suffrage and politics had been replaced by low key chatter, intended to keep everyone on friendly terms.

Richard sighed from deep within his chest. Yes, he was back in Wonderland. He hadn't yet seen a rabbit wearing a waistcoat, but what of it? These ladies were of a new ilk, forcing him to remember George's warning about being left behind during changing times. Wasn't it correct to shield females from life's harsher realities? Only a few days ago, his answer would have been yes. Now he wasn't so sure.

∾

After dinner, guests began recessing to the ballroom, where an orchestra played a gentle waltz, and soft candlelight cast fascinating shadows on the rustling gowns, dazzling jewels, and elaborate hair-styles bedecked with feathers. The scene reminded Anna of an exotic bouquet. From across the room Richard smiled in her direction and she glanced away, pretending not to notice.

Daphne leaned in. "He looks at you with unveiled admiration, Anna. I wish you wouldn't ignore him."

Anna took a sip of the fruity punch that had been handed to her by a footman. "I'm afraid he is too old fashioned for my taste. Besides, he doesn't believe women should have the right to vote!"

Daphne's eyebrows pinched into a frown. "He never actually said he's against suffrage, did he?"

"Tiddlywinks. He didn't have to!" Anna marveled at her friend's naiveté. "Didn't you see the disapproval in his eyes while we were discussing it? Women deserve a chance to excel every bit as much as a man, but I can assure you he doesn't believe we should have the right to cast our ballots. She emptied her glass.

Daphne clucked her tongue. "Neither does Edward, but I'm sure he'll come around after we're married."

Anna ignored her friend's remark and lowered her voice. "What happened between Richard and his fiancée?"

Daphne grasped Anna's elbow, leading her to one of the corner Christmas trees where they would have more privacy.

"I'm not exactly sure." She reached to remove a small nutcracker dangling from one of the lower branches, pretending to study it while they talked. "Only a short time before they were to marry, she returned to Chicago and the poor man was devastated. For months, he barely slept or ate." Pausing, she placed the ornament back on the tree. "Uncle George was convinced that his patients were the only thing keeping him alive."

Anna sucked in her breath. "He seemed so sad when Mrs. Wharton brought up the subject. I couldn't help feeling bad for him."

Daphne glanced around casually, as though to be sure no one was within earshot. "According to Uncle George, Julia wanted him to put aside his medical practice."

Anna gasped. "Why on earth?"

Daphne rolled her eyes. "Because she thought he should take his rightful place back in Great Britain as a duke. She didn't know he had abdicated the title to his younger brother, years earlier."

"Are you telling me that Richard Wellington is a duke?" Anna almost choked on her punch. This explained his natural poise, developed over generations of time.

Daphne giggled. "Yes, he really is a duke, and not an impoverished one either. But according to George, he never liked the idea of reigning over his village. Since early childhood he wanted nothing so much as to become a doctor and practice medicine. Hard to believe, isn't it?"

"Yes," Anna said, feeling herself soften. "That's an amazing story, to give up one's title in exchange for a life of service to the sick."

Daphne let out an exasperated breath. "He may be a bit old fashioned, but I still like him. And he's smitten by you. I haven't seen him smile this much in a long time. You seem to have broken through the ice around his heart."

Anna's pulse quickened as the topic of their conversation crossed the ballroom in their direction and Daphne suddenly disappeared.

He offered a slight bow. "I wonder—would you do me the honor of this dance?"

His deep voice sent tingles down her spine. She hadn't danced since her first and only season, seven years earlier. Could she carry out a simple waltz without tripping over her own two feet? She nodded, heart dipping in a confusing mix of fear and delight.

Feeling the heat of his hand come to rest in the small of her back, she placed her left hand on his shoulder, and with all the ease of a man used to leading, he guided her forward and they fell in step with the other dancers, floating away on the soft waves of a Christmas waltz.

He was a good dancer, directing her effortlessly between the other couples while smiling down into her eyes. "What do you think of Biltmore so far?"

His deep and throaty voice caused her heart to drum in hard slow thuds. "It's all quite remarkable really, the way George has managed to create such a beautiful home. So many lovely furnishings and paintings, yet it all blends together artistically."

"George searched for the décor of this house long before Biltmore existed." He broke off, whirling her past two other couples. "Even now, he claims the place is still a work in progress."

She gave a quick glance around the opulent ballroom with its Christmas trees and flower laden tables. The Vanderbilts, the Goelets and their *nouveau riche* contemporaries had managed to raise the bar on society entertainment to the heights of extravagance not previously seen. Anna's late father and her stepmother came from a Knickerbocker background and would judge the scene as gaudy but typical.

As though reading her mind, Richard glanced around once more at their surrounding decorations. "We have an adage in Great Britain that *less is more*, but the American motto seems to be, *the more the better*."

Anna chuckled. "I suppose we Americans do have a tendency towards excess. Perhaps our love of the lavish is a rebellious carryover from the class oppressive system of your country. We like having the freedom to be as flamboyant as your royals."

His eyes glinted with amusement. "When I first came to America, I was disappointed to discover the class order that thrives here, especially in New York. Somehow, I expected to find more of a pioneer spirit and less snobbery than what I left behind in England."

Anna felt her exasperation return. "But you *did* witness that pioneer spirit in Denver, and you didn't like it."

"*Touché!* I walked right into that one, didn't I?" He held up his hands in mock surrender as Tchaikovsky's *Waltz of the Flowers* came to an end. "You are a most remarkable woman, Anna St. James. I suspect if I spent more time with you, I'd soon be marching with women for suffrage."

"Would that be such a bad thing?"

He laughed. "I must admit you make a good case."

The music started up again and Anna turned to walk away from him, wondering how he could not be in favor of suffrage. It seemed ludicrous, especially after what she had shared about the closing of saloons in Denver.

In seconds, he caught up with her. "Are you angry with me?"

She shrugged. "It's difficult for me to understand why you are not in favor of women's suffrage. It seems absurd, especially for someone of your intellect."

He smiled as if he found her words to be refreshing, or perhaps just foolish and immature. She wasn't sure.

"Forgive my old-fashioned attitude." He placed a hand over his heart. "My little sister recently accused me of antiquated thinking and she is probably correct. But sometimes I feel as though I'm running to catch up with all the changes, and sorting them out has become somewhat overwhelming."

The look in his eyes made her feel almost cruel for badgering him. He dragged a hand through his hair, and when one defiant lock fell across his forehead, it was all she could do to prevent herself from reaching up and smoothing it back into place. Instead, she reached for the painted silk fan attached to the belt of her dress, waving it back and forth across her face. "At least you're willing to try."

He smiled. "Would you care to join me for some fresh air?"

She nodded, tucking her gloved hand into the crook of his arm. While making their way through the crowd, Alva Vanderbilt, wearing a black gown that glittered with too many sapphires, stopped them dead in their tracks.

"Dr. Wellington," She called. "How is your dear mother? I simply must invite her to tea during my next visit with Consuela."

"I'm certain she would enjoy your company, Mrs. Vanderbilt," he said with gallantry. You know Dr. St. James, don't you?"

Alva regarded her with glacial indifference. "Oh, of course, Miss St. James. I do hope you are faring well these days." She drew a bit closer, peering at them through a gold-handled lorgnette.

In their world of unspoken meanings, Alva was proclaiming full knowledge of Anna's financial ruin, and for the briefest moment, Anna felt self-conscious. Not wanting the older woman to get the best of her, she replied, "How very thoughtful of you to be concerned for me."

Alva pursed her lips, causing the wrinkles to deepen around her mouth. "I'm rather surprised you aren't in Europe with Claudette."

Before Anna could formulate a reply, Alva excused herself and hurried away to annoy someone else.

As they walked out on the balcony, Anna leaned toward the bannisters, looking out at the snowy mountains and fields that were bathed in moonlight. The light fragrance of hemlock and pine wafted around them, blending with the faint spicy smell of his aftershave.

Richard breathed a long sigh. "Hard to believe that only yesterday we were buried under a snow storm."

She glanced up at him, giving a slow nod of agreement, and her heart came alive as he leaned down, his lips almost touching hers.

"So, there you are!" Mrs. Wharton's voice broke the sweetness between them. "Daphne and I have been looking everywhere for you. Mrs. Vanderbilt will soon read *Twas the Night before Christmas* to her grandchildren and thought you might like to join us in the nursery."

"Yes!" they both answered at the same time.

Richard cleared his throat. "We were just getting—some fresh air."

"Oh, of course." Mrs. Wharton's tone was light, while eyeing them with a little knowing smile. "Ballrooms do tend to grow stuffy. Follow me, and we'll pretend to be children while Mrs. Vanderbilt reads to us."

As they proceeded upstairs to the nursery, Mrs. Wharton noted all the decorations, praising the beauty of Biltmore's architecture, while Anna smiled with distraction. She was unable to push aside her curiosity of how Richard's lips might have felt against hers, and a little tingle rushed down her back. Surely the sugarplums Mrs. Vanderbilt read about were nowhere near as sweet as the kiss that almost occurred on the balcony.

Chapter Ten

When Anna awoke on Christmas morning, her thoughts immediately returned to Richard. Stretching her limbs beneath luxurious sheets, her mind wandered back to the time they had spent together the evening before. The very thought of him brought a surge of warmth throughout her body.

A knock on the door brought her back to the moment. "Come in," she called, pulling the covers up around her neck.

Ellen entered the room carrying a tray. "I thought you might like some breakfast. Miss Daphne wants you to join her and the family in the library at eleven o'clock." She placed a tray on Anna's bedside table and poured her coffee.

Anna took several sips of the hot liquid while the girl added a log to the fire. "Tell her I'll be down shortly."

"Yes, Miss, I'll do that in just a minute. I hope you had a good time at the party last night."

"Oh yes, it was lovely." She was glad Ellen had her back turned and could not see her blush.

"The footmen were all sayin' it was grand. Course, I never cared too much for parties myself. I went to a square dance last summer with my brother and could hardly wait to get back home. All that music and everybody talkin' at the same time made me nervous." She gave the fire a final jab as though to underscore her point.

Anna spread orange marmalade on a triangle of toast. "I know exactly what you mean. Parties can be exhausting, but this one proved most enjoyable."

"I'll be back in a shake to help you get dressed. If you need anything before then, just ring the bell."

Anna finished her breakfast, still thinking about Richard. She would likely see him at the children's Christmas party this afternoon. Perhaps she would wear the blue silk day gown Daphne had loaned to her. It was a lovely color and would bring out the turquoise in her eyes.

Stop that! She chastised herself as the reality of her situation crashed against her conscience. Papa was gone, her allowance had been taken away, and she needed to find work to support herself. This was no time to daydream about a man.

Jumping out of bed, she made a hasty toilette and chose one of her own gowns—a sensible looking navy blue with white cuffs and matching lace collar.

By the time she had placed the last pin in her hair, Ellen was back. "Why, Miss, you're already dressed!" She glanced at the clock on the mantle. "These time regulators must be wrong. I was only gone fifteen minutes."

Anna chuckled. None of her own previous maids had ever been so chatty, nor had they looked her in the eye when addressing her. She liked Ellen's independent attitude. "No worries, Ellen. I work pretty fast when I set my mind to it and besides, you shouldn't be detained from your other chores just to help me get dressed."

"Well, bless my soul, you are in no way like the other guests. Some of em are a runnin' my legs off." The girl bobbed a curtsy and hurried out the door.

When entering the library, Anna's eyes immediately rose to the vaulted ceiling's magnificent painting of angels and clouds that were bathed in light, then gradually moved downward to the two-tiered walnut paneled room with thousands of books lining each shelf. She'd heard about George Vanderbilt's love of literature but had no idea of just how enamored he was of books until now. It would be wonderful to delve into some of the great works of literature during her visit.

"I'm so glad you decided to join us." Daphne interrupted her thoughts. "The other guests are still resting, but I wanted you to celebrate with us." She led her to a seating arrangement adjacent to the giant Christmas tree, where beneath its wide branches lay red and green bowed packages, great boxes of chocolates, fresh oranges and apples in baskets. In front of the long French windows stood a damasked table, laden with cracked nuts, grapes, and molds of cranberry jelly that glistened like huge Cabochon rubies.

Daphne grabbed a handful of cracked nuts before taking a seat. "How did things go with you and Richard last night?"

Once again, Anna felt her face grow warm with the remembrance of their time together. "After we danced, he suggested we go out on the balcony for some fresh air." She leaned closer to Daphne and whispered, "I think he might have kissed me if Mrs. Wharton hadn't interrupted us."

Daphne stopped nibbling on the pecans. "I remember the first time that Edward and I kissed. We were standing on the ship's deck after dinner, gazing out at the sunset over the ocean." She giggled. "My toes still curl when I think about it."

Suddenly, both women noticed Daphne's mother watching them like a hawk surveying her prey. "Do you think she heard me?" The girl crossed both arms, as though to defend herself from the intrusion.

"I don't think so." Anna reached out to touch her hand. "Let's walk over to the other end of the library and view those paintings. It will give us a bit more privacy."

Daphne stood, brushing the folds from her skirt. "I'll be so glad when Uncle George talks to Mumsie and we can get my engagement to Edward out in the open. It's so tiresome having to keep my love for him a secret. I want to shout it from the rooftops."

Anna chuckled. "I'm sure you'll be able to do that soon. Meanwhile, try to relax and keep your senses about you. It wouldn't do to have your mother know what you are up to just now, especially since she is under the influence of your Aunt Alva."

"I'll say," Daphne replied, rolling her eyes. "All Aunt Alva talked about last night was her daughter, the Duchess and cash for class. How disgusting."

"She waylaid Richard and me as we were walking out to the balcony."

Daphne touched her shoulder. "What *about* you and Richard? I believe true love is knocking at your door, and I don't want you to miss out."

"He is very charming. But I need to concentrate on being able to support myself." Anna paused when Daphne gave her a knowing smile. "All right, it is true. I get butterflies in my tummy when he looks at me. But really, I hardly know him, except for our time together on the train. And all of my energy must now be focused on survival."

Daphne frowned. "Are you really planning to move out West? I would hate for you to be so far away. Especially after all that Richard told us about his own experience in Denver."

Anna gazed for a moment at the paintings of Renoir, Monet, and the work of other esteemed artists hanging on the library wall. "I do plan on moving, but I must first get back on my feet."

Daphne patted her on the hand. "You and Richard seem so well suited for one another. Surely, if God wants the two of you together, he will arrange it."

Anna wondered if God really did arrange such things. He hadn't prevented her father's death. He hadn't saved her bank account and ancestral home from being ravaged by Douglas Van Demark. It was hard for her to believe that God might do anything as personal as

Daphne indicated, but she kept those thoughts to herself. No need to be a fly in the ointment with her own personal turmoil. If the job at the clinic didn't come through, her plans to move west would be blocked. How would she live if she didn't get this job?

The children shrieked while shaking packages and guessing what was inside the boxes, as their parents, aunts, uncles, and grandparents watched in amusement. It was incredible to see the little ones playing in such a luxurious space. The children on the Lower East Side were thin and wizened with their noses running from the cold. She felt her eyes glaze over.

Daphne suddenly nodded toward the balcony above the fireplace. "Can you see it?" she whispered.

Anna squinted. "What am I looking for?"

"A hidden door."

Gazing up at the rows of books on the balcony, nothing seemed out of place. Rays of sunlight poured through the upper windows, casting light and shadows on what appeared to be a slim vertical panel of wood dividing two shelves. She gasped. "I would never have noticed if you hadn't brought it to my attention."

"It's a private entrance to George's room." Daphne kept her voice low. "At night he can easily slip into the library for a book without disturbing the servants or making the long trek downstairs."

Anna's gaze returned to the second-floor balcony. "How exciting to have one's own secret passageway."

Daphne gave a throaty chuckle. "There are several throughout the house, and I'll show them to you after the holidays. Can you imagine how much fun the children would have if they knew about them? George says he'd never again have a moment's peace if they were discovered."

Anna nodded as they moved back toward the others. The children, now restless, began demanding to open presents. Two of the nursemaids shepherded them onto a Persian rug before the big fireplace, ordering them to be quiet while the butler and footman served hot drinks from an elaborate Russian tea urn.

The children's laughter rippled through the library, causing Daphne to almost spill her tea. "Goodness," she said, placing the cup back into its saucer. "These wild cousins of mine make me wonder if I could ever deal with a brood of my own."

"I suppose it's normal for them to be excited, especially at Christmas." Anna took another taste of her drink. "We used to make just as much noise when we were little. Remember how excited we were by our matching dollhouses?"

Daphne leaned forward. "I still have mine. I'll never forget *that* Christmas! Both of us asked for the exact same gift, and our mothers must have had them specially built. How old were we?"

"We were five." Anna felt a sudden wave of sadness. "It was the last Christmas I had with my mother. I remember her getting down on the floor and playing with us. I still have my dollhouse too. It was crazy to drag it along with me to my new living quarters, but I couldn't bear to part with it." She felt a sob of melancholy form in her throat and quickly changed the subject. "This drink is most unusual. I like it."

Daphne's eyes sparkled. "Uncle George obtained the recipe and urn while in St. Petersburg last year. It's Russian tea. I think it captures the essence of Christmas, don't you?"

Anna took another sip, savoring the tang of cloves and cinnamon on her tongue. "It really does."

While the children opened their presents, the family laughed in enjoyment at their various outbursts of excitement over cowboy hats, wind-up trains, and baby dolls. There was also a lavish assortment of coloring books with wax crayons, board games, and jigsaw puzzles.

While they were absorbed by their toys, Maria Vanderbilt's personal maid distributed gilded Christmas cards and packages topped with candy-striped bows.

Anna opened her gift to find a beautiful hand-tooled note-book and ink pen. Rising to her feet, she went over to thank the Vanderbilt matriarch who wore a crimson shawl over her shoulders. Her beautiful silver hair was caught up in a bun, with a few escaping waves framing her face.

"Thank you so much, Mrs. Vanderbilt." Anna bent down to give the woman a light peck on the cheek. "I shall always think of you when using these."

Mrs. Vanderbilt regarded her with a twinkling smile, appearing almost girlish. "You are very welcome, my dear. I thought you could use such things in your note keeping." She paused when a grandchild handed her a piece of paper.

"Gwammy, here's Santa. I dwawed him just for you." The little girl's blue eyes sparkled while her grandmother looked over the garish crayon picture.

"This is very nice, Henrietta." She leaned forward to pull the child into her lap. "Santa told me you were a very good girl this year."

The child clapped her hands together. "Weally, Gwammy? Did you talk to Santa?"

Before the woman could answer, Henrietta's nurse appeared and scooped the little girl from Mrs. Vanderbilt's lap. "There you are. I hope she didn't get candy on your beautiful dress, ma'am!"

Mrs. Vanderbilt's lips curved into a smile. "What's a little smudge of candy on Christmas morning? Now run along with your nurse, dear. Perhaps she'll allow you to watch your Uncle George set up the toy train."

Mrs. Vanderbilt turned her attention back to Anna. "Thank you, my dear, for the delightful box of truffles and lace handkerchiefs. I had two of the chocolates with my coffee this morning." She closed her eyes for a moment. "They were divine."

Anna was pleased. "I'm convinced chocolate has curative properties, even though medical science hasn't proven it yet."

The older woman nodded. "I suspect scientists will agree with you someday. Meanwhile, we know that chocolate is good for a woman's soul, if nothing else."

"It certainly is," Anna said. "I'd like to borrow that phrase if I may. Several of my female patients would love it."

"Indeed," she replied. "And of course, moderation in all things."

Daphne tugged at Anna's sleeve. "I have something for you too." Her voice was as gleeful as a child's. "Go sit. I'll bring it over to you."

Excusing herself to Mrs. Vanderbilt, Anna took a seat while Daphne plucked a bright red package from the Christmas tree. "I hope you like it."

Anna carefully untied the ribbon and opened the small box, smiling when she saw the lovely pendant locket watch, nestled in soft white paper. "Daphne, this is exquisite. How thoughtful of you."

Daphne sighed in seeming relief. "I know you're always rushing here and there, so I thought a time piece might help."

"And you're right." Anna leaned forward, kissing her on the cheek. "I shall wear it often and think of you, my dearest friend in all the world."

From her pocket, Anna produced a small package, fastened with a thin red ribbon, and handed it to her friend. With obvious excitement, Daphne unwrapped the box and withdrew a beautiful little string of matched white pearls. She gasped. "Oh, my goodness! These are lovely. I shall wear them on my wedding day." Her eyes became misty.

Anna didn't mention they had belonged to her grandmother, or that she had almost sold them for a tidy sum, but had decided to put them aside, feeling they should go to her best friend for Christmas. "They *would* go well with white satin, although I wasn't thinking of that when I decided to give them to you."

Daphne pressed Anna's hand. "I'm so glad we're spending Christmas together." She dabbed the corners of her eyes with a handkerchief. "What time is your interview tomorrow?"

"Nine o'clock. I've been meaning to ask if you might arrange for a carriage to take me into town."

"I've already made plans for the main coach to be ready for you at eight o'clock in the morning. That's not too early, is it?"

"No, it's perfect. You're a wonderful friend, Daphne. If I'm lucky enough to obtain this post, I will have only you to thank."

Daphne swatted her hand. "Oh shush, you're the one who graduated from medical school. How you managed to take all those horrible courses in math and science is beyond me. If it hadn't been for you, I would never have passed high school biology."

"You did well, dear. I only tutored you."

Her friend circled the rim of her cup with a forefinger. "And helped with all my homework." She frowned. "How I detested that biology teacher we had. What was his name?"

Anna narrowed her eyes, trying to recall. "Mr. Todd?"

Daphne giggled. "Yes, that's it. But we called him Mr. Toad."

Anna shook her head. "The poor man. You and I together were far too rambunctious for any teacher to bear."

Daphne scooted forward in her chair. "Oh, come now, don't tell me you've forgotten how harsh he was."

Anna choked back a chuckle. "Of course, I haven't. Remember how he told all of us that teaching young women was a waste of valuable time and effort? Why he chose to instruct at an all girl's school is beyond my understanding."

The piercing sound of a whistle brought a halt to their conversation. The endless stream of noise continued, until Daphne walked over to the toddler and jerked the object of their misery out of his mouth, placing it into her pocket. A nurse scooped up the crying child, while Anna let out a huff of exasperation, wondering how the house, big as it was, could absorb all the noise.

When Daphne returned to her seat, a little boy wearing a cowboy hat patted her on the arm. "Betcha can't catch me, Aunt Daph!"

A smile played around her lips. "Betcha I can!" She stood and smoothed her skirts. "Meet me in an hour for the children's party."

"Meet you where?"

Her friend glanced back, blonde curls bouncing off her shoulders as she raced after her young cousin. "In the banquet hall."

⌒

Richard was greeted at the door by a distressed looking Bosworth. "You were missed at this morning's family celebration, sir." The butler glanced around with what appeared to be anxiety.

"I'm afraid I was detained at the clinic," he said, handing over his hat and gloves. But last night was quite wonderful, and the food superb."

Bosworth helped him out of his cloak. "I'll be sure to send your compliments to Cook."

Two little boys wearing cowboy hats clattered through the entrance hall, pulling a bright red wagon. Richard glanced at the grandfather clock in the corner and frowned. It was only noon, and Daphne had said the party would not begin until half past. "Have the children already arrived?"

"Oh no, sir." The butler gave a weary shake of his head and glanced over at the children with trepidation. "Those are the young Vanderbilt cousins, still celebrating." He clapped his hands. "Run along now, youngsters. You aren't supposed to be out here." He turned back to Richard. "I expect their nurse will soon hustle them upstairs for naps, then we shall begin a second celebration with the children of our staff."

Richard studied him through narrowed eyes. "You look all in, man. Why don't you take a strong cup of tea and put your feet up for a few minutes?"

The butler's countenance immediately cleared. "Oh no, sir, I'm fit as a fiddle. It's just the holidays, you know. They can be quite taxing, but we're all having a lovely time."

Bosworth's smile did not quite reach his eyes. Richard thought he looked exhausted from all the revelry.

"Mr. Vanderbilt suggested you set up your clinic in the salon, so I have taken the liberty of placing a privacy screen in the far corner of the room." He whisked Richard's cloak and hat into a nearby closet. "The footman brought up a couple of tables for you to use with your patients. Be sure to let me know if you require anything further."

A qualified assistant, Richard thought. Usually he brought along Nurse Cartwright from the clinic because she could always get children to do as she wished without argument. Just one look from her was all it took to get a child's undivided attention. Unfortunately, she was out of town, visiting her sister for the holidays. "That won't be necessary, Bosworth. You may tell Mr. Vanderbilt I am here."

The butler disappeared, and Richard proceeded to the salon where he set up his examining table and laid out several lollipops alongside the tongue depressors. Glancing up, he saw Anna enter, looking almost as though she were lost. She stopped to gaze at the chess set in the opposite corner of the large room. The sun streaming through the windows cast golden highlights in her hair as she picked up a carved ivory bishop.

"I see you have discovered Napoleon's chess set." Richard walked over to greet her.

She turned with startled eyes and then smiled. "Oh—pardon me, I didn't see you. Did this really belong to Napoleon?" She placed the bishop back on the game board. "It's charming, isn't it?"

"Yes, quite unique. Napoleon used it while in exile at St. Helena's Island. Interestingly enough, the table itself served as a temporary resting place for his heart during the autopsy."

"What?" Her face went sober. "Are you serious?"

Although Richard wasn't a big Napoleon enthusiast, he experienced a twinge of pleasure informing this intelligent woman of something she didn't already know. He picked up a knight, turning it around in his hand. "Napoleon was paranoid and believed he was being poisoned. While in exile, and under British guard, he insisted that after his death an autopsy be performed on his heart." He placed the decorative piece back on the table and continued. "When surgeons removed it during the procedure, they temporarily deposited it into an urn where it remained on this very table before being returned to his body for burial."

She leaned forward to study the table a bit closer, as though looking for any remaining signs that might have been left behind. "How bizarre." She straightened. "Do you think he was actually poisoned?"

"Doctors who performed the autopsy stated that he died from stomach cancer." He shrugged. "But another physician who also examined the heart, felt certain Napoleon was the victim of arsenic poisoning."

She gave a slow nod, as though the story was coming together in her mind. "The toxins from arsenic could have been administered over a long-time. Napoleon may have had good reason for his suspicion."

He placed both hands into his pockets and smiled. "You're right. If the arsenic was sprinkled into his food over an extended phase it could have taken the poison months to bring about his demise."

She drew her delicate brows into a frown. "Perhaps it was just enough to make him slightly nauseous most of the time. Do you think that's why he suspected someone was poisoning him?"

"More than likely," Richard said, flicking a speck of dust from the table. "Perhaps he wasn't paranoid at all."

A pucker wedged at the bridge of her nose. "How peculiar for George to keep such an item. I'm not superstitious, but I don't think I'd want something like this in my home."

He waved a hand toward the huge ceiling draped in rich burgundy tenting, a feature inspired by Vanderbilt's passion for Oriental and Moorish decorating styles. "George has a fascination for the exotic—or in this case, the macabre." He lightly touched a sixteenth century tapestry of angels that hung on the wall above the chess set. "He can see art in the most unusual combinations."

She glanced up at the tapestry and then back to the chess board, a slight furrow still in her brow. "I see what you mean. Perhaps it is befitting after all, for Napoleon's board game to reside here along with the table that once held his heart. It brings a touch of mystery to Biltmore."

When she smiled, his heart gave an inadvertent jump. He was standing close enough to smell the rose scent of her hair. Once more, his eyes wandered down to her lips.

He cleared his throat. "Biltmore is filled with all sorts of curious collections. Of course, George realizes he can't take all these exquisite trinkets with him into the hereafter. His hope is for them to be passed down for future generations to enjoy."

She picked up a queen from the chess board and studied it for a moment. "Do you play?"

His earlier twinge of pleasure turned to uneasiness. "It's been quite a while. During my last trip abroad, I engaged in a game of chess with my father. To say that he won would be an understatement."

"I find a good game of chess to be stimulating. Even if one loses, the game itself is worth the effort."

"I wouldn't have guessed you to be a chess player," he replied. *But then, I wouldn't have guessed you were a doctor either.*

She placed the queen back on the game board. "My father and I used to play." Her tone became wistful, and Richard pictured her as a precocious little girl with braids.

Then the amusement vanished from her eyes. "My stepmother believed the game unladylike and put a stop to it. Papa and I never played another match of chess after that."

Richard felt an immediate hostility toward this unknown woman who had caused her pain. "Do you play now?"

"I'm far too busy with my patients. Chess requires practice, you know, and I simply don't have the time to put into the necessary training."

"You wouldn't just do it for the sake of simple recreation?"

She raised a brow. "Is that a challenge?"

"Indeed not. After being clobbered by my father, I decided I might never play again unless I had a more interesting opponent."

Her laughter reminded him of little silver bells, joyful and easy on his ears. "I'm afraid we are in the same boat." Her eyes sparkled. "I'm not sure I could effectively compete in a simple game of croquet anymore."

"That's what happens when one practices medicine. It has a way of taking precedence over everything else." He turned and motioned to the makeshift infirmary. "Come, see the examining room. I think I have everything in order, but it never hurts to have another pair of eyes look things over." *Especially eyes as beautiful as yours.*

They walked toward the far corner section of the salon where Bosworth had assembled a privacy screen and her gaze roamed over the delicate blue birds painted on the Japanese partition. "So, you are the official doctor for Biltmore?"

He gave a self-deprecating chuckle. "I suppose I am. George asked me to fill in until he finds someone else. As his friend, I could hardly say no, but an estate of this proportion requires a doctor's services quite often."

She brushed against his shoulder while reaching to straighten a tongue depressor, and his heartbeat accelerated. "I could use some help today." He hoped she didn't notice the slight quiver in his voice. "There are more than fifty children to see, and some of their parents may need medical attention as well. Would you mind assisting me? I'd be grateful."

Her face lit up. "I'd be delighted. Just excuse me for a moment while I run upstairs to get my medical bag."

Richard watched her disappear, still smiling over the obvious joy in her eyes. What had happened to the man who only a few days ago had been adamantly opposed to female physicians? Would he ever be able to climb out of the rabbit hole and put his world straight again?

Chapter Eleven

Anna retrieved the medical bag from her room, all the while thinking about how nice it was of Richard to ask for her help. How she
loved the practice of medicine. Now if only Dr. Becker would hire
her tomorrow, her feet would be firmly planted on the pathway
of her dreams. The thought rejuvenated her while descending the
stairs.

She stepped into the foyer just in time to witness a drove of
laughing children being herded into the banquet hall by the weary-
eyed butler and a parlor maid. Bundled up in colorful hats, coats,
and mittens, the little ones sported exposed faces that bore rosy
cheeks the color of holly berries.

Adjacent to the entrance hall was the solarium, and she stopped
for a moment to gaze at the golden rays of sunlight illuminating the
poinsettias that surrounded the fountain. The natural light lifted
her spirits.

Assuming Richard would not require her assistance until after
the party, she placed her medical bag among the flowers. As she
wandered into the banquet hall behind the children, her attention was immediately drawn to a little girl with a cherubic face
and wheezing cough, clutching a tiny baby doll. A regal-looking
woman with a crown of golden braids patted the child's back, and
when at last the little girl caught her breath, the woman shook her
head, appearing distressed.

"I sorry, Mamma." The little girl's voice was hoarse from croup.

The woman bent down and kissed the child on her forehead before turning her attention to Richard who had entered the room. "I was greatly afeared of bringing little Nellie out in this bitter weather, but my husband said you'd be at the party and might could help her with a modern remedy."

The woman's thick Elizabethan speech was melodious like the other staff members at Biltmore. But instead of a uniform, this woman wore a simple green gown with a white lace collar. There seemed a certain dignity about her stature, reminding Anna of a princess in some old portrait.

Richard reached down, placing a hand on the child's forehead. "She feels a bit warm. What medicines are you giving her?"

The woman lifted her chin. "Right now, I'm a dosin' her with wild cherry cough syrup and groundhog oil."

Anna's smile faltered. She understood how the syrup of wild cherries might help to ease a cough, but groundhog oil as a medication? She had never heard of it, but Richard nodded in a matter-of-fact way, as though familiar with the treatment.

"How old is Nellie?" He reached to lift the child up into his arms, but she scampered away from him, taking refuge behind Anna's skirts.

The woman paused. "She'll be three, come the Ides of March."

The expression on Richard's face remained unchanged as the woman listed various remedies she was using to treat her daughter's cough: burdock root, elderberry tea, and onions fried in butter. "All of those things are fine." His voice was kind. "But I need to get a look at her throat. Do you think you might coax her into the salon? I've set up an examining room there."

The woman turned her attention back to the child. "Nellie, get ye'self away from the lady's skirts so the doctor can help you."

Nellie shook her head with vigor, tears filling her big blue eyes. "N-no. D-docker give shot."

The child broke into a seizure of coughing, attracting the attention of other mothers who drew their own little ones closer. Anna reached down and scooped Nellie into her arms. "There now," she crooned, as the toddler sobbed into her bosom. "Let's look around and see if we can find some candy to ease your throat."

Daphne hurried toward her with a questioning look. "Whatever on earth is wrong?"

Anna pushed a strand of hair away from the child's eyes. "Oh, just a bad cold, I think. Did Santa bring any peppermint? It might soothe her throat."

Daphne rushed over to a big table filled with refreshments and picked up a stick of red and white striped candy from an elaborate red dish. "Will this do? It's soft peppermint."

Anna nodded. "Oh yes, thank you, Daphne. This should give her some relief."

Nellie clutched her tiny baby doll in one hand, reaching for the candy with the other. "Don't want no docker," she said, slurping the peppermint. "Docker give shots."

Daphne laughed. "Oh, sweetheart, you don't have to worry. I'm not a doctor. But you're in good hands." She patted the little girl's back and threw Anna a wink before returning to the other children who were waiting to play another game.

Anna retrieved a handkerchief from her pocket and wiped away the little girl's tears. "Let's go over to the salon and look at your throat. Your baby might need some medicine, too."

Nellie held up the miniature doll wrapped in a tiny pink blanket and nodded in agreement while sucking on the stick of candy. Her eyebrows furrowed when she spotted Richard walking behind them. "Docker give shot," she said through a wheezing gasp.

Richard playfully reached out to touch her golden braids. "Nellie, dear, I've never given you a shot."

The child's mother gave an audible sigh. "Oh, she heard some of her elder cousins a talkin' about doctors givin' shots. Their tongues are a mile long, and I think they about scared her ta death, talking about needles and such-like."

Anna chuckled, still fascinated by the woman's dialect. "You have a beautiful daughter. She's very bright for her age."

"Yes, she's my bonnie girl and she's really taken a shine to you." The woman touched Anna's shoulder. "Name's Maggie. Dr. Wellington tells me you're a doctor. Nellie's used to havin' a woman doctor care for her when she's sick, and I guess that's why she's took up with you."

Anna was surprised by the woman's nonchalant manner concerning female physicians. "Oh, are there many women doctors here in Asheville?" She glanced at Richard, but his gaze was on Nellie.

Maggie narrowed her lovely gray eyes. "Well, I don't rightly know about that, but my granny was a doctor, and she brought little Nellie into this world. Granny didn't have yore type training, o' course, but she delivered nearly all the babies on this side o' Asheville." Her eyes misted over. "She passed on up to heaven a few months ago."

Anna's heart went out to her. "I'm so sorry to hear that. So, your grandmother was a midwife?"

Maggie lifted her chin. "You could say that, I guess. She treated anybody needin' her and could cure most any old disease with poultices and remedies that her grandma brought from over yonder in Scotland." Her eyes filled with tears. "Granny always took care o' my little Nellie when she was sick, and now I don't know what I'll do." Her voice faded, and she drew a lace-trimmed hankie from her sleeve, dabbing her eyes. "I'm greatly sorry for carryin' on so, Miss, but my hearts not mended proper just yet."

Anna patted the woman's arm. "Please don't apologize, Maggie. My grandmother passed on a number of years ago, but I still think of her every day."

Maggie nodded. "Oh, I shall always be a ponderin' on the remembrance of her." She shook her dainty head. "But, the Good

Book says to everything be there a season...a time to be born, a time to die; a time to mourn, and a time to dance."

"That's a beautiful scripture." Anna returned her smile.

Maggie had a faraway look. "It was Granny's favorite. She had her earthly time with us, and now she's a havin' her eternal season in heaven with the Lord."

"I suspect she's watching over you and little Nellie," Richard said thoughtfully.

"I'm much obliged for your kind words," Maggie said, while following them to the examining area. "I hope Granny really does watch over us down here. I need all the help I can get."

Nellie squinted her eyes with suspicion when Anna lowered her to the table, then giggled when Richard pulled a red rubber gadget out of his pocket and placed on the tip of his nose, tweaking it to make the sound of a horn. He squeezed the clown-like nose again and then waggled his eyebrows at the laughing child.

"That's a beautiful dress," Anna commented while unbuttoning the top of the little girl's red jumper so that Richard could listen to her heartbeat.

"Momma made it." Nellie smacked her lips on the candy and giggled when the doctor drew a pair of bright red glasses from his pocket.

"Your momma is a very talented lady," Anna remarked. "I wish I could sew like that. My goodness, what a gift you have, Maggie."

"I make dresses and such-like." The woman's long tapered fingers reached to smooth her daughter's hair. "I wanted Nellie to have a fancy outfit for the party."

Anna admired the neatly stitched appliqué of Santa on the bib of the little girl's dress. "Are you a seamstress?"

The woman gave a shy smile and nodded. "I make all the uniforms for the maids here and have a few other customers from town. If ever ye might need anything, I'd be happy for yore trade. My husband's the gamekeeper at Biltmore, and any of the servants can tell ye how to find me. We live on the grounds."

Anna studied the fine simple lines of the dress Maggie was wearing. "Do you create your own designs?"

"Oh, yes. When somebody tells me what they want, I picture it in my mind and then draw it to see if they like my ideas or not. I also spin wool, weave my own cloth and dye it with wild berries, hickory nuts, and such-like from the estate."

Anna felt as though she'd been transported back in time, caught up in an Elizabethan enclave with Shakespeare himself hovering all around them.

Richard brought out a thermometer and handed it over to her. "Do you think Nellie would allow you to take her temperature? She seems quite taken with you."

She slipped the instrument beneath Nellie's arm and the child's mouth puckered for a moment, but Anna diverted her by pulling a stethoscope out of her medical bag. "Do you mind if I listen to your baby's heartbeat while Dr. Wellington listens to yours?"

Nellie hesitated, as though thinking it over, then nodded. She watched with eyes alight as Anna placed the instrument beneath the doll's minuscule white gown while Richard put his own stethoscope on the little girl's chest.

"Your baby's heartbeat is very strong." Anna whispered. "Would you like to listen to it?"

Nellie's intelligent eyes brightened while placing her tiny hand on the end of the stethoscope and moving it around on the doll's chest. "Baby's heart berry stwong."

"I need to get a look at her throat," Richard murmured.

Anna leaned in closer to the child. "Would you ask your dolly to open her mouth for me?"

Nellie peered down into her dolly's eyes. "Open mouf!" she ordered. "Girl docker don't give shots."

Everyone laughed. Then Anna tried a different approach. "Maybe if you will open your mouth for Dr. Wellington, your baby will open her mouth for me."

The little girl deliberated for a second or two, as though having serious doubts about the reasoning behind such a request. Finally, she opened her own mouth wide, showing all her tiny baby teeth and pink tonsils.

Anna watched in suspense as Richard peered into the child's throat. If Nellie had diphtheria it would mean a quarantine for everyone there. How would she ever make it to her interview tomorrow if unable to leave Biltmore?

"Her throat is fine." There was a ring of triumph in his voice as he turned to address the child's mother. "Nellie has bronchitis, but her lungs are clear, and she doesn't have pneumonia."

"Nor diphtheria," Anna said.

"Nor diphtheria." He echoed her sentiments.

Maggie expelled a deep breath of relief. "Thank the good Lord! I've nigh wearied myself to death about this baby."

Anna handed Richard the thermometer and buttoned up the bib on the child's dress while he scrutinized the numbers.

"She's running a fever, but it isn't high enough for us to worry about." He scribbled down a few notes on the child's chart. "Well, Nellie, my girl, it seems you have a cold with bronchitis."

"And a kawf!" her voice squeaked.

He laughed. "That's right, and we need to get that cough under control so that you can get some rest." He placed the thermometer into an alcohol solution on the table beside them.

Nellie furrowed her brow. "Don't want no shot." She waggled a tiny finger at him and then glanced back at Anna for support.

He shook his head. "No shot. I'm going to give you some cough syrup instead."

The child watched with suspicious eyes as he took a bottle of codeine from the medical bag and dispensed a few ounces into a small glass bottle with a dropper attached to its lid. Then he showed Maggie the red line on the tiny dispenser. "Give her four drops, twice daily. It is very powerful medicine, so do not go beyond this line. She'll need a dose before breakfast, and then at bedtime. No more," he stressed. "If she doesn't improve in three days, contact me. Dr. St. James will administer the medication now, and you may give her another dose tonight before bed."

Maggie nodded. "What about the wild cherry cough syrup I have ta' home? Should I be dosin' her with that too?"

He straightened. "Just this remedy for now. We don't want to give her too many different medications. It might make her worse."

What a wonderful answer. Anna pretended to give the dolly a dose of medicine before administering the drops to Nellie whose mouth was already open. The little girl wrinkled her nose in disgust after swallowing.

Richard looked up from his scribbling. "Maggie, do you have any lemons and honey at home?"

The woman nodded. "Yes sir, Mr. Vanderbilt gave us a bushel of lemons and oranges for Christmas. I tend the bees here on the estate, and he lets me keep part o' the honey."

"That's good," he said. "I want you to give her some lemon water with honey, several times throughout the day. Just squeeze the juice into water, and then stir in the honey. It will soothe her throat. You can warm it if you like. Also, let her have as many oranges as she wants."

Maggie buttoned Nellie's collar.

"Should I keep a dosin' her with the groundhog oil?"

Anna wondered about the groundhog oil but refrained from asking. As though reading her thoughts, Richard turned to her with a smile. "The groundhog survives on roots and herbs that many of the mountain people use for medicinal purposes."

Maggie lifted her chin. "The groundhog eats from the purest of all herbs, way high up in the hills where man can't reach and destroy. My granny swore by its healin' ways."

Anna nodded, not quite knowing what to say. Most doctors gave their patients herbal remedies from time to time. Perhaps groundhog oil might contain some curative benefits, but she shuddered to think of the furry little creature being killed for that purpose.

Richard handed the bottle of medication to Maggie. "You can continue with the groundhog oil after she has finished with this medicine."

He scooped Nellie up into his arms. "Now, young lady, I think we should return to the party. We wouldn't want to miss Santa's visit, now would we?" The child tweaked his clown nose and giggled.

By the time they reappeared in the banquet hall, he had to coax Nellie into joining the others for ice cream and cake. The little girl seemed content in his arms. No wonder, Anna thought, as she observed him with the child. She still remembered the strength of his arms when he had saved her life.

While the children enjoyed their refreshments, Daphne told them about the very first Christmas, the night when baby Jesus was born in a stable. Then she asked the children if they wanted to add anything to the story, and a handsome blond lad with curls stood up. "When Jesus growed up he died on the cross, so we'd get saved from our sins."

Daphne brought her two hands together. "Very true, Homer." Her gaze roamed over the sea of children seated at the little round tables set up by the footmen. "Would anyone else like to share what they know about Jesus?"

"Mama says if we take Jesus as our Savior then we go up ta' heaven when we die a-cause he makes our sins whiter n snow."

Daphne nodded to the little girl with red braids and freckles. "That's true, Pearl. Jesus really does cover all our wrongs with his love. Who else?"

A little boy with jet black hair stood and gave a solemn gaze around the table. "When Jesus growed up, he beat the stuffin' plum out of the devil, so we could be saved." A few of the children giggled, and he gave them a scathing look. "If ye' don't get saved, you'uns will all go down to hell when ye' die."

"Ah hesh up, Plato." A stout little boy in overalls glared. "You're always a runnin' your tongue at both ends, tryin' to scare somebody. You ain't no preacher, so just you hesh and sit down."

"Hesh your own mouth, Glenn," the boy glowered back. "My pa says we don't need to be goin' down there to hell a' cause life on this here earth is shore hard enough. I'm jest learnin' the young'uns about hell so they won't go there!"

Glenn stood up and clenched his fists, leaning closer to Plato. "Well, yore a scarin' em with your talk about fire and brimstone. We all know about hell, so keep it to ye-self."

The children grew quiet, their eyes round with fear. Some nodded their heads in agreement with Glenn, while others appeared frightened.

Anna gulped. Would the two older boys get into a fist fight? Their discussion of the afterlife was harsh, especially when expressed by children so young. Daphne's own mouth dropped open with surprise, but she quickly recovered and walked over to both boys. "We respect all opinions here, but we don't want a fight. I want you boys to shake hands and make up. After all, it is Christmas and I think God would want us all to be friends, don't you?"

"Yes ma'am," both boys said at the same time, and with reluctance they shook hands.

"Now, that's being a good sport." Daphne smiled at the boys. "Come with me, both of you. I want you to help me pass out gifts to the younger children. Would you do that for me?"

Both boys nodded and trudged along behind Daphne to the front of the banquet hall, each casting a scowling glance at the other.

The room filled with chatter once more, and Daphne clapped her hands to get everyone's attention. "Children you are very dear to me, and God loves each of you." She turned to the table where a big red shopping bag waited. "Glenn and Plato will help pass out these gifts. "I know you have family Bibles for home worship, but I want you to have one of your very own." She held up a children's Bible and flipped through the colorful pages, pointing out pictures, including one of Joseph in his coat of many colors, and another of David slaying Goliath.

"I know that story," one of the boys shouted as he recognized the scene. "David kilt that giant with a wee rock from his slingshot!"

Daphne smiled. "That's true, Johnny. He put his entire trust in God."

"David cutted the giant's head off."

Daphne nodded. "Very good, Clyde. All of you know the stories quite well. Now you will have pictures to go with them."

The children giggled as Glenn and Plato passed out Bibles to the younger children. Some were turning the pages and reading the Scriptures aloud. A few minutes passed before Daphne interrupted their chatter once more. "Now we have another special surprise for you. Nell and her brother, Clayton, brought their dulcimer and guitar to play for us today. Come on up, children, and let us hear your Christmas music."

A hush fell over the room as a dark-haired boy around the age of ten, and his younger sister, whom Anna judged to be seven or eight, walked to the front, carrying their instruments in cloth cases of patchwork design. The little girl sat down in a straight-backed chair that Daphne provided, and placing the dulcimer on her lap, she looked down at the instrument as though in communion with the strings. Some of the boys in the audience snickered, as the brother placed the guitar strap around his neck. He paid them no mind and stood close beside his sister.

Anna was captivated by their lilting composition of *Silent Night*. As the melody wafted through the room, she closed her eyes in an attempt to absorb the magnificence of the children's talent. The little girl plucked the dulcimer strings, creating a poignant melody, while her brother provided perfect background rhythm with his guitar. After a few minutes, the little boy began to sing *Silent Night,* and his little sister joined in with alto, their voices were pitch perfect, their timing precise.

After singing a few more Christmas songs, the children put away their instruments and shyly walked back to their chairs as everyone applauded. They had barely taken their seats when a loud knock on the door echoed through the room and everyone became silent.

Daphne raised her eyebrows. "Do you think that might be Santa?" She hurried over to the entrance. "Who's there?" She called.

All the children let out a gasp as they eyed the door.

"'Tis Santa Clause!" a deep male voice bellowed.

"Santa!" The children's voices resounded through the great hall. "It's Santa Clause!"

Richard went to open the heavy double doors, and in walked Santa, carrying a huge red sack over his shoulder. Daphne giggled and led him to a chair in front of the fireplace where he began opening the bag and withdrawing toys.

After Santa's grand entrance, Richard returned to stand beside Anna at the back of the room. A tingle went down her spine as he leaned down and whispered: "George is playing the role quite well, don't you agree?"

She nodded, clearing her throat. "Let's just hope the pillow for his belly remains in place. Otherwise, he'll be the skinniest Santa this world has ever seen. I understand Daphne's original pick for Santa is in bed with influenza."

"I can assure you, only a dire emergency would have placed George in that red suit." His smile was replaced by a worried frown. "And yes, you are correct. I stopped by to see the ailing Santa on my way here. He'll be in bed for at least another week."

"Have you had many cases of influenza this year?"

He gave a weary nod. "It's a bit above the normal range, but hopefully nothing to worry about."

After Santa finished passing out toys, Daphne and the children sang *Away in a Manger*. Richard nodded toward her. "We should go over to the examining area now. Our patients will arrive soon."

While walking back over to the salon, Anna inhaled the scent of pine from surrounding wreaths, trees, and other Christmas embellishments that were scattered throughout the entry hall.

"I've never known a family who took such pleasure in celebrating Christmas." She bent down to pick up an ornament of hand painted red birds that had fallen off a tree, tucking it back onto a lower branch.

"I thought Christmas was the height of New York," Richard remarked. "When I left the conference, a part of me wanted to remain to capture the holiday essence."

She waved a dismissive hand. "Most of the Christmas parties in New York are crowded affairs where everyone talks *at* one another and never *to* one another!"

He nodded. "I loathe the empty chatter that passes for conversation in most circles. It seems such a waste of precious time."

Their eyes met, and she averted her gaze to the nativity scene beneath the tree. "I love the spiritual component of the Biltmore festivities."

He smiled as they entered the salon. "No one can say George Vanderbilt doesn't love the true spirit of Christmas. By the way, you were wonderful with little Nellie. I've never seen a doctor examine a doll and make it look so authentic."

Her cheeks grew warm. "But it was your clown act that really saved the day. That is—I mean ... well ... you really do have a magnificent bedside manner."

Again, their eyes locked. Bosworth entered, and she turned to straighten the examining table, not wanting to reveal her flushed face.

"Sir, may I have a word?" The butler's tone was edged with anxiety.

"Of course, Bosworth, what is it?"

The man smoothed an invisible wrinkle from his sleeve. "Should I send the patients in, one family at a time? The children are quite a handful, and I think it might be a problem for so many of them to be milling about in this room all at once." He lowered his voice. "There are a good number of breakable items in here, you know."

Richard nodded. "Of course, do whatever you think is best."

"Very well, sir, I shall allow the first family to enter now. It seems that one little boy hurt his knee while playing in the banquet hall. I offered his mother a bandage from the medical kit downstairs, but she was adamant that her son see you instead."

Richard waved a hand. "Send them in."

Several children with an assortment of ailments showed up for an examination. The little boy that Bosworth mentioned required general first aid and a bandage, while the remaining patients were treated for a variety of minor sniffles and sore throats—none as debilitating as Nellie's.

While Anna assisted, her mind kept replaying the long look they'd shared just before Bosworth had entered the salon. His eyes had worn the same expression the prior evening, right before Mrs. Wharton interrupted them. Or had she imagined it?

The two worked steadily for more than three hours, until finishing up with all the patients. Just as they completed packing the things in the examining room, the butler returned carrying a tray of tea and scones. "I thought you might like some refreshment after this busy afternoon." He held the tray aloft while another servant covered a table near the window with a white cloth.

Anna closed her medical bag with a snap and walked over to the basin and pitcher of hot water that the parlor maid had brought them for hand washing. "Bosworth, you are most perceptive." She turned to Richard who was packing his leftover medical supplies into wooden crates. Once again, she felt her face grow warm when he returned her smile.

"A strong cup of tea would hit the spot just now." He held both arms up in a long stretch. "At this point, I would gladly drink it standing up. It's amazing how energetic children are. Even when they aren't feeling well, they can run circles around healthy adults."

"Indeed, sir." The butler nodded, indicating the crates with a slight lift of his chin. "Shall I have a footman carry those to your carriage?"

He nodded his acceptance of the offer, and Bosworth rang for a footman.

Almost immediately, a strapping young man in livery entered the salon, whistling *Jingle Bells*. He immediately became silent when seeing the butler's frown.

"Jeremy, please carry those items to Dr. Wellington's carriage."

"Yes, sir." The young man lifted one of the boxes without effort, then hurried out of the room with Bosworth on his heels saying, "Look sharp, my boy! Look sharp!"

Chapter Twelve

Richard gratefully sipped the hot drink, hoping to unwind after working with so many patients. "I was relieved that none of the children had influenza."

She nodded. "Most of them seemed quite hearty. Nothing of a serious nature, thank goodness. Of course, we must keep a close watch on little Nellie."

"Indeed," he replied. "But I've no doubt that Maggie will pay you a visit if her little girl needs additional care. It would have been a very strenuous day without you, Anna. I only hope I haven't taken advantage of your generosity, especially since you are on holiday and would probably prefer to be relaxing."

"Oh, but I love my work," she said right away. "And this really is an extraordinary place."

Breaking a scone in half, he bit into the flaky tartness of a blueberry. "I've been here only a few years, but I now call it home."

She chuckled. "Your love of this place is understandable. I'm fascinated by the dialect of the people here, and had no idea the Elizabethan language was still being vocalized outside of Shakespearean theatre."

He gazed at her for a moment, taking in her unusual turquoise eyes and creamy complexion. She appeared radiant, even after spending several hours with a bunch of rowdy children. "I'm impressed you recognized their speech as archaic and not corrupt."

She dabbed her mouth with the napkin. "Listening to them made me feel as though I'd stepped into the pages of Chaucer or Shakespeare."

"I'm rather impressed by your keen observation of the language. Many newcomers to the area view the mountaineers with disdain, deeming their outdated dialect as a sign of ignorance. Almost all the so-called *bad English* used by natives of Appalachia was once employed by the highest-ranking nobles of the realms of Scotland. I find it refreshing that you viewed them without prejudice."

A sparkle came into her eyes. "And the beautiful music provided by the brother and sister. I don't believe I have ever heard anything quite so lovely. Did they study here in Asheville?"

Richard laughed good-naturedly, shaking his head. "No music lessons. Those kids have a God-given talent, like their parents and so many other mountaineers. Their instruments came with their ancestors from Scotland, passed down to each new generation."

"Oh, now that is amazing. They seemed courtly."

"I know what you mean." He brushed a crumb off his sleeve. "Many are descendants of the nobility who fled Scotland during the Jacobite uprising. The Riddles and MacNeals, along with several other families whose ancestors supported Bonnie Prince Charlie, settled here in the 1700's because it was so similar in appearance to the land they'd left behind."

Anna traced the lacey edge of tablecloth with her forefinger. "I vaguely remember reading about the Scottish uprising while in school. I didn't realize they settled in Southern Appalachia."

He nodded. "There were other immigrants who chose to put down roots in these mountains. Some German and English, but most were Scottish. When I first arrived in Asheville, it wasn't at all unusual for a patient to show me relics belonging to their great-great-grandparents from Scotland. Old land maps, kilts, even paintings of castles belonging to their ancestors, stowed away in attic trunks and gathering dust." He leaned forward. "And I never fail to be amazed by the way these mountaineers honor the classics by the names they give to their children."

Her laughter trilled out around them, lifting Richard's spirits. "Thank you for explaining that to me. One of the little boys at the party was named Plato. I couldn't help thinking that was an unusual name for a child. Now I understand why."

He chuckled. "And don't forget Homer."

She finished a scone and wiped the crumbs from her fingers, a glint of amusement lighting her eyes. "Are the mountaineers actually familiar with the classics?"

"Some are. Their ancestors would have studied them while living as nobles, passing them to future generations by oral tradition. As time passed, the stories were watered down until the names, language, and songs were all that remained."

Her eyes filled with sudden sadness. She toyed with her spoon for a moment before placing it on the saucer. "The children at the party talked a lot about the devil and hell. It seemed so real to them. Why is their doctrine so fierce?"

He gave a wry smile. "Not all the mountaineers hold such rigid dogma, but those who do are well-acquainted with hardship. Perhaps their own harsh experiences with poverty and struggle has given them an uncanny knowledge of how horrible hell might be. They don't want to take a chance on a hereafter that could be far worse than the severity of their present existence."

Her features softened in sympathy. "The poor little dears. I do wish things were easier for them."

The warmth of her compassion settled within him and he longed to reach for her hand. "Well, you certainly won them over today and that alone is quite a feat."

Her beautiful eyes searched his face. "Do you think so? I enjoyed being with the children and talking to their parents, but do you really believe that was enough for them to like me?"

"I know so. The mountaineers are as clannish as their Scottish ancestors. Proud and loyal to a fault. But when they like someone, they'll go out of their way to befriend them. On the other hand, if they don't take a fancy to you, they'll never change their feelings."

Her lips parted. "Never?"

"Never," he said.

Anna chuckled. "Well, I'm glad to have passed a test I didn't study for."

"With flying colors," Richard said, pouring himself more tea. "The women hung on to your every word and all the kids adored you."

A gleam of warmth lit her eyes. "I'm glad," she said, reaching for another blackberry scone.

He nodded. "So am I. George says that the people here remind him of his grandfather, Cornelius Vanderbilt. He was a stubborn sort who hated the New York upper classes but was often invited into their homes to discuss business matters. He chewed tobacco and developed a reputation for deliberately missing the spittoons in their palatial mansions. The mountaineers are more genteel than Cornelius. They would never go that far, but their stubbornness is comparable."

Her eyes sparked with humor. "How very funny. Cornelius must have infuriated them!"

"Wonderful story, isn't it? I can well imagine how the London Ton might have reacted. At least The Four Hundred allow great-grandchildren of the *nouveau riche* into their fold. In Great Britain, commoners are seldom admitted into the parlor of an aristocrat. It's absurd."

She drew a deep breath. "Mrs. Astor allows no one into her circle unless their money is at least three generations removed from menial labor. There have been few exemptions, the Vanderbilt's being one of them."

"Are the Vanderbilt's considered *nouveau riche*?" he queried.

She nodded and lowered her voice. "Alva Vanderbilt was determined to be part of the Four Hundred and gave a lavish party several years ago. Mrs. Astor's daughter wanted to attend, and she begged her mother to call upon Alva so that she might be invited." Anna paused for a moment as though hesitant to continue.

He chuckled. "Don't stop now. What happened?"

"Well, according to my stepmother, Mrs. Astor gave in to her daughter's wishes and after that, the Vanderbilt's were officially part of New York Four Hundred."

Richard leaned back in his chair for a moment. "Alva was the lady who spoke to us last night. Her daughter married Charles Churchill, or Sunny, as I grew up calling him."

"Yes, her daughter, Consuela, is now a Duchess."

He took another sip of tea. "And not a very happy one from all I hear. Would she be what some might call an *American money princess?*"

"*Money for a title* is all the rage these days, especially among the *nouveau riche.*" She shrugged. "It's their way of getting even with New York Society. The Four Hundred bows to royalty and loves inviting them to parties, so it's an easy in for those who have been previously shunned."

He shook his head. "Mrs. Astor sounds like a difficult woman to deal with."

A frown wrinkled her brow. "Especially if one does not follow her rules and customs."

"You sound as though you have firsthand experience."

"I admit that I have balked at some of her silly rules." Her tone hardened. "My time in medical school caused quite a stir."

Richard wasn't surprised to hear this. "How did the Four Hundred react when you announced your plans to become a doctor? I imagine you must have shaken their foundation a bit."

Anna put aside her cup. "Papa was supportive, but my stepmother, Claudette, thought it was a ridiculous idea. During my medical training, I missed all of the parties and summer gatherings in Newport." She looked down at her hands. "Claudette thought I should flutter my eyelashes at the prospective husbands that she and Mrs. Astor chose for me." She closed her eyes for a moment, as though to block out the memory. "But when I persisted with my studies and passed my courses, they began referring to my medical profession as a 'nice little hobby'. I suppose the sarcasm was preferable to being ostracized, but still ... "

"You must have missed several coming out parties while studying so hard." Richard paused for a moment, wondering if he should ask her what happened to all the young men who would have been clamoring for her attention. He decided to reword his thoughts. "What became of those beaus who had their hopes dashed by your decision to ignore them?"

She reached to touch a small bouquet of red roses Bosworth had placed on the table. "All happily married and I'm quite certain they are each better for it. I'm fortunate there was no major scandal surrounding my decision to become a doctor."

He nodded. "My younger sister, Emily, recently announced she is planning to pursue a career in law and wants nothing to do with marriage. Mother is beside herself with worry. In the end, I'm sure Emily will have her way, for she is quite stubborn, but I'd much prefer to see her happily married and raising a family, rather than reading dusty old law books."

Anna fiddled with the spoon on the table, her heart a curious mixture of apprehension and anticipation. "I don't understand why our culture forbids a woman to have marriage *and* a career. Don't you think it is unfair for your sister not to be able to have both?"

Richard appeared puzzled, as though he found her question difficult to understand. "Who would rear and comfort the little ones if

both parents spent all day away from them? His tone was disbelieving. "As much as I respect your own courage and intellect, I believe
a *married* woman's place is in the home."

"But what if a woman has gifts that go beyond keeping a house
and caring for children? Would you forbid her from becoming all
that God created her to be? Think of Deborah the judge, who led
her people to freedom and peace. And what about Queen Esther
who saved the Jewish people? It's pretty obvious that God created
them for more than tending their homes." Anna trailed off as his
eyes narrowed with disapproval.

"I admit you have a point about talented women, but you are
the exception. What about all the common ordinary women who
were meant to be wives and mothers?"

She gave a little wave of her hand. "Most wives and mothers are
no different than me. I just happened to have a supportive father who
paid my way through medical school and believed in my abilities."

He put aside his cup. "A Godly woman chooses to make her
husband and children a priority," he said, as though searching for a
way to make her understand biblical principles. "Scripture clearly
teaches that a man is to be head of the home, and his wife must
submit to him. And in turn, a husband must submit to his wife.
And cherish her," he quickly added.

She placed her elbows on the table and leaned forward. "I don't
dispute the scripture about husbands and wives submitting *equally*
to one another, but really, that has nothing to do with whether a
married woman should have a career. What say you about widows
who must support themselves, or a woman with a disabled husband? Are they to be tied down in a factory, or taking in laundry and
sewing when they might better support their families with a career
in law or medicine? If a man is to cherish his wife, would he not also
encourage her to use and develop the gifts God gave to her?"

His jaw tightened. "Well, first, it is the responsibility of the
church and family to assist widows and orphans. And as for disabled

husbands, again, it is also the role of the church to help out those families in need."

Anna felt so flustered. Why couldn't he understand? "But how many pastors really pay attention to the needs of their own church family? I see women everyday who are struggling to survive, with or without a husband, and they can barely afford to make ends meet."

Richard seemed to wince at the truth in her statement. "I agree with you—the church hasn't done a very good job on that end. Who knows? Perhaps in time, our society will become more comfortable with your viewpoint, but it is hard for me to imagine a world where married women leave their children every day for a career. In fact, I shudder at the thought."

Anna shook her head. "It may be hard to imagine, but I think time will support my views. I pray for the day when women can freely develop their gifts in whatever way they choose."

An uneasy silence filled the room. Anna bit her lip, wanting to ease the tension between them and suspected she'd already said too much. But why shouldn't she be able to express her opinion? Why did women have to keep quiet all the time, while the men shared their thoughts freely?

When the clock began chiming the hour, he rose from the table. "I regret having to end our visit, but I must get back to the clinic." He seemed to have recomposed his feelings, but she felt sickened by the knowledge of how he really felt, as she stood to bid him farewell.

He cleared his throat. "Perhaps we shall meet again before your return to New York?"

"Possibly." She nodded. "I plan to remain at Biltmore, at least through the New Year."

He started to say something more, but Bosworth entered the room. "May I get you anything else?"

"No, thank you, Bosworth." His smile appeared forced. "After having tea, I feel equal to any task, though unfortunately, I must take my leave."

The butler nodded. "Very well, sir, I shall gather your belongings."

Richard turned to face her. "Thank you for assisting me today." Then, as though to lighten the moment, he grasped her hand. "Merry Christmas!"

"Merry Christmas to you as well, doctor." Her voice sounded a bit hollow, even to her own ears.

After his departure, Anna climbed the stairs with a heavy heart. In the privacy of her room, she berated herself. When had she become the irrational and romantic fool? This man had no respect for her rights as a woman and she was an idiot to have thought otherwise.

Biltmore was merely a stopover on her way to the western frontier. There she would be able to fulfill her dreams with a thriving medical practice and the right to vote. Why then, was her heart so tender from his scathing words about married women with careers?

It isn't wise for a girl to be too clever. A previous warning from her stepmother rang in her ears.

She inhaled a deep breath, determined not to give in to the hot wetness springing to her eyes.

"Oh, be quiet," whispered Anna to her stepmother's voice. "He is nothing to me. Nothing at all."

Chapter Thirteen

Once settled inside the coach, Richard let his breath out with a groan. How could the day have started off so joyful, only to end on such an unpleasant note? Everything was going well until he brought up his sister's desire for a vocation in law. Rubbing his forehead, he wished he'd never mentioned it. The radical opinions of Anna St. James went against the grain of everything he believed regarding God's perfect will for the family. Why couldn't women simply allow men to lead?

He had to admit amending his thoughts on women doctors, especially after witnessing Anna's skill at delivering the baby, and then assisting him with the children at Biltmore. Even his views on suffrage had been transformed to some extent, particularly after discovering what the women voters had accomplished in Colorado. But the very idea of a married woman with a career was bizarre and against all biblical principles.

The surrounding mountains, cloaked in smoky blue and green, usually gave him tranquility, but not today. The only thing he could see in that lovely vista was the color of Anna's eyes that had deepened in hue while defending her viewpoint. Suddenly, her remark about poor widows attempting to make ends meet loomed before him like specters rising from an unearthed grave. It was true, the church had in many ways failed these women. He had seen the bread lines filled with mothers and their children, as they waited for a bite of food that barely stood between them and starvation.

Richard shifted in his seat. Aside from her concern for the poor, it was obvious that her own plans were set. She would go to Colorado just as she had mentioned last night at the dinner party. There had been a resolute sparkle in her eyes when she spoke of starting a practice in Denver. Yes, Anna St. James would leave Asheville after the holidays, and he would never see her again. He didn't care. Then he had to ask himself, *If I don't care then why am I so upset?*

A red-tailed hawk swooped over the coach, the explosive ruffle of wings causing the horses to stop and complain with loud, high-pitched whinnies. "Walk on," the coachman's calm voice ordered.

Walk on, indeed! Richard straightened his shoulders. *That is exactly what I need to do. I need to walk away from this entire infatuation with Anna St. James.* He leaned toward the window, eyes gazing up into the sky for comfort, then down into the gorge where the French Broad River wound its way around the valley like a silver ribbon rushing along on its journey to the next town or village.

"Father," he whispered. "Help me to move on in your grace. I need you now more than ever before."

⌒

Anna rose early the next morning, still weary from her conversation with Richard. The depth of his dislike toward married women with careers had left her melancholy. She shook her head, as if the movement itself might free her mind from the disappointment she felt.

Well, despite his old fashion ways, he *had* saved her life. Without his heroic effort, she would not be here. He was a marvelous physician who had accepted her as a colleague—at least to a point. But none of that could erase his uncompromising view of a woman's place.

Trying to shake off the lingering distress, she went to the closet to choose a dress for her interview. Among the two nicest outfits she had brought along, she decided upon a tailored green suit. The un-boned jacket and separate blouse allowed far more freedom of movement than the constrained style of earlier decades. How glad she was to be living in modern times, even though some people refused to escape the dinosaur era!

Her rising frustration was interrupted by a brisk tap on the door. Ellen entered with a tray. "Nothin' like a good breakfast and strong coffee to get a body goin' in the right direction." She placed the silver service near the window. "I see you're already dressed." She appeared frustrated. "Why didn't you ring that little bell? It's my job to help you, Miss."

Anna gave the girl a smile while securing the last pin into a stray wisp of hair. "I saw no reason to disturb you on the day after Christmas. I know you must be exhausted from the parties." She glanced over at the silver coffee pot. "But thank you for bringing the tray. I can certainly use the coffee."

Ellen's green eyes crinkled into a grin while pouring the fragrant brew. "Just look up yonder at that sky," she said, gesturing between the open drapes. "No tellin' how much snow we'll get this time."

Anna applied butter and marmalade to her toast while glancing out at the dark clouds that had settled over Biltmore. "I really didn't expect to see snow this far south. Do you always have such stormy winters?"

"It comes in spells." Ellen made the bed while she talked. "My cousins live in Charleston, South Carolina, and they've never even seen a snowflake. But these here mountains are a different story. Once the cold sets in, it stays awhile." She smoothed a blanket. "It's a blessing I can stay at Biltmore where it's warm, and not have to be worried ta' death about how to get back and forth to work in a blizzard."

Anna became suddenly curious. "Where would you work if not at Biltmore?"

"Oh, I guess I'd be slavin' away in that old cotton mill down river. That's where Daddy and Momma work." She shook her head dolefully.

"Your mother works, too?"

"Oh, yes, ma'am. We all have to pull together." She brightened. "But I've almost got enough money saved up so that Momma can quit her job and stay home if she wants to. Mill work is hard on her. My little sister, now that's a different story. She's in college."

"How wonderful." Anna was somewhat surprised. "Which University does she attend?"

The girl lifted her head with pride. "Berea College in Kentucky. It was built for the Southern Appalachian people. There's no charge for tuition, but the students have to work a certain number of hours each week in exchange for their education." Ellen picked up a pillow and gave it a punch. "I was mighty sorry not to see her over the holidays this year, but she had to help out around the campus til right up on Christmas Eve, and that means we won't get to see her before Easter. We miss her, but she's gonna make something good of her life."

"What is she studying?"

"Music Education." The girl's eyes sparkled with pride.

"That's marvelous, Ellen. I know you must be proud of her. Has your family always lived in Asheville?"

"My grandparents came here from Scotland during the 1820's gold rush." She paused to straighten the ruffled bedspread. "Of course, most of the mountain people have been here since the early 1700's. My folks didn't find much gold that I know of." She smoothed a ruffle on one of the pillows before stopping to catch her breath. "Granny said they made a decent living minin' for rubies and other precious stones. This here necklace belonged to my grandmother." The girl proudly displayed a small ruby on a chain around her neck. "It came out of the mountain right behind my house."

Anna took a close look at the deep red gem. "Why, it's as lovely as any I've seen displayed in a jeweler's case."

Ellen smiled, tucking the necklace back under her blouse. "Yes, ma'am, it's mighty special to me. I wear it for good luck. Makes me feel like all my ancestors are watching over me. They're angels now, and I guess they can fly around any place they like. From what mama told me, all of em were saved, so I guess I'm bein' well-protected."

Anna leaned forward with interest. "Ellen, may I ask you something?"

"Why yes, ma'am. What is it?"

"When you say that your ancestors were saved, what do you mean exactly?"

Ellen tucked a strand of hair behind her ear, giving Anna a curious look. "Why, saved from their sins and the fires of hell, ma'am. Being saved means you know Jesus as your own personal savior, and that you're fit to go on up to heaven when you die." She grimaced. "The good Lord knows how hard it is here on earth, so I shore don't want to spend eternity with the devil in that awful lake of fire, do you?"

Anna shuddered, sorry to have asked, especially since it all seemed so agonizing. "Of course not," she murmured. "But is being saved the same thing as being born-again, or inviting Jesus into your heart?"

The girl's smile returned. "Oh, why yes, ma'am. I'm pretty sure that's what it means." She paused. "I guess it's different for everybody, cause we're all special in the eyes of the Lord. Well, I'd best be gettin' on to my other chores." She poked the fire log with determination before bobbing a curtsy and backing out the door.

Anna gazed out the window. The new birth carried with it a message of innocence and hope, while being saved from the fires of hell sounded desperate and frightening. But Richard had said the mountain people lived harsh lives, making them even more cautious of avoiding a hellish hereafter.

Finishing her coffee, she stepped back over to the mirror, smoothing an unruly curl into its proper place and then reached for her hat with soft green plumes. After trying it on, she changed her mind and decided on a smaller one of green felt that appeared better suited to her business-like appearance. Just as she finished straightening her collar, Ellen peeked in. "Your coach is waiting, ma'am."

She took a deep breath. "Thank you, Ellen. I'll be right down."

Anna secured her hat with a pin and took one last look in the mirror. Feeling confident, she hurried down the stairs where Bosworth was waiting with her cloak and gloves. The butler opened the door and a footman took her arm. Just as they descended the front steps of the grand mansion, a gust of wind pulled wickedly at her skirt, blowing a dusting of snow on her cape.

Once inside the coach, the footman placed a bear skin rug over her lap, and she relished its warmth as the horses clomped down the narrow winding drive. In the distance, she heard the mournful cooing of a dove and shivered, hoping its sad song was not an omen of the day ahead.

Richard shrugged out of his cloak and hung it on a peg behind the conference room door before hurrying over to the fireplace. Laying another log on the blaze, he prodded the seething coals to warm up the room.

He'd made a point of arriving earlier than usual. Dr. Becker had requested his presence at an interview. As chief of staff, Richard knew he could not refuse the request of his boss, but hoped the man would hurry along soon. He had a house call later in the morning and wanted to make haste before snow made the mountain coves impassable.

After thawing his hands, he walked over to the window. A harsh wind shook the treetops, raising a fine veil of snow from the ground around them.

Becker was a fine doctor, though lately he seemed to have problems making up his mind. Before the holidays, he announced that he would hire the first man they had interviewed, promising to have him in place before departing for Europe. Then, another vitae arrived from New York. Becker was so impressed with the fellow's training that he decided to do one more interview. Richard hadn't had a chance to review the New York doctor's application, but trusted his colleague to make the right decision, feeling that his own energy was best used elsewhere.

If the snow maintained its present pace, his carriage would never make it up the mountain for a house call. Turning away from the window, he took a seat at the round conference table. As the grandfather clock struck the quarter hour, he heard the clomping of horses that signaled Dr. Becker's arrival. Moments later, his colleague came huffing into the room, carrying a stack of folders and an overflowing briefcase.

"Sorry to have kept you waiting, Wellington, but the wife needed help securing some last-minute details—something about how many formal parties we'd be attending so she would know the exact number of gowns to pack." He glanced at the clock, taking out his pocket watch to synchronize the time.

"That's quite all right." Richard was cordial. "I haven't been waiting long."

The portly man gave a brisk nod. "It's a good thing you're an uncomplaining sort, for should you ever take a wife, your patience will be tested far more than you can imagine." He ran a hand through his steely gray hair and placed one of the folders on the table. "I have always been bewildered by the quantity of clothing a woman requires for traveling. The number of trunks my wife has packed for our trip would fill this entire room." He blew out a puff of air. "And she is only half finished."

Richard gave a slight smile while the doctor pulled out an eye glass from his coat pocket and began polishing it with a handkerchief. "Women are most unusual, my boy. They presume to have the answer to everything, but cannot see beyond the next ball gown, or even dismount from a horse without a man's assistance." He sighed, sinking deeper into his chair. "Such helpless creatures."

Richard shifted in his seat, uncomfortable with Becker's comments. They seemed excessive.

He'd dined with Dr. Becker and his wife on Thanksgiving, less than two months ago, and the man hadn't appeared quite so domineering then. How could he have changed so much in such a short time? *Or am I the one who has changed?* He shook aside the thought. No, it was his colleague who had changed, becoming crankier with age.

Becker adjusted the glass and peered down at the sheaf of papers in his hand. "I still view Dr. Smith as a strong candidate, but I didn't make him any promises. I'll wire him tomorrow with my final decision." He held up the resume. "Now *this* young man is from New York. He graduated from medical college first in his class, did post graduate work in Germany, and studied obstetrics for a short time while in Russia." He tapped his pen on the table. "Not that we would require his skill in obstetrics, but I think it speaks well for a doctor to have a well-rounded education, don't you?"

"He may be the best man for the job." Richard nodded. "As I recall, Dr. Smith had quite a bit of knowledge surrounding tuberculosis but lacked the rigorous training and experience one receives while abroad."

Dr. Becker rubbed his chin. "I'm hopeful this new man could relieve some of the burden on you while I'm away."

"I look forward to meeting him."

The grandfather clock started to chime. "His appointment is at nine o'clock sharp. Would you like to glance over his resume?"

"That won't be necessary. I prefer to see what he is all about in person."

⌒

The horses turned onto a narrow road leading uphill to a Queen Anne-style house with red gables. Anna's heart jerked with sudden dread when reading the clinic sign, Blue Ridge Sanitorium. Dr. Becker would be expecting a man to show up for the interview. She clenched her hands, hoping the decision to use only her initials would not have a disastrous outcome.

When the coach came to a halt, the footman opened the door and helped her out. She ducked her head while hurrying up the steps before the snow could ruin her soft felt hat. "God be with me, and give me strength," she murmured, before stepping into the entry hall.

I am always with you, whispered a still small voice that wrapped around her like a soft cloak. The first thing she noticed about the clinic was the absence of strong antiseptic odor. One window was cracked, and fresh mountain air billowed the white lace curtains in the reception area. A fire roared from within a cast-iron stove, sending tendrils of warmth out into the room.

Walking over to the nurse's station, she rang a bell for assistance. Within seconds, a small, dark-haired woman, wearing a white pinafore and nurse's cap appeared.

"How may I help you, Miss?" She spoke with a refined Southern accent.

"I have an interview with Dr. Becker."

A frown ridged her brow.

Anna cleared her throat. "I'm Dr. St. James."

"I see. I-we weren't expecting a lady doctor."

Anna swallowed the lump in her throat. If this starched nurse was shocked, how might Dr. Becker react?

The next instant, the nurse's surprise transformed to a smile as she held out her hand. "I'm Henrietta McFalls. Doctors Becker and Wellington are waiting for you in the conference room. It's their policy for each applicant to have a brief tour of the clinic before interviewing a prospective employee."

Her heart tripped over itself. "Did you say Dr. Wellington?" She felt a sudden urge to run out the door and never look back. Could she possibly face Dr. Wellington after their disagreement last night?

The nurse gave a friendly nod. "Yes, Dr. Richard Wellington is the chief of staff here. Dr. Becker established this clinic but focuses most of his efforts on research. Now, if you'll follow me, we'll begin your tour."

Her mouth felt dry. What on earth would Dr. Wellington think when discovering she had applied for a position at *his* clinic? Did he know she was the applicant? Of course, he had mentioned his work at a TB sanatorium, but how could she have known which one? Doubts and embarrassment threatened to steal her nerve. *Of course, I had to go and offend him at our last meeting, she scolded herself.*

Following through the quiet halls, Anna's heart thumped in rhythm with the padded tap of the nurse's soles. The whispered routine of the clinic went on around them and in a distant room came the sound of a cork being removed from a medicine bottle, followed by the rustling starched skirts of a nurse delivering the curative to her patient.

The double doors of the wards stood open, and Anna caught glimpses of resting patients tucked under mounds of blankets. Many of their delicate faces were framed by silver hair, while other countenances clearly belonged to young adults. All of them were bound together by the shared pallor so common among sufferers of tuberculosis. Even so, the atmosphere appeared cheerful. The walls were covered with bright paper, and airy white curtains moved back and forth in the brisk mountain air.

"Everything is very uplifting." Anna glanced around at the yellow wallpaper.

The nurse nodded. "We really try to keep the patients' surroundings as bright as possible." They entered a parlor and Nurse McFalls hurried over to the sofa and straightened a pillow that had lost its place in the colorful line-up. "Several church choirs drop in every Sunday afternoon to sing hymns." She hesitated, as though weighing her words carefully. "Melancholy often accompanies tuberculosis, so we do everything possible to raise their spirits."

Anna nodded. "There has been quite a bit of research on the therapeutic benefit of music. It does seem to encourage the infirmed."

The nurse smiled. "Yes, it seems that music is of some value to our patients, and they also enjoy the company of those who sing. Many are here from other states and do not have families close by. We try to ease their loneliness as much as possible."

Anna followed her down a corridor to a stairway. "Our patients rise each morning at seven o'clock," she explained as they climbed steps to the second floor. "At that time, they are given bed-baths and served breakfast. That's all finished by half-past eight."

As they approached the wards, the nurse's tone became hushed. "After their morning meal, the patients are wheeled out into the sunlight for deep breathing treatments—unless it is severely cold or snowing as it is today. When spring arrives, our patients are encouraged to stay outdoors for a longer period of time."

Double French doors led to a big screened-in porch that wrapped around the entire house. Various partitions were set up to simulate semi-private rooms. "By early summer, patients can sleep out here and fully saturate their lungs with healing air."

Anna drew a deep breath. "Yes, the air is very pure here. I'm sure this porch must be delightful in warmer weather."

The nurse's demeanor seemed to lighten, now that they were outside. "Dr. Wellington would prefer all of our patients to be brought to the sleeping porches much earlier than June." She shivered and pulled her white sweater closer. "But we don't get a real thaw until the middle of May. I suppose we should go back inside for your interview now." Her voice was brisk while leading the way on rubber-shod feet

Stopping before the heavy double doors, Anna moistened her lips and braced herself for meeting Richard in his professional setting. What on earth had she gotten herself into?

Chapter Fourteen

Richard's jaw dropped when Anna entered the room. What was she doing here? She couldn't be applying for the post, could she?

As he slammed his mouth shut, continuing to stare at Anna as she stared back at him, the pieces fell into place.

Why wouldn't she apply for the position of Assistant Clinical Director? She *was* an MD, wasn't she? But she'd said she was visiting Asheville on holiday. If she was here for employment, why hadn't she mentioned it? Surely, they had spent enough time together over the last few days for the subject to have come up. His jaw hardened, feeling betrayed despite himself.

As the silence in the room deepened, Becker cleared his throat. "What can I do for you, Miss?"

She blinked, as if waking from a dream, and turned her stunning turquoise eyes on Dr. Becker. "I..." Her voice faltered. Then she drew her shoulders up and began again. This time her voice was firm and in control. "I have an interview this morning with Dr. Becker." She glanced at the grandfather clock in the corner, as though to confirm her punctuality.

Dr. Becker, a confused look on his face, looked beyond her. "I am expecting Dr. St. James. Is he your husband?"

"I am Dr. St. James." Her eyes seemed to challenge him.

A stony silence filled the room. Dr. Becker put in his eye glass as though that might help him to understand the state of things. "*You* are Dr. A. M. St. James?"

173

She gave a curt nod. Whereas a lesser woman might have cowered, she lifted her pert chin and a sparkle lit her eyes. It was a glimmer Richard recognized; it meant she was rising to the challenge.

"Yes. Dr. *Anna Michelle* St. James. It's a pleasure to meet you, doctor." As she spoke, she advanced into the room, her right hand held out.

While Becker looked intently at her, as though willing her to disappear, Richard stepped forward to give his colleague time to recover. "Forgive my poor manners, Dr. St. James." He shook her hand as if they were meeting for the first time, his tone all business. "Allow me to take your cloak. Please have a seat." He waved her toward one of the wing-back chairs at the table. "I didn't realize you had applied for this post, so I take it you understand my surprise at seeing you here today."

She gazed up at him, the first sign of regret in her eyes. "I had no idea worked at this particular clinic."

While the answer didn't satisfy Richard completely, it did help him to overcome his initial feeling of betrayal. He managed a reassuring smile, though he was still feeling confused and at odds with her appearance here in his clinic. "I suppose with over fifty such hospitals in and around Asheville, it is understandable."

Dr. Becker clenched his jaw until the tendons in his neck protruded like taut ropes. He turned his steely gaze toward Richard. "Am I to understand that you and this young lady are acquainted?" His shaggy brows drew closer. "Wellington, if this is one of your dry British pranks, it isn't funny. I have many things to accomplish before my trip abroad, and this entire situation is wasting precious time." He brought his hand down on the table with such force that the prisms on the chandelier above them jangled in disharmony.

A pulse began to beat in Richard's temple. Did the man have no more sense of decorum than to lose his temper in front of a lady? And an applicant at that.

Anna's face grew pale. Richard walked toward his colleague, in a quiet attempt to protect her from further verbal assault. "Dr. St. James and I met a few days ago, on the train from New York. She's a guest at Biltmore, and a highly competent doctor, I might add. You saw that from her resume." He hoped the reminder would help Becker to get his temper under control.

A highly competent doctor? Richard could hardly believe he had said such a thing. But hadn't she saved the lives of both mother and child on the train? And didn't the children at Biltmore love and trust her? Yes, she was highly competent, even if he did not agree with all her views.

Dr. Becker sat back down in his chair and took a folded handkerchief from his pocket to mop his forehead. "How long have you known the Vanderbilt family?" He directed his words to Anna, his voice stern, as though he had the right to arraign her for some crime.

Her eyes were steady. "Mr. Vanderbilt's niece and I were in school together." She paused, as though to count out the precise amount of time. "Actually, I have known the Vanderbilt family for most of my life." Her voice had a slight wobble but her beautiful face remained unruffled by the conversation.

Richard had to admire her spunk—especially in the face of the unpropitious beginning presented to her by his forcible colleague. He'd seen more than one young nurse run away from Becker in tears.

It suddenly occurred to Richard that George Vanderbilt made regular donations to the clinic. This might present itself as a problem should Becker refuse an interview to a friend of the Vanderbilt family. On one hand, hiring a female physician would go against the very grain of Becker's principles. But not hiring her might cause a financial loss he simply did not need—particularly on the eve of his grand excursion to Europe.

Richard folded his arms, beginning to feel a certain amusement at his employer's dilemma. The next second, he sobered, catching a glimpse of Anna's serious expression. Had she found herself in similar situations before? Yes, he remembered something she'd told him about being turned away from prospective jobs without the benefit of an interview. Could Becker rightly fault her for using only her initials when signing the inquiry? He wasn't certain that he should. Male doctors used their initials all the time on patient's records and other official documentation, so what gave them the right to hold it against her? It wasn't deception. It was more like self-preservation.

Becker cleared his throat. "I will tell you in advance, this position is not appropriate for a woman. However, since you are a friend of the Vanderbilt family, I will grant you an interview." He rustled through some documents on the table and thrust them in her direction. "Miss St. James are you familiar with the use of Dr. Forlanini's *artificial pneumothorax* procedure?"

Richard's heart wrenched with the inequity of the question. Most physicians had never even heard of the new treatment, and Becker certainly hadn't queried previous applicants on the subject. To his surprise, she nodded and drew off her gloves to freely rifle through the pages of documents, giving them a quick perusal. Then she moistened her lips and placed the papers back on the table in a neat stack.

"I'm actually quite familiar with this discourse. I visited Dr. Forlanini's clinic a few summers ago to observe the temporary lung collapse procedure. I was interested in perhaps implementing it with some of my TB patients."

Becker appeared astonished. "You—er—you say that you have met with Dr. Forlanini?"

"Yes. When studying abroad, I visited his clinic, and the method he uses is most intricate." Her eyes took on a soft light as she began to describe in detail something that Richard and his colleague had only heard about.

Becker leaned forward, as though temporarily forgetting all about her gender, causing Richard to see that her personal association with the world-renowned doctor had made an impression. "What are your thoughts on this new method? Did you observe the entire operation?" There was now an interesting blend of excitement and curiosity in the older doctor's voice.

"Yes, I witnessed the complete procedure." She spoke with authority. "But as much as I admire Dr. Forlanini's medical genius, I find his surgery to be invasive—especially for patients already weakened by tuberculosis." She lifted her chin. "Clearly, he has enjoyed a certain degree of success with his work, but until more extensive research is done on his method, I must hold fast to a more conservative course of treatment."

Richard suppressed a smile. How like her to always give an honest opinion without first examining what it might cost her.

Becker snorted. "You dare to insult Dr. Forlanini?" There was a thin note of cruelty in his voice.

"Certainly not," she said, a quick color flying into her cheeks. "I have tremendous respect for him. It's just that I happen to believe his method needs a little more refinement." She shrugged. "He knows my opinion on the matter and in no way considers it an insult. In our recent correspondence, he was even considering one of my suggestions for improving the procedure." She sat back in her chair.

Seeing the spark of anger in the older man's eyes, Richard came to her defense. "Actually, I agree with you about the procedure being too invasive." He turned to Dr. Becker. "You and I were having a similar discussion about Forlanini's methods a few days ago, were we not?"

Becker grunted, giving him a sharp glance before resuming his questions. "Since you are in collaboration with the experts, what are your special recommendations for patients with tuberculosis?" His mouth lifted sardonically. "Would you like to add anything of your own?"

She seemed undeterred. "Nurse McFalls gave me a thorough tour of your facility and I greatly admire the work you are doing here." She pursed her lips before continuing. "As for any special recommendations, I have none to offer. But in the future, I *do* believe that Dr. Conrad Roentgen's recent discovery of the X-ray will serve as a great stride forward in the monitoring of TB."

Becker sneered. "That X-ray business just came out a few weeks ago. Are you also corresponding with Dr. Roentgen?"

The barbed comment brought an even more vivid color to her cheeks that swept up to her brow. "Certainly not. I've only read of his work." She made a quick recovery and continued. "But perhaps within the next few years, we'll be able to actually *see* what is going on inside the lungs. What a difference that would make, especially for those patients in the early stages of TB."

Becker slapped the table, saying through a guffaw, "X-rays! Now there's a fly-by-night invention for you. Dr. Roentgen's picture-taking machine is no more than a curiosity."

The man was acting like a buffoon, and Richard was revolted by his colleague's behavior. Glancing at Dr. St. James, he noticed the only sign of consternation was the whitening knuckles of her folded hands on the tabletop.

Richard cleared his throat. "Perhaps the technology will prove more helpful than we suspect, Dr. Becker. The X-Ray uses a mild form of radiation that might help us get an inside view of the lungs and bones. If we could actually *see* what was going on in a patient's lungs through Roentgen's new invention, we would get an immediate diagnosis of the patient's condition possibly saving valuable time."

Her eyes lit with eagerness. "Just imagine being able to take a picture of the internal organs. Wouldn't it be marvelous to see what we were up against? Surely that would help us better know how to treat many other problems besides TB."

Richard couldn't help but smile at her enthusiasm. "Yes, it would be a giant step forward in our work."

Becker gave an impatient wave of his hand. "The American Medical Association observes all advancements in science, and so far, they haven't embraced Roentgen's magic picture making machine."

Her eyes widened a fraction. "But Dr. Becker, any new development in medical science is well worth watching, don't you agree?"

Dr. Becker harrumphed. "As I said, young lady, the AMA keeps us apprised of such things."

Richard caught the look of annoyance on her face and remembered her remarks on the train about the American Medical Association not allowing female physicians into their membership. He was relieved she did not express her opinion.

Becker's gravelly voice grew sharper. "Working with TB patients is very tiresome, Miss St. James. The doctor for this position will work twelve to fifteen-hour shifts. It will also be necessary to make numerous follow-up house calls for discharged patients." He leaned back in the chair, his expression smug. "I'm afraid this job would prove too distasteful and rigorous for you, my dear. Women are susceptible to hysteria, you know. Such an intense position could leave a harmful mark on your stability."

Her dazzling irises sparked. "I do not suffer from hysteria, Dr. Becker, and my work at the Women's Charity Hospital required the same rigorous routine as does your clinic." She paused to draw in a breath. "And for the record, I do not view my profession as distasteful. I'm honored to help patients suffering from tuberculosis, influenza, diphtheria, pneumonia, and even cholera."

When she finished speaking, all the while maintaining a perfectly modulated tone, she eyed Dr. Becker with all the bearing of a young queen who had successfully reprimanded a disobedient subject. Richard almost stood and applauded her poise amid Becker's tyranny.

Dr. Becker drummed his fingers on the table. "I admit you have excellent qualifications, Miss St. James; and when I first read your resume, I was quite prepared to offer you a position." He shook his head. "But hiring a woman doctor is something I couldn't do."

She drew back with a wounded expression. "What does my gender have to do with your choice, sir? You just stated my qualifications are excellent." Her voice betrayed a hint of impatience for the first time. "I do not have a family to support, and my salary would be nowhere near the amount a male physician would require."

The expression on Becker's face softened, as though he'd suddenly caught the brass ring. He picked up her resume and glanced over it again, studying over a paragraph here and there before placing it back on the table. "Well, I do need to fill the position," he said in a begrudging tone. "And I admit that you have numerous qualifications that I admire."

Richard could not believe what he was hearing. Was the old grump going to hire her after all?

Becker made a steeple of both hands, holding them just below his chin. "I propose to hire you as Dr. Wellington's assistant—as a nurse. Because of your extensive training, I am willing to offer you a higher salary than our other nurses on staff."

Anna stared at him as if she didn't comprehend what he was saying. Richard found it hard to believe Becker would insult a medical doctor with such an offer.

"A nurse, you say?" Her voice was faint.

"That's right." He sat back with a satisfied air. "Take it or leave it."

She moistened her lips. "Could I give you my answer tomorrow morning?"

"I need to know now," snapped Becker. "My ship sails for Europe tomorrow, and I must get this wrapped up quickly."

Richard's heart wrenched at the audacity of his demand and watched with attentiveness as Anna glanced down at her hands, then over to the clock as though it might offer a solution to her dilemma. "I accept." Her voice wavered. "When do I begin?"

"Talk to Wellington," Becker said, shoving out of his chair. "Now if you'll both excuse me, I have other matters to attend."

⌒

The clock chimed nine times, as though in celebration of the scowling man's departure. Richard interlaced his fingers. "I apologize for my colleague's behavior. He was in rare form today and I'm afraid you got the brunt of it."

Anna drew a deep breath and blew it out slowly. "I've been through horrible interviews before, but never with an ally. Thank you."

Concern creased his forehead. "I don't understand why you approved his offer. You turned down a nursing job in New York because you didn't want to roll bandages for the rest of your life, yet you accepted Becker's proposal that you work here as a nurse. Might I ask why?"

Anna debated how much to disclose. The support he had shown her during the grueling interview had proven his friendship, and he deserved an explanation. "I—" her voice faltered. "I accepted the offer because I need the money."

His eyes narrowed as she plunged ahead. "When my father passed away, he left a large amount of debt—more than his estate could absorb. His business partner forced me out of my ancestral home and froze all bank accounts. For the last year, I have been living in a boarding house near the hospital, with a salary barely enough to maintain the most frugal lifestyle."

She paused for a breath, gathering courage to continue, but her chest felt tight and she could feel hot tears springing up behind her eyelids. Try as she might, Anna couldn't stop them. She tried never to cry. Tears were misinterpreted as a sign of weakness, especially for a female doctor. But they were now rolling down her cheeks, one right after the other like an avalanche and she couldn't hold them back.

Richard scrambled to his feet and handed her a fresh handkerchief. "Take your time." He clasped her shoulder, prompting a surge of comfort throughout her body.

For a moment, she thought of how nice it would feel for him to hold her. She shivered. "Forgive me. I never allow myself to lose control like this, but it seems I am not having the best of days."

"Warm yourself," he said, ushering her to a chair in front of the fireplace. "And please do not feel you must apologize. You deserve a medal after what you've just been through. I'll get us some tea."

She nodded, not trusting herself to speak as he led her to a wingback chair near the fire.

After he left the room, Anna wiped her eyes and blew her nose, hoping to regain her composure. What must he think of her outburst? Would he conclude, as would his colleague, that her tears were proof of a woman's tendency toward feminine hysteria?

A few minutes later, Richard returned with a teapot and two cups. He placed the tray on a table between the chairs and poured her portion first. Although her mind was an emotional whirlwind, she was flattered he remembered how she took her tea—with a dollop of milk and two sugars.

She took several sips of the strong hot liquid before finishing her story, stopping a few times to draw a ragged breath. She even told him about Van Demark's marriage proposal and how she'd turned him down.

By the time she finished, the teapot had grown cold and they sat in silence. A log in the fireplace collapsed, scattering rosy coals throughout the ashes before flaming up into bright colored gold. Anna looked down and smoothed a wrinkle from her skirt, then glanced back up. "I know my situation could be worse. At least I have a means of supporting myself, and for that I am grateful."

His head moved in a slow nod. "I wish I could convince Dr. Becker to hire you as a physician, but by now you must realize he is almost impossible to budge. He seems to have grown more unreasonable over the last month or so." He shrugged. "I hardly know what to say to the man anymore."

"You've already proven such a help to me, Richard. I wouldn't want you to speak with him on my behalf."

He waved his hand in a dismissive gesture. "Nonsense. What are friends for? You've been through quite an ordeal. Most people would have never finished the interview, but you didn't let him get the best of you. You can be proud of yourself for that. As for the tears, don't apologize for those either."

She rose from her chair. "When would you like for me to begin my work here?"

He retrieved her cloak from behind the door.

"Monday morning, seven o'clock sharp." He helped with her wrap. "Dr. Becker's ship sails tomorrow, and the rotating staff will still be here on Sunday."

She pulled on her gloves. "How long will he be away?"

"A year, possibly longer." His lips curved into a boyish grin. "You won't have to see him again anytime soon."

She suddenly felt a spark of hope. "Very well, I shall see you on Monday morning, bright and early."

Richard walked her to the door and Anna took the waiting footman's arm. She didn't like the idea of working as a nurse but was thankful for God's provision. As the carriage rolled away from the clinic, she felt reassured that somehow all would be well.

Chapter Fifteen

Richard watched as the Vanderbilt coach rolled out of the courtyard, the sound of hastening hooves muffled by the snow. He turned away, still thinking about everything Anna had shared. How horrible it must be to have lost both her doting father and her fortune. He clenched his fists when thinking of the business partner who had proposed marriage in exchange for clearing her family's debts. An obvious rake who would like nothing more than to use her beauty and good breeding to make himself look good in society.

For the first time, he felt genuinely relieved she could support herself as a physician. Her education and skills had shielded her from becoming a pawn in the hands of that devious man. He cringed at the thought of her living in a lodging house near the hospital which was probably in the Lower East End of New York. Well, the mountains of Asheville would be a safe place for her, even if she did have to work as a nurse. Though she would be exposed to TB, it would at least be contained in a sterile environment.

The snow was growing deeper and had already outlined the finely penciled branches of trees in the courtyard below. He would need to leave posthaste to make that house call.

A little later, as he made his way up the mountain on horseback, his thoughts returned to Anna. He was amazed the way she had dealt with his colleague. There was nothing phony or insincere about her. In fact, he knew she was everything he wanted in a wife.

He shook his head, knowing she would never give up her career for him or any other man. And he wasn't about to set himself up for another heartbreak. But that didn't mean they couldn't remain friends. Friendship with her would indeed be for the best all the way around, yet a small voice in his heart begged to differ.

While Richard was making his house call, the storm dumped another eight inches of snow, making it barely possible for him to return. When he finally rode into the courtyard of the clinic, a groomsman met him and led his horse into the stable. As he stomped the snow from his boots, Nurse McFalls opened the door and took his coat before ushering him into the kitchen.

"Get yourself warmed up, doctor." She handed him a cup of tea. "How is Mr. Owen?"

Richard took a seat near the fire, holding the cup with both hands. "A bit better, but now his wife has influenza. Thank goodness, their teenage daughters are able to care for them. Otherwise, they'd be in a serious predicament."

Nurse McFalls placed the kettle on the back burner. "I'll take them some chicken soup later today."

He raised a warning hand. "Better wait until the storm settles down. I barely made it into their cove on horseback and had to walk a half mile to their cabin. George really needs to do something about that road. It's part of his property, but unfit even for a horse to navigate in this weather."

The nurse wiped down the surface of the stove with a wet cloth and took a step back to make sure she had removed all the grime. "Mr. Vanderbilt probably doesn't know what shape it's in. Didn't he buy over some hundred-thousand acres?"

Richard nodded. "One-hundred and twenty-five thousand, to be exact. It would take at least a week for him to inspect it by horseback. I'll mention the road when I see him again. I'm sure when he realizes the poor condition it's in, he will repair it."

Suddenly, Dr. Becker entered the room and Nurse McFalls placed the dish rag on a peg behind the stove and scurried out, saying something about the need to make rounds. Richard wished he could disappear too. He was in no mood to talk with his opinionated colleague.

Becker cleared his throat. "I presume you were able to work everything out with Miss St. James?"

There was a sarcastic gleam in his eye. Richard poured himself another cup of tea and prepared to choose his words with care. "I'm rather shocked you didn't ask about her practice in New York. I know her identity caught us both by surprise, but from what I've gathered, she works mostly with the poor on the Lower East Side." He shook his head. "Only the most dedicated doctor would venture into that part of the city."

Dr. Becker gave him a sidelong glance, helping himself to the remainder of what was left in the teapot. The fact that he was listening emboldened Richard to continue. "I think you should reconsider hiring her as a physician. We could use a doctor with her experience."

"You know how I feel about women doctors." He gave Richard a curious look. "I thought you shared my views. You seem like a different person nowadays. What's come over you, man?"

Richard placed his spoon back on the saucer. "It's funny. Only a few weeks ago, I would have agreed with you completely about female physicians." *And several other things,* he thought, while staring down at his teacup. "But, now—" He shrugged. "I'm not so certain, especially after working alongside Dr. St. James."

Becker jerked his head toward him. "You've actually *worked* with her? You didn't mention that during her interview."

Richard nodded. "She delivered a baby that was breech while we were on the train to Asheville. No caesarean procedure. Just forceps." He cleared his throat before continuing. "Then, yesterday at the Biltmore party, she assisted me in examining all the children who were sick. I watched her win the heart of a frightened toddler who had a severe case of bronchitis. The child adored her. She has the best bedside manner of any doctor I know."

"So, she delivered a baby and crooned over a child." Becker dismissed his words with a wave of his hand. "That tells me she might make a good midwife and mother. Don't go soft on me, Wellington." He narrowed his eyes, pulling his brows close together. "I find no fault with your attraction to Miss St. James. After all, she is a beautiful woman. Just don't make the mistake of confusing her magnetism with competence."

"Oh, come now," said Richard, exhaling a long slow breath. "I assure you I am neither confused nor going soft. I have the utmost faith in Dr. St. James's capabilities as a physician, and I feel that you made a mistake by not hiring her as such."

Becker's jaw tightened. Without a word, he walked over to the window. "If she's as capable as you say, she'll make a fine nurse."

Richard placed his cup and saucer into the sink. Why should he bother to argue with this stubborn man? Their conversation was eating up valuable time. "If you'll excuse me, I have several patients to attend." Swallowing his exasperation, he left the room.

Anna took hold of her skirts and hastened up the long staircase at Biltmore, still beside herself after the grueling interview. She was glad the thick hallway carpet muffled her steps. As much as she loved Daphne, she didn't want to face her just now.

When reaching her room, she bathed her face in cold water, hoping to erase any sign of tears. Over the years, she had learned to hide her innermost feelings from the world, burying annoyances in her heart and grieving over them in silence. She wasn't happy about getting a nursing position at the clinic, but at least she would be well paid and could save some money.

But oh, how kind Richard had been to her. She was glad their disagreement yesterday had not shaken his belief in her abilities as a physician. He had shown himself to be a true friend during the harsh interview, and she would never forget it. She sank into a soft cushioned chair and closed her eyes. Lifting a hand to her neck, she wished she weren't so dependent on getting this job. If only she had the money that Van Demark had stolen, she could catch the next train to Denver and pursue her dream. But what would her life be like without Richard and the Vanderbilts?

Her thoughts were interrupted by a gentle tap on the door. "Come in," she called, feeling ready to face her friend.

Daphne strode into the room and dropped onto the floral divan before the fire. "I couldn't wait any longer to find out how things turned out. Did you get the position?" There was excitement in her voice.

Anna felt her lips quiver. "Dr. Becker refused to hire me for the position of doctor at the clinic. He did, however, offer me a nursing job, which I accepted." Her voice sounded flat, even to her own ears.

"He what?" Daphne's smile disappeared. "Anna, how is that possible? You aren't a nurse, you're a full-fledged doctor."

Anna shrugged. "He believes women are prone to hysteria and shouldn't be allowed to practice medicine. A nurse, on the other hand, is under the complete supervision of a male doctor, so he decided I should work in that capacity."

Daphne clasped a hand to the ruffled collar of her dress. "Well, the very nerve of that man! Did he really say that to you?"

Anna grimaced. "That and more. He said women were prone to hysteria and that my acting in the capacity of a physician might push me over the edge. I suspect he would be very much in favor of all women having an ovariotomy."

Daphne wrinkled her nose. "What on earth is that?"

"It's the removal of normal ovaries, a somewhat fashionable European treatment for menstrual madness. I'm adamantly against it, as are most sensible physicians."

"It—that sounds horrible." The girl clasped a hand to her mouth as though she might become ill by the thought.

"It's appalling, and most of the women, or I should say *victims*, of this surgery have no say in the matter." Anna brushed a stray tendril of hair behind her ear. "If a man decides his wife or daughter is getting out of hand, or becoming too emotional, some doctors will perform the surgery without hesitation."

Her friend's pleasant face was now a study in frowns. Anna felt a twinge of guilt for her rant.

"I detest the thought of you having to be anywhere near that mad man." Daphne rose and began to pace back and forth in front of the fireplace.

Anna walked over to the window and gazed at the falling snow that had already covered the grooves of the carriage wheels that were fresh only a few minutes earlier. The scenery projected a determined kind of silence that matched her feelings. "I didn't have a choice." She turned to face her friend. "Oh, Daphne, I need to earn some money as fast as possible."

Daphne regarded her with eyes of compassion, her taffeta gown swishing as she crossed the room to place an arm on her shoulder. "I have plenty of money, and Uncle George won't mind your staying with us indefinitely—here at Biltmore. And with Grammy living here, everything will be on the up and up."

Anna opened her mouth to protest, but Daphne shushed her and continued. "I'll set up a special bank account, and you won't have to ask me for anything. It will be in your name and at your disposal. Later in the year, we'll travel to Europe and it will be just like old times."

Her friend's generosity was overwhelming, but she couldn't accept it. "I appreciate your thoughtfulness more than you know," she said. "But it wouldn't be right for me to rely on you for my support."

Daphne arched a golden brow. "And why not? You'd do the same for me, wouldn't you?"

"Yes, of course I would. You *know* I would. But you're going to be married soon, and I won't jeopardize your union by tagging around like a fifth wheel." She shook her head. "Besides, I don't mind working as a nurse, at least for a little while. I'll be assisting Richard. I didn't realize he worked at the same clinic where I applied, so you can imagine my surprise when I saw him there with Dr. Becker."

"I *knew* Richard worked at one of the TB clinics. I didn't know *which* one." Daphne's voice was filled with distress. "I should have made it my business to find out where he was employed. Oh Anna, I feel as though I've let you down." Her eyes misted over with tears.

Anna patted her friend on the arm. "Don't be a silly goose. You certainly aren't to blame for any of this. The only thing left for me to do now is work as a nurse-at least until I can get back on my feet."

Daphne's expression fell. "But won't it be just horrible to see Dr. Becker every day? Especially since he hates women doctors."

Anna smiled. "Actually, he is leaving for Europe tomorrow and won't return for a year. Hopefully, I'll be able to save some money and move to Colorado before he returns."

Daphne furrowed her brow. "Colorado? I want you to stay here, in Asheville. Won't you please allow me to ask Uncle George for help? I'm almost certain he donates to the clinic where Richard is employed. Perhaps he could put pressure on Becker to hire you as a doctor." Her voice trailed off.

"Absolutely not!" Anna shook her head, adamant. "Besides, trying to change things now would only serve to make it worse."

Daphne released a deep breath. "God can help with all of this."

There was a long pause, with only the snapping sparks from the fire spreading its warmth amid the silence between them.

"I know you're right, Daphne." She spoke in a broken whisper. "But I really don't know how to pray in this particular situation. I know God cares, but I don't know what to say. Does that make any sense at all?"

Daphne took her hand. "We all feel that way from time to time. I'll pray, and you can join me in agreement. The scripture says where two or more come together agreeing in the name of Jesus, they can ask whatever they wish, and it will be done for them."

Anna nodded. "I'd like that very much, and yes, I'll come into agreement with you." The women knelt in front of the divan, hand in hand, while Daphne prayed.

Anna noticed that her friend didn't use a formal tone of voice as she had during their school days. This prayer was straight forward and bold.

"Father, you have called my friend to be a medical doctor, and now she has been hired at the clinic as a nurse. If this is what you want, then please give her the grace to accept it. But if it's not, we implore your intervention in the matter so that she may use all of her gifts on your behalf." She paused. "And Lord, about Douglas Van Demark. If there was anything illegal about his dealings with Anna's father, please shed your light on the matter. We completely trust you to make everything as it should be, Father, and we ask this in Jesus' name. Amen."

"Amen." Anna said, rising from her knees. "Thank you, Daphne. I am learning how to pray all over again. It's as though I've been holding a treasure in my heart for many years and am just now opening it up."

Dimples creased Daphne's cheeks. "I know what you mean. I have always been a believer, but Edward helped me obtain a better understanding of God's unconditional love." She gave a little lopsided grin. "And speaking of Edward, I have some very good news."

"Then by all means share it."

Daphne's eyes sparkled. "Uncle George talked with Mumsie yesterday, right after the Christmas party. She was resistant about my marrying Edward, but when he told her none of the family wanted a repeat of what had happened to Consuelo, she gave in. The wedding is set for August tenth in the garden here at Biltmore. Isn't it wonderful?" She clasped both Anna's arms and they whirled around the room until they both fell back down on the divan, laughing and out of breath.

"Now, how could we have gone to Europe with your wedding so close at hand?" Anna waggled a finger.

"Your good sense has always helped keep my feet on solid ground. We may not be going to Europe, but I still intend to help you financially, whether you like it or not."

Anna opened her mouth to protest, but Daphne raised a warning hand. "Shush now, we'll discuss it later. It's almost time for lunch and I want to show you a picture of a wedding gown I've fallen in love with!" She rolled her eyes. "Mumsie says it's too modern, and would prefer that I wear her dress. But I want a wedding gown of my own. Could you look at it before lunch? It's in the Parisian Magazine."

Anna couldn't resist a smile. "I'd love to see it."

The women looped arms while walking down the hall to Daphne's room, and for the first time since her father passed away, Anna felt a new sense of peace.

Chapter Sixteen

When Anna arrived at the clinic for her first day at work, Richard was waiting for her on the front porch. He held up a warning hand as the footman opened the carriage door. "Don't come any closer," he called as she started to dismount.

Had he changed his mind? Dark bristles covered his chin and jaw. What was going on that would so adversely affect his appearance. Her gasp was the only sound for a long moment.

"We had an outbreak of influenza over the weekend, and the Health Department placed us under quarantine. The other two physicians are at home in bed. All the nursing staff, except for one, left early last evening with chills and fever. Everything is in chaos."

"Oh no," she breathed.

He nodded. "I'm the only doctor here. And only one nurse is left?"

"Yes, Nurse Cartwright is as hearty as ever, thank goodness. And we still have cook, and our cleaning lady." He studied her for a moment. "I could really use your help, but I wanted you to be aware of the quarantine, so you'd at least have the option of changing your mind. I'd never put pressure on anyone to begin a new job under these conditions." He rubbed his forehead.

Anna felt a sudden euphoria. He needed her. The sentiment was immediately replaced by a conviction of guilt when she thought about the suffering patients. "How many are infected?"

"Fifteen are displaying symptoms. I sent word to The Sisters of Mercy, asking them to lend us some of their nursing students."

She frowned. "How advanced are they in their training?"

"The Sisters have strict requirements, so they'll be up to speed. Besides, you can show them the ropes—er—that is, if you decide to climb aboard this sinking ship."

She chuckled. "I have every intention of doing so. But first, I'll go back to Biltmore and pack a bag."

"Are you sure? He offered a half-hearted smile. "It could be several weeks before things return to normal."

"This isn't my first quarantine, and I doubt it will be the last. Do you need for me to pick up any special supplies or medicines?"

He rubbed the stubble of his jawline, as though thinking it over. "Cook has the cupboards well stocked, but it wouldn't hurt to add a few things to our medicine chest. If you don't mind, could you stop by the Asheville Dispensary and order some of the basics. Just be sure to tell the pharmacist we're under quarantine and to deliver the provisions at the back gate."

She nodded. "I'll return as soon as possible."

"I really appreciate your help." His smile was brilliant.

"Of course," she called over her shoulder while boarding the coach once more.

Her ride back to Biltmore seemed longer than normal. The horses plodded along, as though enjoying the scenery and with no intention of missing such a lovely morning. When they finally reached their destination, she opened the carriage door without waiting for the footman and rushed up the front steps. Bosworth met her at the door with a concerned look in his eyes. "I didn't expect you back so soon, Dr. St. James. Is everything all right?"

"There's an influenza outbreak and the clinic is in quarantine. I've returned to pack a bag."

"Quarantine?" The butler raised his eyebrows. "Is there anything we can do to help?"

She stopped at the foot of the stairs. "Could you arrange to send some oranges over? It would be splendid for the patients to have fresh fruit."

The butler nodded. "I'll see to it right away. We still have several crates of fruit leftover from the holidays. There are plenty of lemons too. Would you like some of those as well?"

She gathered her skirts to climb the staircase. "Yes, lemon tea would be excellent for the patients. Thank you, Bosworth."

She met Daphne half way up the stairs. "I overheard your conversation. Can I do anything to help?"

Anna hurried past her down the hall. "I can't think of anything at present, dear, but I'll let you know if something comes to mind."

Daphne was practically walking on her heels. "I could visit you at the clinic later today and find out if you need anything." She followed Anna into her room and dropped into a chair.

Anna paused. "Oh, no dear—You mustn't visit me there. The clinic is under quarantine and if you enter the premises you'll be exposed to influenza germs and cannot leave." She paused, picking up her toiletries from the dresser. "If you must get in touch with me, have one of the servants deliver a note to the back gate."

Daphne's beautiful face grew tight with obvious concern. "But you can't be isolated indefinitely. This ruins all my plans!"

"What on earth were you planning?" Anna flung her travel case on the bed and began rummaging through the trunk she'd brought from home.

Daphne inched forward in her chair. "A trip to Hot Springs. I made reservations at Mountain Park Hotel for the entire weekend." She rolled her eyes. "Gram is going with us because she thinks we need a chaperone."

Anna held a partially folded dress in mid-air. "Where is Hot Springs?"

Daphne slumped back in her seat. "Just north of Asheville—about an hour by train—I planned for us to spend the entire weekend relaxing and taking the waters."

"That *does* sound lovely." Anna finished folding several simple day dresses she had brought along for her new job. Thank goodness, they could be easily washed and pressed without aggravation. "Perhaps we can go after the quarantine has been lifted."

"You don't think the quarantine will be lifted by week's end?"

Anna gave a deep sigh. "It could go on for several weeks—even months." She snapped the suitcase closed, giving a rueful shake of her head. "Influenza lasts longer among those with tuberculosis."

Daphne drew her delicate brows into another frown. "Well then, I'll reschedule the trip for later. It wouldn't be any fun without you."

Anna stopped packing and gave her friend a hug. "Daphne, I really think you should go. The healing properties of those mineral springs would be good for you and your grandmother, especially with this influenza epidemic. Perhaps you and I can go later, after the quarantine is behind us."

Daphne sighed. "I suppose we *could* go without you this time, but I shall miss you. Do promise me you won't get sick while during all that horrible influenza."

Anna shook her head. "I wish I could make such a promise, but I give you my word to at least try and remain healthy while under quarantine."

Daphne rested her chin on her palm. "How can you do that?"

"By washing my hands often and eating the right foods. Getting plenty of rest helps too, though I doubt there'll be much of that available, especially since the clinic is so short-staffed."

Daphne's mouth formed an *O* of surprise. "Do you really think doing those things can make a difference?"

Anna headed for the door with her friend following. "Oh yes—especially washing your hands. You should also drink plenty of orange juice and get lots of fresh air."

Bosworth met up with them in the hall and took the suitcase. "Let us know if there's anything we can do to help you through this difficult time. I'll be sure to get those oranges and lemons delivered by early afternoon."

"Thank you, Bosworth. Just be sure to have the driver leave them at the back gate. He mustn't have personal contact with anyone there or he'll be drawn into the quarantine."

"Dear me," said Bosworth, smoothing an invisible wrinkle from his tie. "I'll be certain to tell him that."

As Anna boarded the coach, the bright winter sun was almost halfway to its zenith. When the footman placed the lap rug across her knees, she asked, "Is it very far to the Asheville Dispensary?"

"No Miss, it's right on our way." He jumped down and closed the carriage door.

Settling into her seat, she felt a sudden determination to enjoy the ride. It could be weeks before the quarantine was lifted, so why not take a bit of pleasure in the beauty of her surroundings? As the coach wound its way through the forest, she filled her lungs with the delightful fragrance of hemlock and pine that bordered the drive. She was starting to relax when the carriage lurched and stopped for a deer that bounded into their path. Her heart thumped, as the beautiful creature with big-branched antlers leapt past the horses and disappeared into the snowy wood. She was suddenly reminded of the scripture she'd read the evening before.

Whatever things are pure, whatever things are lovely—-meditate on these things.

The coach eventually moved into an open valley where a pasture filled with munching cows looked up in surprise as the horses passed. Anna leaned back, thankful to God for providing her with this position, even if it wasn't what she specifically wanted.

Her mind wandered back to Daphne's prayer, asking the Divine to shed light on any wrongdoing between Van Demark and her father. Could it be that Van Demark had swindled her father out of money, or had Papa ran up more debt than he could afford?

When reaching the city of Asheville, a streetcar buzzed down the middle of the thoroughfare, causing the horses to give a high-pitched cry of fear at their monster competitor on rails. The driver reassured the matched thoroughbreds in low tones until they settled down.

A few minutes later they passed a trundling hay wagon that was holding up traffic. As she peered out the window the driver of the buckboard grinned at her, tipping his hat in a courtly manner. She lifted one gloved hand and returned his smile, amazed by the way the small city reflected both a rural and sophisticated society which managed to coexist.

At last, the coach stopped in front of the pharmacy and Anna pulled the list from her purse to look it over once more. Everything seemed to be in order. Quinine, Willow Bark, extra bandages, and antiseptics—she took out a pen and added cough drops to the list. As she stepped from the carriage, a sobbing wind snaked around her ankles, causing her to shiver as she took the footman's arm.

When entering the establishment, a bell jingled above the doorway, and the scent of bromide and alcohol filled the air. A jovial voice called from behind a curtained partition: "Be with you in a minute. Just look around and make yourself at home."

"Yes, I will. Thank you," Anna called back, eyeing the colorful peppermint candies in fanciful jars beside the cash register. While browsing the shelves, she heard the clicking sound of a glass bottle being opened, then a spoon mixing up some medicinal concoction.

A large stock of items appeared in the cabinets on either side of the big room, and a soda fountain near the back was filled with multicolored syrup dispensers. Above the colorful display was the picture of a smiling lady, wearing a blue hat with white plumes and holding a glass of Coca-Cola. She noted the drink sold for only a nickel in Asheville, while it was a pricey dime in New York.

Anna continued to peruse the store for a few minutes, looking over the various liniments and headache cures. Most were syrupy combinations of cocaine and opium, with caffeine. Many of her colleagues freely prescribed them, but she avoided their use as much as possible, reserving them for only the most serious illness. Too many people were dependent on these medications through the carelessness of misleading ads in magazines, and she preferred to treat her patients in a more conservative manner.

At last, a tall man with dark graying hair appeared from behind the curtain. "How might I assist you today?" He peered over the rim of his spectacles while drying both hands on his apron.

"I have an order for you." She smiled and handed him the list. "We need it delivered by early afternoon, if at all possible."

He gave a slow nod while looking it over. Then he glanced back up at her with a quizzical look in his eyes.

"I'm Dr. St. James," she spoke haltingly, studying his reaction. "We've had an outbreak of influenza at Blue Ridge Sanatorium and are under quarantine."

The stern expression on his face relaxed and was replaced by the look of admiration. "I didn't know they had lady docs over at Blue Ridge. I'm David McKlean, the pharmacist here. A pleasure to meet you." He inclined his head.

Anna gave him her most pleasant smile, relieved that he didn't rebuke her for being a doctor. "This is my first day." She didn't mention she would be acting as a nurse instead of a physician.

He laughed with pure mirth. "First day and you're in detention? My goodness, how did you manage to escape?" His blue eyes twinkled.

Anna chuckled along with him, amused by his sense of humor. "I haven't entered the clinic yet, but when I do, I'll be there for the duration." She nodded toward the colorful candies. "While I'm here, I'd like to purchase a half pound of those peppermints."

"Why sure. Did you want the red or the green?"

"Green. I had enough red ones during the holidays."

He continued to smile, scooping the candy from its ornamental jar with a tiny shovel. "I know what you mean," he said, weighing them on the scales. "I did the same thing, but regardless of their shade, these little candies are the best thing on earth for fighting off infections." He poured the colorful confections into a small box.

Anna gave him a coin. "I try to keep some on hand at all times."

"Good for you." He nodded, placing her money into his cash register before counting out change. "They really do ward off illness. I suggest you have several each day." He closed the lid on the box and tied it with a green strand of yarn. "I sure hope your quarantine doesn't last too long. What a shame it would be for a patient to die from influenza while in a tuberculosis clinic."

"That *would* be terrible," she said, placing the change back into her purse. "Hopefully we won't lose anyone."

He gave a sober nod and walked out from behind the counter. "Tell Dr. Wellington I'll have those supplies to him around noon." He glanced at the wall clock above the window. "My delivery boy is out on another errand, but he should be back soon." He accompanied her to the door, handing over the box of peppermints. "A pleasure to meet you, my dear, and don't you go getting sick with that influenza, now, you hear?"

She smiled. "I'll do my best."

As she walked out, still smiling, a sudden stiff gust of wind tugged the corners of her cloak. With one free hand, she pulled it tighter against her body, thankful she'd securely pinned her hat on, or it would have blown away. She almost giggled out loud at the thought of it landing on some high mountain peak to be discovered someday by a woodsman or scout.

The footman assisted her into the carriage and placed the bear-skin rug over her lap. Before another blast of air could besiege them, he jumped on the back of the coach and signaled the driver to begin their journey once more. "Walk on!" The driver flicked the reins, and the horses arched their graceful necks at his command, trotting away from the pharmacy.

⌒

Richard was in the medical supply room when the sleek Vanderbilt coach returned to the front entrance. He stepped back from the window in time to prevent her from seeing him. *Get a hold of yourself,* his inner voice reprimanded. *You can't be gawking out the window like a school boy in short pants. You must work with her for several weeks. Maybe when the quarantine is over you will no longer feel this impossible lure.*

He shook his head in effort to clear the troubling thoughts of his attraction to this woman who could never belong to him. A few moments later, she stood at the open door of the supply room, her cheeks flushed. "I'm afraid it took me longer than I expected. The pharmacist and I got involved in a long conversation about peppermint candies. But the medical supplies will be delivered early this afternoon."

Richard chuckled. "David McLean is a nice chap, but he'll talk your head off. I'm actually surprised you made it back so soon." He scanned the shelves once more before signing the inventory sheet.

Her lips curved into a slow smile. "I like him."

Richard grinned, picking up her valise. "He is indeed a personable character. He can chat about his family tree for hours on end, going all the way back to his forefathers in Scotland." He nodded toward the staircase in a gesture for her to precede him. "I'll show you to your quarters."

While climbing the stairs, Richard had sudden doubts about placing her in the plain little room on the third floor. It was used by the rotating doctors for an occasional respite, but now he felt embarrassed by its austerity. "It isn't Biltmore, but it will offer you a place of rest when you need it." He opened the door, positioning her suitcase on the dresser.

"Thank you, Richard." She cast a swift glance in his direction and smiled while hanging her wrap inside the wooden wardrobe. "This is *more* than adequate."

His concern for the room's insufficiency was replaced by a surge of admiration. In her soft blue dress, she reminded him of some extraordinary bird of paradise that had landed in the midst of dry land. "Good," he said with a smile. "I'll leave you to get settled." He glanced at the mantle clock. "Meet me in the parlor in fifteen minutes, and I'll go over a few things with you."

"Certainly," she replied. "Where are the aprons?"

"In the closet across the hall," he called over his shoulder.

While descending the staircase, he heard the nasal voice of Nurse Cartwright giving the Sisters of Mercy nursing students a tour of the facility. He said a quick prayer of thanks for sending this additional help and continued to walk toward the kitchen. Cook had left a fresh pot of coffee warming on the stove, and he filled two cups, adding cream and sugar to both before going into the parlor.

Just as he was about to sit down, Anna entered. The apron completely covered her dress, making her small and delicate form appear much younger. He nodded to the chair nearest the hearth and handed her the cup after she was seated.

Her face brightened. "I smelled the coffee when I walked in the front door." She inhaled an appreciative sniff of the brew before lifting the cup to her mouth.

Richard nodded. "Cook has a fresh pot going at all times." He seated himself in a chair directly across from her. "I want to bring you up to date. As I mentioned earlier, fifteen of our patients have influenza. That leaves twenty patients who are healthy, relatively speaking, and we've moved them into a separate wing." He stopped talking for a moment and ran his thumb along the edge of his cup. "It's doubtful their isolation will do any good after already being exposed, but it certainly can't do them any harm."

She took a long drink of coffee before placing the cup back into its saucer. "Did the health inspector say how widespread the influenza has become?"

He drew a deep breath. "They've placed quarantines on all the hospitals and orphanages throughout the region. Apparently, it is far more pervasive than I realized."

Anna brushed a tendril of hair away from her forehead. "I shall never forget that horrible siege of influenza we had in New York a few years ago." She closed her eyes for a moment, as though envisioning the outbreak. "I was just out of medical school. So many people died ... including some of my own colleagues."

He nodded. "As I recall, it affected mostly those between the ages of twenty and forty."

She drew a sigh that seemed to rise from the depths of her soul. "Most of the children and elderly remained unscathed. I thought it strange at the time, especially since it's usually the young and elderly who are most vulnerable."

There was a long gap of silence between them, broken only by the logs snapping in the hearth. Richard took a sip of coffee and cleared his throat. "Because we are in a state of emergency, I'm promoting you to the position of doctor. Nurse Cartwright will oversee the students from The Sisters of Mercy, and you will assist me."

The color of her eyes turned a deeper shade of blue. "But— Dr. Becker—he made it clear that I am not to practice medicine here." She interlaced her fingers.

He leaned forward. "Dr. Becker had no idea anything like this would happen. According to the policies of this establishment, my responsibility in his absence is to review the larger canvas, doing whatever is appropriate for the safety and health of our patients." He shrugged. "Besides, I can think of no one more capable than you."

Two pink spots appeared on her pearly complexion. "I promise to prove myself equal to the task, doctor."

If he had not already witnessed her skills, he would have laughed at the absurdity of her statement. Little wisps of hair waved around her face, and the tiny white rim of her dress collar peeped out from beneath the apron. She looked more like a princess in disguise than a physician. In no way did she *appear* capable of practicing medicine, but he knew she wouldn't back down in the face of adversity. Even so, he felt a sudden urge to send her back to Biltmore where she would be safe. How could he live with himself if she became ill or died? His heart lurched at the very thought of losing her. But as much as he wanted to protect her, she was not his to shelter or to lose. He would have to keep his heart in check. Besides, she was already exposed to the influenza germ and could not leave the premises.

"I am grateful for your help," he said, draining the last of the coffee and rising from his chair. "Now, if you'll excuse me, I need to catch up on a few things."

"Thank you," she called to him as he walked out the door.

"Don't give it a second thought. You've earned it."

Chapter Seventeen

Anna sat down in the chapel and closed her eyes. Ten days had passed without any new cases of influenza. Everyone at the clinic hoped the forced isolation would soon end.

Richard had requested the entire staff to dine together this evening, promising to make an important announcement, which she suspected had something to do with lifting the quarantine. Their friendship had grown over the last several weeks. A glimpse or smile here and there and their shared fight against influenza seemed to draw them closer than ever.

Whether a patient lived or died, Richard always praised the goodness of God. His steadfast devotion prompted her to begin reading the Bible during her breaks. Just a verse or two of the Psalms helped to calm her worries and renew her strength.

She smiled, remembering Daphne's prayer that she might function in the clinic as a doctor. Anna was still in awe of the quick affirmative answer, and was thankful to have used her training throughout the long quarantine. Even so, she found herself helping the nursing staff in their tasks of rolling bandages and emptying bedpans. These humble acts had helped her to develop a new awareness that no one task was greater than another.

Anna pulled the mail from her apron pocket. Two letters had arrived earlier in the day and she was determined to read them before dinner. Taking a deep breath, she opened the official-looking envelope first, barely breathing while scanning the page. It was a summons from the probate court where she was to appear for the final hearing of her father's estate. Though all bank accounts had been frozen for over a year, Mr. Van Demark wanted things finalized as soon as possible. She was somewhat surprised by this formality. Why should she be forced to attend a hearing that would tell her exactly what she already knew? Hadn't she been through enough? What difference would a hearing make now?

Anna refolded the letter and brushed a tear from her eye, remembering Daphne's prayer that God intervene if there had been anything underhanded on the part of Van Demark. Would a last-minute miracle occur?

Turning her attention to the next piece of mail, she recognized the decorative script of her stepmother. Inside the classic ivory envelope was a long epistle about her time in Europe. She had secured temporary apartments at the New York Waldorf-Astoria Hotel, begging Anna to return home from the *wilds* and help her to secure another house. A generous check had been enclosed for travel expenses, along with the promise of another installment upon her return to the city. She shoved both letters back into her pocket, unable to deal with this news now.

The clock was chiming as she ran upstairs to make a hasty toilet and change into a simple blue gown. How she wished Claudette had taken her advice and searched for a place to live before running off to Europe to escape the scandal of their financial loss. Anna did not want to return to New York. She wanted to keep working alongside Richard and the nurses at the clinic.

While surveying herself in the mirror, she sighed a quick little shivering breath of conviction, knowing it was her obligation to help Claudette. It was what her father would expect.

She consoled herself by deciding she might as well get it all officially done so she could put it behind her. Still, she hated to leave her work at the clinic. Suddenly, she felt weighted down by cares and responsibilities. It could take weeks to get Claudette settled into a new place. With a frown, she realized there was no way of knowing how much time would be required in resolving all that lay before her.

She might as well give notice to Richard as soon as possible. The money she had saved, along with the loan Daphne had insisted upon giving her, would pave the way to Denver as soon as business matters in New York were reconciled.

This was her dream, and she needed to see it through. But a wave of sadness washed over her at the thought of leaving Richard and the clinic behind. Funny, how she once regarded the western frontier to be the land of opportunity and excitement—now it all seemed far away and unimportant, as her life had taken on a new direction. A vision of Richard's strong, handsome face appeared. *You have fallen in love with him,* accused a little voice inside her head.

For once she did not argue, but shook aside the disquieting thought and hurried downstairs.

After everyone was seated for dinner, Richard made the announcement they had all been waiting for. "I have good news," he said. "The health inspector has agreed to lift the quarantine very soon."

There was murmur of excitement among the staff. "When can we return home to our families?" asked one of the student nurses.

"Tomorrow morning, if—" he held up a hand to silence their excited chatter, "*if* there are no new cases of influenza between now and then."

He felt his lips curve into a smile as they applauded once more. "All of you deserve great praise for the excellent care you've given our patients. I can never thank you enough!"

As they began the first course, Richard noticed Anna had a worried look in her eyes. "Would you like to take a stroll after dinner?"

She glanced up from her plate. "I'd like that very much."

Nurse Cartwright gazed at them over the rim of her cup. "Be sure and bundle up," she said. "We can't have our doctors getting sick." She lowered her voice. "Are you going to tell them about Nurse Brown?"

"Indeed," he replied, rising from his chair. "I have one more announcement, everyone." There was a sudden hush. "Miss Brown received a proposal of marriage by mail today from her sweetheart." He glanced down the table at the young woman with bright red braids wrapped into a crown on top of her head. "We all wish you and your fiancée the very best."

The young nurse blushed and bobbed her head while everyone applauded.

Anna smiled and unfolded her napkin. "Will you be finishing your nursing course, Miss Brown?"

The girl's eyes grew misty. "Oh no, ma'am, my fiancée has already put his foot down about that." She sighed. "He'll let me finish up my work here at the clinic, but then I'll be going ta' the house."

Another student nurse giggled and made a face. "He couldn't stop you from finishing your work *here*. We're under quarantine, and they ain't nobody allowed in nor out of this place."

Miss Brown gave her colleague a sidelong glance. "You don't know Billy. If he didn't want me at the clinic, he'd march straight up here to get me—even if he had to bring his daddy's shot gun."

Anna's eyes widened. "He would actually come here with a gun and force you to leave?"

"Oh yes, ma'am." Her voice cracked. "When Billy makes up his mind about something, that's it." She took a long drink of water. "And there ain't no use in arguing with him. He made up his mind to marry me when we were just young'uns and I finally said yes."

Anna picked up a roll from her bread plate. "It's too bad you won't be able to finish your training."

Richard found himself in agreement with Anna. How could Miss Brown's fiancé be such a brute to his future bride, especially when only a few short weeks stood between her and graduation.

"You should talk to him." Nurse Cartwright's voice drummed out in a tone not to be ignored. "Finishing the training would benefit your entire family, and if you have children, you'd certainly know what to do if one of them were to become ill. Your future husband might even benefit—not to mention his parents and yours who will grow old and need special care."

The girl looked down at her plate. "Billy believes a woman's place is in the home, and I guess I'll be a mindin' his wishes from now on. I don't want to end up an old maid, like—" she stopped in midsentence.

"Like me?" Nurse Cartwright snorted. "Well, young lady, I may be an old maid, but I don't have to worry about some man telling me what to do." She reached for her knife and began aggressively cutting the roast beef that was on her plate.

"I know how these mountain men are," she continued. "Once they get a noose around their sweetheart's neck, she can no longer speak without his permission. That's why I never married." She glared across the table at the nursing students, who appeared shocked that Nurse Cartwright might ever have had a beau. "Yes, I was young once." She tore her roll in half. "And I had my share of suitors. But Pa supported my desire to become a nurse so that I wouldn't have to be dependent on anyone." She popped the roll in her mouth, turning her attention back to her plate. A hush fell over the evening, and everyone continued their meal without saying another word.

Richard combed his thoughts for something that might lighten the atmosphere but came up short. At last the cook and waitress brought in dessert trays and Anna broke the silence. "I really think we should commend Cook for providing us with this delicious meal. Everything is just scrumptious, isn't it?"

Everyone applauded, agreeing the food was wonderful, and to his relief, the atmosphere lightened. Soon the nurses dove headlong back into their chatter about the forthcoming weekend without quarantine, and Richard said a silent prayer of thanks while wondering if there was anything that Anna St. James didn't know how to do.

⌒

Anna marveled at the evening skyline that displayed an assortment of pinks and blues, melting into the twilight. The tall pines rustled in the breeze as though to welcome her and Richard while strolling the grounds.

"Anna, I can't thank you enough for coming to my rescue back there." He rubbed the back of his neck. "Your precise timing broke the tension over dinner."

The way he said her name sent a delightful little shiver up her back. "Actually, it's Cook you should thank. She arrived at exactly the right moment with chocolate soufflé."

His lips curved into a grin. "Nevertheless, I am sorry if Nurse Cartwright's feelings were hurt. I don't believe Miss Brown meant for her words to come out quite as she expressed."

"Oh, I don't think Nurse Cartwright's feelings were hurt," Anna remarked, as they stepped around a mound of dirt left by the gardener earlier in the day. "I think she made a good point regarding her warning to Miss Brown and the others."

He gave a sharp laugh. "Nurse Cartwright never fails to make her point. Still, I cannot see how it could hurt for Miss Brown to finish her nursing courses."

"Indeed," she said. "What could it possibly hurt?"

He paused for a moment, as though in self-reflection. "I never realized how much Nurse Cartwright's career meant to her. To think that her father encouraged her to pursue it. Maybe the younger nurses will think twice from now on before allowing a sweetheart to tell them what to do."

"I can't believe you actually feel that way." The words slipped off her tongue before she could take them back.

Richard chuckled. "I have changed my thinking about many things, thanks to you." He gestured toward a picnic table beside some low pruned bushes. "During the summer months, I often eat my lunch over there beside the rose garden. Perhaps you will join me when it is a bit warmer."

Anna's chest tightened with sadness, knowing she would not be there when the roses bloomed. How could she tell him she was returning to New York? They continued to walk, their steps crunching the small scattered stones along the trail until they eventually came to a bench and sat beneath the stars while the full moon rose.

"You're worried about something." His voice was almost a whisper.

"Am I so transparent?"

His gaze held hers. "I can see it in your eyes." He reached out and caught her hand in his, holding it for a moment longer than necessary before letting it go.

Anna willed her nerves to be still, sucking in a deep breath before answering. How she would miss these evening walks with him. They had become a source of solace in the last several tense weeks.

She cleared her throat and looked away. "I received word from New York today about the final hearing on my father's estate."

He appeared shocked. "So, you'll need time off."

She released a sigh. "There's more. My stepmother needs my help in finding a place to live, and it could take weeks to get her situated." She rushed ahead. "I have decided to give you my notice."

Richard searched her face with intensity. "Why would it take so long to get her settled? Can't you help her find a place and hire movers to take care of it? I don't think I can manage that long without you. And from the way you explained things earlier, it doesn't seem as though you owe your stepmother anything." He straightened his shoulders. "Go to the hearing of course, but afterwards you should return to Asheville where people care about you."

Hope rose in her heart like bubbling champagne. Still, she couldn't turn her back on Claudette. She shook her head. "No, I must help her, and I'm afraid it will take much longer than one week."

He sighed from deep within his chest. "Then I will save the post for you. Take whatever time you need."

She paused, tempted to accept his offer. "It wouldn't be fair to ask that of you. No, I shall leave tomorrow afternoon—if that is all right with you, just as soon as the quarantine is lifted."

A troubled expression crossed his face. "What happens after you get things settled in New York? Will you return to Asheville?"

She tried to summon a gleam of a smile. "I might. I'm just not sure at this point."

Rising from the bench, he pulled her up by the hand and tucked it into the crook of his arm. "I hope you will consider returning to Asheville. I've actually been thinking of starting my own clinic and I could use your expertise as a doctor."

She felt her jaw drop. "You would hire me?"

He nodded. "I certainly would. And not as a nurse either."

"That would be wonderful! I mean—we work together so well."

He nodded. "Of course, it would be after Dr. Becker returns from his trip abroad."

"That would give me time to straighten out all my business matters in New York," she said slowly, still trying to reconcile what he had told her.

The moonlight cast a silvery ribbon onto their path as they climbed the steps to the clinic entrance. When reaching the door, he paused to gaze down at her in the flickering shadows.

Was he going to tell her what her heart longed to hear? She almost closed her eyes in anticipation of a kiss. Then he spoke, very softly. "No matter where you decide to go, I ... well ... I just hope you will stay in touch. You are very special, Anna. I count you as my ... very dearest friend."

His dearest friend? Anna swallowed, feeling the color of embarrassment rise to her cheeks. Thankful for the cover of darkness, she turned to open the door. "Of course, I'll stay in touch." She feigned a joyful laugh. "That's what all good friends do."

Too emotional to say anything further, she escaped up the stairs and into her room. But long after going to bed, she dwelled on his words. She *was his dearest friend!*

The following morning buzzed with excitement as the other medical personnel returned to work. Anna busied herself most of the day, updating notes on patient files and making certain she left everything in order.

As the clock chimed two, she put away her work and walked over to the window. Bluish gray clouds scurried around in the sky as if uncertain of their direction, and she found herself empathizing with their tentative path. The Vanderbilt coach was due to arrive in half an hour, and she would be leaving on the noon train to New York tomorrow. As for whether she would return to Asheville, she was not sure. How long could she conceal her feelings for him? Did she want to spend the rest of her life drawing energy from a friendship that could never offer her a lasting relationship?

She was about to turn away from the window, when a sleek black coach drove up to the entrance and stopped. A liveried footman jumped off the back to open the door for a woman dressed in a royal blue velvet coat, plain in cut, but the severity of it was offset by a beautiful mink collar. As she disembarked, a blast of air pulled at her hat, causing several dark curls to escape from beneath its wide brim. A faint blush had been whipped into her cheeks by the wind, reminding her of a porcelain doll.

Richard entered the room, carrying a chart. "I wanted to ask you about Mrs. Bonesteel's medication adjustment," he remarked.

"In just a moment," Anna replied.

As she opened the door, the woman rushed toward Richard, as though her very life had not begun until that precise moment.

"There you are, my darling," she crooned.

There was a surprised look on Richard's face as the woman threw herself into his arms. "Julia, what on earth are you doing here?" He gazed at her, as if seeing a ghost.

"Oh, silly man. I'm back to plan our wedding!"

Anna made a quick exit, leaving the two lovers in an embrace. So, this was Julia, the woman who had left him at the altar. Questions whirled through her mind. Had the two reconciled their differences? She strove to remember the last time Richard had brought up her name, but could not recall any conversation of a recent nature.

She ran up the stairs before anyone could see how upset she was, knowing that at all cost, she must leave this place as soon as possible. Locking the door behind her, she began flinging dresses, camisoles and nightgowns across the bed and shoving them into her suitcase. After putting on her coat and bonnet, she saw the envelope on her desk and picked up the brief goodbye message she had penned to Richard the night before. Slowly, she opened her door, glancing up and down the hallway before making a mad dash to Richard's office, leaving the note on his desk.

Taking the backstairs, she slipped out the kitchen entrance and hurried down the narrow road, hoping to reach the end of the driveway before the Vanderbilt Coach arrived. Just as she made it to the sidewalk, the coach appeared, and she waved at the driver to stop before making the turn. A footman jumped down from the back and opened the carriage door and they were soon on their way back to Biltmore. She sank into the seat, tears pooling in the corners of her eyes before trickling down her cheeks. No wonder Richard hadn't proclaimed his love for her the evening before. He had never stopped loving Julia, and now they were back together! She took a deep breath, knowing she should feel happy for her friend, but all she could do was think of how foolish she had been for allowing herself to fall in love.

⌒

Darkness stole over the clinic as Richard entered his office and picked up an envelope propped against a stack of books on his desk. When breaking the seal, a hint of fragrance escaped the contents and he closed his eyes to inhale the lovely scent.

My dear friend,
I will never forget you and shall keep you always in my prayers.
Thank you for believing in me.

Sincerely,

Anna St. James

Richard studied the correspondence for a moment, hoping to squeeze something more from her words. Why had she left so suddenly, without saying goodbye? Still holding the letter in his hands, he gazed out the window and into the night, recalling their stroll from the evening before. His face grew warm with remembrance of her pleasant laughter, and he could almost feel the pressure of her little hand inside the crook of his arm.

He turned away from the window and dropped into a nearby chair. It had been a day of insanity. Could anything else possibly go awry? If so, he couldn't imagine what it might be.

Chapter Eighteen

The next morning, after packing her belongings for the noon train, Anna went downstairs and found the Vanderbilt family in the breakfast room enjoying a relaxing meal.

Daphne jumped up from the table when she entered, giving her a hug. "I'm so glad you are back. Does this mean the quarantine is finally over?"

Anna nodded while taking her seat. "Indeed, it is." She covered her lap with a napkin. "It lasted much longer than any of us expected."

"We were fortunate not to have been afflicted by the influenza outbreak here at Biltmore," George remarked, taking a sip of coffee.

"You young people always look so fresh in the morning." Mrs. Vanderbilt beamed at her from across the table.

Anna wondered how she could appear fresh. She had barely slept at all, and couldn't seem to get the disturbing picture of Richard and Julia's embrace out of her mind.

"I do wish I slept like a youth." The matriarch reached for her glass of orange juice. "When my children were small, I felt as though I could never get enough rest. Now, I consider myself lucky to sleep just a few hours, and spend most of my evenings reading and catching up on correspondence. It's the only thing I know to do in the middle of the night."

Daphne chuckled. "All of our Christmas guests were night owls, like you, Grammy. Edith Wharton rarely sleeps at night either."

"That's because she's a writer." George buttered a triangle of toast. "Many creative people do their best work in the evening, and I presume she is one of them."

"Oh, she is." Daphne nodded in agreement. "She showed me her little lap desk that she uses to write on while in bed. It was adorable."

Mrs. Vanderbilt raised a brow. "Perhaps I should take up the pen too, or better yet, the paintbrush. When I was a young girl living in Paris, I created some lovely pictures. My teacher said I was quite talented." She shrugged. "Of course, I gave all that up when I married."

"I don't see why you had to give anything up," Daphne said. "That doesn't seem quite fair to me."

Mrs. Vanderbilt smiled. "Oh, I didn't *have* to give it up my dear. It's just that getting married and starting a family left me little time to do anything else. I kept hoping to get back to my painting but moved on to other things."

George turned his attention back to Anna. "So, the influenza epidemic is over at last. I hope you'll be able to rest up for a few days and recover from all that hard work."

Anna dabbed her mouth with the napkin, knowing it was time to announce her departure. "I've been subpoenaed to a hearing in New York concerning Papa's estate. It's been over a year since his death, and I'm hoping to get everything settled."

Daphne's jaw dropped. "How long will that take? I'd hoped we might do some shopping together for my wedding."

Anna picked at her food. "I'm not exactly certain. I also received a letter from Claudette. She has returned from Europe and needs my help securing a place to live. After that, I suppose I shall search for new employment."

"New employment?" Daphne leaned forward. "Don't tell me you're going to Denver."

Anna fiddled with the handle of her fork, not meeting Daphne's eyes. "I'm not sure just now, dear. I'll have to get through these other hurdles first and see how things turn out. But my train departs at noon today and I'll need a ride to the station."

"It sounds as though you have far too many things to do," Mrs. Vanderbilt remarked. "I hope you won't neglect your need for proper rest. You look a bit peaked, and you mustn't forget you have been through a horrible influenza epidemic."

Anna forced a smile to her lips. "No, I'm not apt to forget that anytime soon. It was one of the worst cases I can remember. We were fortunate to get through it without too many losses."

George took a long drink of orange juice and placed his empty glass back on the table. "I might help you shorten that list. I need a full-time doctor here at Biltmore, and I hope you might consider the post."

Anna's coffee cup stopped in mid-air. Last night, before going to sleep she had asked God and the angels to open the right door for her. Was this the answer? She placed the cup back into its saucer. No, she decided. It couldn't possibly be. It was too close to Richard and she didn't want to see him again because he would be with Julia. But George was trying to help her, and she decided to hear him out. "What exactly does the job entail?"

Mrs. Vanderbilt spoke first. "I would be your first patient, dear, for I simply cannot abide the thought of running up to New York every time I need to see my physician." She gave a prolonged sigh. "Besides, I want a doctor who will listen to me instead of patting me on the shoulder and prescribing laudanum."

Daphne had a radiant smile while helping herself to more whipped cream over a bowl of strawberries from the Conservatory. Suddenly, Anna wondered if George was offering her the position as a favor to his niece. Even though she had no plans to accept his offer, she didn't want to feel beholden to this gracious family. They had already done so much for her.

George leaned forward, as though reading her thoughts. "This is something I've been planning for quite some time." He rubbed his chin. "You see, I promised Richard I'd find a replacement for him as soon as possible. Truly, he doesn't have the time to fill in here. I've been thinking we could set up an infirmary downstairs, and of course, I shall offer you a salary equivalent to that of the best male doctors in New York."

Anna turned it over in her mind. If George had offered her the post when she first arrived, she would have taken it without a second thought. Knowing her emotions were in a frightful mix, she decided to stall. "I have no idea how long it will take to get Claudette settled. I'd like some time to think it over, if you don't mind."

George nodded. "By all means, I shall hold the position open until you decide."

Mrs. Vanderbilt smiled. "It would be wonderful having you for my doctor."

"I promise I wouldn't patronize you, or prescribe too much laudanum," Anna said.

The older woman flourished a dismissive hand while rising from the table. "I know you wouldn't. Now, if you will all excuse me, I am going back upstairs to my room." She pulled her blue dressing gown closer. "This area of the house is far too drafty for a woman of my age."

George's straight brows drew into a troubled line. "Why, Mother, you should have said something! I'll arrange for the furnace to be placed on a higher setting."

The lovely matriarch reached over and patted her son's dark, wavy hair. "You've always been such a considerate young man. But there's no need to turn up the heat on my account." She turned to Anna. "Have a safe journey back to New York, my dear, and be sure to give Claudette my best. I would love for her to visit me here at Biltmore. Do you think she would accept an invitation?"

Anna nodded. "I'm certain she would. It would do her good to get away from New York. Especially after all she has been through."

Mrs. Vanderbilt nodded with understanding. "Wonderful. I shall make it a priority."

After Bosworth ushered Mrs. Vanderbilt out of the room, Daphne turned to Anna. "Grammy really needs a doctor like you. It would really set my mind at ease, knowing she was in your care."

George nodded in agreement. "If you decide to accept my offer, I'll arrange a time for you to meet the staff and their families. The house servants live here with us, of course, but a good number of my employees reside around the estate and in Biltmore Village." He paused while buttering another slice of toast. "Richard can show you around and bring you up to date on everything you need to know."

Anna's throat tightened with uncertainty. Was this what God wanted for her life? She needed a decent salary, she loved Biltmore and the people of Asheville. But could she bear seeing Richard and Julia together? She forced a smile. "I promise to let you know just as soon as I conclude my obligations in New York."

Chapter Nineteen

March 12, 1896

Richard seldom ventured downstairs and knew little about the inner workings of his own kitchen. But after prowling around for a few minutes, he found some matches behind the stove and lit a few candles, before taking a few seconds to glance at the calendar that hung above the sink. It had been weeks since Anna left for New York, and he hadn't received so much as a postcard letting him know she had arrived safely. He struck another match against the stove with more force than necessary, to light the oil lamp. The warm glow cast a lacy pattern onto the ceiling from the tablecloth, almost hypnotically taking him back in time.

For over two years, he had hoped and prayed that Julia would return to him. So many times, he had prayed to see her walk back into his life, but when she had, it was far too late. The woman he had thought so beautiful, was little more than a spoiled brat who always had to have her own way, no matter what the cost.

What hurt him the most was his own selfish desire that had drawn him to her in the first place. How could he have pined away for someone who only wanted his title and fortune?

He harrumphed. When her courtship with the Chicago Tycoon ended, she thought they could pick up where they had left off. How shallow he had been to have ever fallen for her. His friendship with Anna had taught him what he wanted in a woman. Someone mature, who could see beneath the surface without a need to glide along on top of it.

Glancing at the calendar again, he narrowed his eyes as though to divine an answer as to why he had not heard from Anna. His thoughts had never strayed far from her since she left Asheville. She had woven herself into the fabric of his life. Would he ever see her again? That question had become a litany for which there seemed to be no answer.

The delicious smells emanating from the stove brought him back to the present. Grabbing a potholder, he opened the oven door and found a beautifully cooked leg of lamb, with carrots and roasted potatoes surrounding it. A whole chicken waited in the warmer, along with two appealing apple pies, their flaky crusts bearing witness to the culinary skill of his cook, who had prepared enough food to last during her absence.

His servants were very efficient, and he had given them a week off in appreciation for their service during the influenza outbreak. Even when the clinic's stores had run low, they had taken the time to deliver home cooked meals and other supplies to keep them going. Now that things had settled down, it was only right for them to have time off to spend with their families.

Richard filled the kettle with fresh water for tea and stoked the dying embers in the stove, adding a few sticks of wood until the flame caught. When the kitchen became smoky from his efforts, he opened the back door and stepped outside for a breath of fresh air. March was like a ferocious lion, but he ignored the chill and walked into the night, inhaling the frigid wind.

There was a light dusting of snow on the ground, but it hadn't stopped the daffodils from blooming. He walked over to the flowers for a closer look at the elegant blossoms, nodding their heads on stalks that remained miraculously upright in the bitter wind. How they managed to flourish in freezing temperatures was beyond his comprehension.

Somehow the flowers reminded him of Anna. Her delicate beauty was the first thing he had noticed after rescuing her from the team of runaway horses. As their friendship developed, he'd grown to know that she, too, was like a blossom bowed by hardship, refusing to break under the harshest conditions.

Had she found her stepmother a place to live? Did the probate court rule against her and on behalf of her late father's business partner? But most of all, did she miss him as much as he missed her?

He gazed up at the full moon and stars. Did God understand the dull pain of loneliness in his heart? "Heavenly Father," his voice was lifted by the wind. "I miss Anna." He paused for a moment. "Please, help me to stop thinking of her. Or show me how we can be together." He knew his prayer was futile. She'd made it clear she would never give up her career for a husband and family, so how could they possibly be together under those conditions? He couldn't find a scripture verse in the entire bible that would support such an arrangement, and he doubted she would ever change her viewpoint.

For a moment, he fixed his eyes on the galaxy, feeling almost able to see the Most High within that faraway band of light. Then he heard a small, still voice within his heart. *The truth will set you free.* Another burst of glacial air whipped through the valley, and Richard shouted above the roaring wind. "Show me your truth. Reveal it to me, and I promise to abide by it."

The starlit sky seemed to bow lower, and for a moment he stood still, breathing in the resinous tang of pine and hemlock that mingled with the wood smoke curling from his chimney.

I will lead you to it, said the still small voice in his heart. Richard exhaled a deep breath, knowing the truth could sometimes be as painful as it was liberating. Even so, he felt a serenity in his heart after returning to his kitchen and sitting down to eat. Dining below stairs was something he'd always enjoyed. When he was a boy, it had been a delight to have a snack with cook, or a sip of tea with the servants, for it had created a deeper understanding of their lives, while enhancing the foolishness of his own class.

Just as he'd taken the last bite of roast lamb, he heard the soft grinding of stones beneath carriage wheels. Thinking it was an emergency courier from the clinic, he vaulted from his seat and hurried up the back stairs.

Throwing open the front door, he was shocked to see George Vanderbilt. "You look as though you've seen a ghost!" Vanderbilt smiled, stomping the snow from his feet.

Richard chuckled, stepping aside for his friend to enter. "That raging wind is too fierce for any ghost worth his salt to survive. Pray tell, what brings you out on this bitter cold night?"

George dusted the snow from his cloak. "I was in the neighborhood. Only a week ago, I thought winter was over. Now, it's all started up again."

Richard took his wraps, stashing them into a nearby closet while George scanned the foyer with a puzzled frown. "What's the matter, old chap? Can't you afford a butler anymore?"

Richard laughed at his friend's wit. "I've given my staff the week off. They usually take a holiday after Christmas, but this year they kept my home fires burning during the long quarantine. Have a seat while I get us some tea." He motioned him into the study.

When he returned a few minutes later, George was looking over the shelves filled with medical and pharmaceutical books.

"Don't you ever read for entertainment?" He raised a brow and placed the volume he had been perusing back on the shelf.

"Some of us must work and study for a living," Richard countered good-naturedly. He placed the tea service on a table near the hearth, while George eased his lanky body into a chair near the fire.

"Actually, I had some business matters to attend downtown and decided to stop by." George wrapped both hands around the cup. "I wanted you to know I offered Anna the post of doctor at Biltmore."

He added quickly, "I'm sorry for not telling you sooner, but I have been in a whirlwind, getting ready to plant the vineyards this year."

Richard sat down opposite his friend, his spirit rising by the news suggesting Anna's return. "Of course, I don't mind. When will she begin?"

George set his tea aside, pulling a pipe from his pocket. "She hasn't accepted my offer yet."

Richard's heart fell with disappointment but tried to hide it by forcing down several gulps of tea.

"If she does accept, I'm counting on you to introduce her to all the patients and show her the ropes." George struck a match against the hearth and held the flame close to the bowl of his pipe, taking several puffs until the room filled with a woodsy bouquet of tobacco.

"Certainly," Richard said, feeling paralyzed by his own emotions. How he wanted to see Anna again. But could he live with the conflict she stirred in his heart? The very thought of her brought a fresh wave of pain while recalling his struggle over her departure. Whether near or far, Anna St. James managed to keep him in turmoil. He leaned back into his seat. "Anna would be a perfect fit for Biltmore. By the way, have you heard from her?"

George blew a perfect ring of smoke into the air and admired it for a moment before answering. Then—"Daphne received a short note, letting her know she arrived safely in New York. But I'm sure she's been too busy getting her stepmother settled to keep up her correspondence."

Richard nodded his agreement. "It was a shock when she left so suddenly. I thought she was committed to staying on at the clinic for the duration, but of course I realize her departure was unexpected."

George was quiet for a moment, as though attempting to discern how much he could say about the subject. "I must admit I was surprised that the two of you didn't spend more time together outside of the quarantine." He took another long puff. "Anna is a remarkable lady. Bright as a button. I remember when she and

Daphne graduated high school. All the young men were vying for her attention, and she hardly noticed." He shook his head. "When Daphne explained to me that Anna had her head set on becoming a doctor, I thought it strange. But I've since grown accustomed to the idea. The work suits her." There was a tinge of admiration in his voice.

Richard nodded. "I know what you mean. At first, I was a bit put off by the fact that she was a physician. But after working with her at the clinic, my viewpoint changed. Now she has my complete admiration and respect."

George leaned back in his chair and smiled.

Richard rose to tend the fire and they were quiet for a few moments with only the sound of crackling flames biting into the logs.

Finally, George broke the silence. "I presumed your admiration for Anna would have led to something more."

Richard sat back down. "I have changed my views. Yet in some ways I feel even more confused."

George raised a brow. "Oh? Why is that?"

Richard shook his head. "Her devotion to our patients during the quarantine was outstanding. It's just that—well, according to the Bible, a man is supposed to be the head of his house. He earns, and the woman oversees the home. How can there be order in a family when the wife is running about with a career?"

George grinned. "Indeed, it seems that many upper-class ladies who were once content to want nothing more in life than marriage now want to use their minds in other pursuits. But perhaps we shouldn't be so hasty in deciding they are wrong to want more. After all, there are several examples of women in the Bible who had successful careers." He waved a hand around the room as though trying to remember a name. "Lydia was one." He gave a triumphant smile. "She supported the Apostle Paul in his ministry."

Richard pressed his fingertips together, remembering that Anna had once pointed to biblical women to make her case too. "Didn't she sell purple cloth?"

George nodded. "It was a premium commodity in those days. There was also Dorcas, who made coats and garments for the widows in her town. She was a seamstress."

"Sounds like you have been doing some Bible study."

"Daphne has us gathering in the library every evening for family worship. Mother and I are really enjoying it." He tapped out the contents of his pipe into an ashtray on the hearth. "Back to your concerns, I don't think there's anything so horrible about a woman having a career. The Bible doesn't condemn women like Dorcas and Lydia."

Richard shrugged. "Likely, they were single women. But a married woman's duty is to focus exclusively on her husband and children."

George raised his brows, and Richard suddenly grew aware of just how peevish he was sounding on the topic.

"You're wrong about that. The thirty-first chapter of Proverbs speaks of the godly *wife* who has a career."

Richard laughed. "Oh, come now, there's nothing in the Bible about a married woman with a career."

George straightened. "Oh, yes, there is. And if I were a betting man, I'd wager my fortune on it. Daphne read it at our Bible study last week. I wouldn't mind hearing it again."

Richard was already in route to the Bible that resided solemnly on the table under the window. "Did you say Proverbs thirty-one?"

George gave a solemn nod. "Starting at around verse ten."

Richard leafed through the pages and cleared his throat. "*Who can find a virtuous woman?*" he read. "*For her price is far above rubies. The heart of her husband doth safely trust in her, so that he shall have no need of spoil. She will do him good and not evil all the days of her life.*"

He glanced up. "So far this virtuous lady sounds like a great woman who is loved by her husband."

George leveled an unwavering gaze at him. "Don't stop there."

Richard continued with some uncertainty. *"She seeketh wool, and flax, and worketh willingly with her hands. She is like the merchants' ships; she bringeth her food from afar. She riseth also while it is yet night, and giveth meat to her household, and a portion to her maidens."* He stopped reading aloud for a moment to skim over the next few verses.

"Go on." George urged as he blew another perfect smoke ring into the air. "You need to hear all of this."

Richard narrowed his eyes to make certain he wasn't imagining the rest of the text, and then resumed reading aloud in a softer voice. *"She considereth a field, and buyeth it: with the fruit of her hands she planteth a vineyard. Her husband is known in the gates, when he sitteth among the elders of the land. She maketh fine linen, and selleth it; and delivereth girdles unto the merchant."* He drew in a deep breath and blew it out slowly. "I don't think I've ever really read this scripture before tonight."

George placed his pipe in an ashtray on the hearth. "When Daphne read it during our Bible study last week, it banished any doubts I might ever have had about married women having a career." Vanderbilt reached for the Bible and scanned over the words. "I heard a portion of this passage at a wedding last summer, but the minister only read those first few verses about the virtuous woman doing her husband good and not evil for the rest of her days."

"I wonder why he didn't read all of it?"

"I'll tell you what I think," George replied, stroking a fingertip across the page as if to outline his thoughts. "I believe he may have been uncomfortable with the entire text, and used those first few verses as a charge to the bride." He gave a little wave of his hand. "You know, sort of an official order from the pulpit that she be a good little subservient wife."

Richard shook his head, trying to banish any unpleasant thoughts toward the unknown minister. "But that would change the meaning of the verse altogether, wouldn't it?"

George nodded. "Well, it certainly throws everything out of context." He glanced back down at the Bible. "Because after those first few verses, the text becomes more specific, saying the godly wife purchases a field with her own money and transforms it into a vineyard. She creates and sells and apparently provides for her family and a staff of servants."

Richard took the Bible back, looking it over once more. "And she does it all while her husband sits among the elders at the gates."

George nodded. "That would mean her husband had a prestigious position in the community. It's not as though he's a lazy fellow who won't support his own family."

Richard shook his head. "Proverbs certainly doesn't seem to support the traditional role assigned to women in our set." He frowned, realizing for the first time how many of his peers treated their wives more like trophies than competent life partners. "Perhaps I have been like the Pharisees Jesus spoke about—the ones who broke the commands of God for the sake of following tradition."

"Most all of us are guilty in that regard," George replied, placing the pipe back into his pocket. "That's why we mustn't expect ministers to interpret the Bible for us. It's really our duty to study it for ourselves and follow our own conscience."

Richard nodded. "I cannot believe how selfish I've been." He placed the Bible back on the table. "All this time I've avoided telling Anna how I feel about her, because I was afraid she wouldn't give up her career to marry me. It was all about me. And I used God to validate my demands."

George smiled with some amusement. "I've known you were in love with her since the night of the Christmas party. But I wondered why you were hesitant."

"The truth has set me free," Richard replied with sudden clarity. "I realized, while working with Anna at the clinic that I was over Julia. But I still tried to protect myself from a future heartbreak, and I used the scriptures to back up my own fear. Anna clung to her career and I saw it as a good reason not to pursue a relationship with her. Now I can only hope and pray that she will have me."

George nodded. "There's one sure way to find out, my friend, and that is by asking her."

"Yes, I intend to do that," he said, with determination.

"When are you leaving for New York?" George rose from his chair.

"Not sure just yet. I need to think about all of this and ask for guidance."

George gave him a slap on the back. "Let me know how it turns out, old boy. I'll even send up a few prayers on your behalf!"

"Please do," said Richard. "I need all the help I can get."

Chapter Twenty

March 15, 1896
Waldorf Astoria Hotel

In the parlor of Claudette's hotel suite, Anna settled into a favorite chair and glanced around the luxurious room with its burgundy and blue furnishings. The colors usually had a calming effect on her, but not today. Her hands trembled as she opened an official document bearing the probate judge's seal that a courier had delivered only a few minutes earlier.

Her eyes skimmed down to the final paragraph.

The estate in its entirety, including land, home, bank accounts, and all holdings of the deceased, William Jefferson St. James, shall hereby and immediately be released to his daughter and rightful heir, Anna Michelle St. James. The deceased's wife shall maintain lifetime ownership of the home with complete access to specific funds in trust. Upon her death, residual monies shall be returned to the estate and distributed to the direct heirs of William Jefferson St. James.

Anna placed the letter in her lap while massaging her forehead. *Thank you, dear Lord!* She closed her eyes and mentally went over everything that had occurred over the last eight hours. The excitement began before ten o'clock that morning when a distinguished gentleman who carried a bulging briefcase was ushered into the parlor by Claudette's maid.

"Mr. Henry Culligan is here to see you, Miss. He says it's about the estate."

Anna wondered who the man was and what he could possibly want. Had he been sent by Mr. Van Demark?

"Are you Dr. Anna St. James?" His eyes roamed the plush hotel room.

"Yes, what do you want?" Her voice sounded cold, even to her own ears, but she wasn't in the mood to be especially nice to anyone that Douglas Van Demark might send her way.

"I'm Henry Culligan with the New York Pinkerton Service." He gave a slight bow and handed her his card.

In confusion, Anna studied it for a moment and Mr. Culligan broke the silence by giving her a kind smile. "George and Daphne Vanderbilt recently retained my services to investigate the background of Douglas Van Demark."

Surprised, Anna fell back into the chair, then apologized for her lack of manners, asking her guest to have a seat.

He gave her a sympathetic nod. "If you can spare a few moments of your time, I should like to go over some paperwork pertaining to my investigation. There are some important things you need to know as quickly as possible." He glanced at the grandfather clock in the corner as though a race with time had officially begun.

She cleared her throat, still feeling flustered. "This is a good time, Mr. Culligan. Would you care for some tea?"

"Yes, thank you," he replied, settling into the leather chair. "A strong cup of tea might be—" He stopped.

"Just what the doctor ordered?"

He chuckled. "I was just about to say that before realizing it might not be appropriate."

Anna waved a dismissive hand while ringing for the maid. "Nonsense," she said. "I appreciate good humor."

The investigator opened his briefcase to begin sorting through file folders, placing them in neat stacks on the coffee table.

After tea was served, Mr. Culligan leaned forward in his chair. "I want you to look over these documents, but first allow me to brief you on what my investigation has uncovered."

Gooseflesh prickled Anna's skin as she forced herself to remain calm.

"The man who foreclosed upon your late father's estate is not the person he claims to be."

She shook her head, trying to grasp the full impact of this information. "Who is he then?"

"His real name is David Silas. Mr. Silas is wanted in the state of Illinois for murdering an heiress by the name of Abigail Butterfield."

Anna blanched. "Murder?" Her father's business partner a murderer? She could hardly grasp the fact.

He interlaced his fingers, giving her a curt nod. "Apparently, Silas swindled millions from Miss Butterfield for a charity he pretended to create for her. After a number of months passed, she wanted to visit the center for orphans bearing her name. Since there was no such establishment, he poisoned her—all this is alleged, of course."

Anna moistened her lips. "And you have proof of these charges?"

He gave a solemn nod. "I do, and there's more. Your father paid back his loan in full to Silas on the day he collapsed. The transaction between them was witnessed and notarized by a postal clerk who saw your father place the official document in his coat pocket before walking across the street to have lunch."

Anna shook her head. "I don't understand. There was nothing on Papa's person except for his wallet."

Culligan nodded. "I'm coming to that. When your father collapsed, Silas stole the notarized document while waiting for the doctor to arrive. A waiter saw him remove something from your father's coat pocket and thought it seemed unusual, but had no reason to report the matter." The detective leaned back in his chair and took a sip of tea. "When I went back to the restaurant and questioned everyone, asking if they'd noticed anything odd that day, the waiter happened to remember Silas had tucked an envelope into his coat. Pity he didn't recall that little detail sooner."

Mr. Culligan picked up two papers from the table. "These are notarized affidavits: One is from the waiter who witnessed Silas's actions, and the other is a sworn statement from the postal clerk who handled the monetary transaction. Earlier today, the police arrested Silas on the murder charges stemming from Chicago, and they discovered the document he had stolen from your father among a stack of papers in a basket beside the fireplace. We were lucky to have confiscated them before they were burned."

For a moment they were quiet.

Anna's heart raced. "Why did he go by the name of Douglas Van Demark?"

Culligan shrugged. "I'm not sure. Perhaps he thought using a Dutch name might place him in better standing with some of New York's more fashionable society."

She nodded, remembering the odious man's claim to be a descendant from Dutch aristocracy. "What happens now?" she questioned, still trying to digest all the information.

He cleared his throat. "This morning I met with the District Attorney. He made an immediate motion to the court for your late father's estate to be released to you. He also issued warrants for the arrest of David Silas. You should be getting a notification by courier from the clerk of court sometime later today, alerting you that all of your late father's assets are now unfrozen."

Anna unclenched her hands from the arms of the chair. "What about Van Demark? Do you think he will attempt to block the court from releasing my father's accounts?"

The detective shook his head. "No, my dear. Mr. Silas has been proven a fraud and is now being expedited by U.S. Marshals to a Chicago prison. He will be held there until trial. I guarantee he will not bother you again!"

For a few minutes the room was still while Anna read over each document, amazed by the Pinkerton's ability to uncover Van De Mark's trail from Chicago to New York. "I cannot thank you enough for all the work you have done on our behalf. My stepmother will be elated."

He smiled, placing the papers back into his satchel. "Believe me, it's been a pleasure putting this man behind bars." Mr. Culligan closed his briefcase with a snap. "I'll have my secretary type up copies and send them to you by courier." He gave her a slight bow, and a softer tone colored his deep voice. "All of this will soon fade away like a bad dream."

After he left, she went over to the picture window and gazed out at the lovely day. Daffodils in full bloom lined the street, and a nurse pushed a pram along the sidewalk. She would immediately send George and Daphne a telegram, thanking them for their help. On second thought, she would return to Biltmore on the midnight train and thank them in person. Her heart gave a painful lurch at the thought of seeing Richard and Julia together, but somehow, she would face it all with God's help. She knew she had to see Richard one more time before going to Denver.

She was wiping away tears of joy when Claudette entered the room. "I have the most wonderful news." Anna gave her stepmother a big hug. "We haven't lost our home after all. Sit down, and I'll tell you all about it."

Chapter Twenty-One

The coach slowed to a stop on the town's square and Richard leaned closer to the window for a better look at a group of young women, wobbling along in a big circle while a news reporter took pictures.

Richard felt the corners of his lips lift into a smile as he heard the girls laughing. Only a few months earlier, the sight of these women publicly pedaling around on one of those contraptions would have caused him great distress. But now, as the breeze stole into the coach and cooled his cheeks, he felt relaxed, even pleased for these young ladies who were having fun and taking their exercise in the fresh air.

His new way of thinking had a great deal to do with the realization that it was the spirit of the law that mattered. He closed his eyes as the squeak of carriage wheels bumped against the brick streets. How he hoped Anna would accept his apology and marriage proposal.

⌣

A deep throated bell from a nearby church steeple began ringing in the distance. Anna closed her eyes for a moment, thanking God once again for all His blessings. A chickadee landed on the window sill, serenading her with its flute-like voice, flying away when a sharp tap on her door interrupted the concert.

"Dr. Wellington is here to see you," Bosworth announced. "He's in the salon."

A lump formed in her throat. "Tell him I'll be down shortly."

The butler nodded. "Very well, doctor."

Anna hurried over to the mirror and smoothed her hair in an effort to calm herself. *He's a friend and colleague, nothing more. And when he announces his forthcoming wedding with Julia, I will smile and extend my congratulations.*

⌒

When Anna entered the room, Richard's heart began to beat like a kettle drum. As she told him all about her trip to New York and how everything turned out, he smiled. "I'm so thankful it went well for you."

"So am I." She glanced down at her hands and silence fell between them.

"Anna," he cleared his throat. "I've come to apologize."

She looked back up at him and frowned. "Whatever on earth for?"

He swallowed the lump in his throat. He wanted to tell her everything at once, but first he needed her pardon. "I've acted like a Pharisee and I can only hope you will forgive my arrogance."

Her gem-like eyes widened. "I'm not sure what you mean." She glanced around the room, as though attempting to find the answer. "You allowed me to work as a physician at the clinic, even after Dr. Becker forbade me to do so." Her voice grew softer. "More importantly, you taught me how to rely on God for everything."

Richard's heart swelled with admiration for this woman. How he loved her open-mindedness and compassion. "I am honored you feel that way," he said. "But I long believed that women—particularly married women—should stay home exclusively, never developing any gifts outside those necessary for being a wife and mother."

He shook his head. "I now understand my ideas were founded in tradition and *not* scripture.

Her eyes widened. "But I'm not married, Richard. I am aware that my career may prevent me from ever becoming a wife and mother, so you have no need to apologize."

Richard realized he was making a mess of things and removed the Bible from his coat pocket. "George shared with me Proverbs thirty-one. The whole chapter is about a virtuous woman. She has both a career and a family. Here, let me read it to you."

"Please do," she whispered.

He read slowly, determined that she hear the entire story of the model wife as presented in the Bible. After finishing, he reached for her hand. "Anna St. James, I have been in love with you from the first moment I saw you. Will you marry me?"

Her eyes widened. "What?"

He leaned forward with urgency. "I promise to cherish you for all my days, and I will never ask you to give up your medical practice *for any reason*," he added quickly.

A weight formed in the pit of his stomach, and the color in her cheeks deepened as she glanced away.

"I have offended you."

She shook her head. "No, you haven't offended me. It's just that—well, what about Julia? The last time I saw you, she was in your arms, planning a wedding, so how is it that you are now asking me to marry you?"

He let out a long sigh. "It's been over between Julia and me for years—I explained that it was too late for us and sent her away. Besides, it is you that I love. From the moment I grasped you away from the jaws of death, I have loved you. Please tell me that you love me just a little."

Her eyes brightened. "I don't think I could ever love you just a *little*." She paused, and his heart fell. If she couldn't love him a little, then they could never be together.

"Then I will not bother you any longer," he said, rising from his seat.

She reached for his hand. "You didn't allow me to finish. I was just about to say I could love you with my whole heart."

Months of tension melted as he took her into his arms. Desire licked through him like a flame as he covered her mouth with his. She quivered as his kiss explored the outer perimeter of her lips, her delicate earlobes, and throat. Some of her hair came loose from its pins, and he buried his face into the silken strands, breathing in her lovely essence.

Her hands timidly touched his face and then caressed the back of his neck.

"Anna, what about your move to Denver? If you still want to relocate, I will happily go with you. We could start our own practice there, and you could vote in the national election, which is only a few months away. We would need to make haste."

"My love for you has replaced Denver. Besides, Asheville has a suffrage movement of its own. Perhaps I can help mountain women secure their right to vote."

He gazed into her eyes. "I am going to love having you for my wife and business partner. You are the perfect combination of beauty and intellect." He pulled her back into his arms. "My sweet Anna! I've wanted to hold you like this for so long."

"I've wanted this too," she murmured. With fingers in his hair, she kissed him with equal demand, until at last, with a heated sigh he pushed her away. "I was afraid you could never love me. I've been such a fool—focusing on things that don't matter. You will marry me, won't you, my love?"

Anna nodded. "Yes, my darling. I would like nothing better than to be your wife."

"Do you think we could find a minister this afternoon?" He stopped short when seeing her look of surprise. "If you prefer a big wedding, I shall be patient. Only promise me you'll be my bride."

239

She tilted her head and laughed. "I don't need a big wedding. But perhaps next week might be better. It would give me time to prepare, and we could send out announcements afterward."

Before he could reply, Bosworth entered the room. "Forgive me for interrupting." His face reddened at the sight of Anna's hair in disarray. "I wondered if you might care for some tea." He focused his eyes only on Richard.

"I think a celebratory toast is more in order." Richard cleared his throat. "Would you ask George and Daphne to join us here in the salon?" He turned to Anna. "We have an important announcement to make, do we not, my love?"

She nodded. "Indeed, we do."

For a second, Bosworth appeared puzzled. Then realization dawned, and he gave them an understanding smile. "Might I suggest another possibility? Why not join the Vanderbilt family for lunch," he glanced at the clock on the mantle, "in precisely one hour? It will give the two of you time to—uh—to discuss things."

"Marvelous idea, Bosworth," Richard replied, turning his attention back to Anna. "Just let us know when lunch is ready, and we'll be there, won't we dear?"

"Of course, darling." She smoothed her hair back into its pins.

Bosworth tiptoed out with a smile on his face while the two lovers snuggled on the sofa, oblivious of the world around them.

Epilogue

December 24, 1896
Biltmore Christmas Party
Anna felt like a princess as she and Richard waltzed across the Biltmore ballroom.

"It seems like only yesterday we were here for the last Christmas party." Richard pulled her close as they navigated around the other dancers.

"It *was* a year ago." She snuggled against his broad chest. "I'll never forget it. Everything was so beautiful that night."

"It's even more beautiful now that we're married," he whispered.

She paused, feeling faint. "Richard, could we stop dancing for a moment? I need something to drink. I'm feeling a bit dizzy."

He came to an immediate halt. "You do look a bit pale. Is it that stomach flu you've been fighting? I daresay you should be over it by now."

"It isn't flu, darling."

Concern filled his eyes as he leaned in closer, his eyes never leaving hers. "What's wrong, my love? You must tell me right away so that we can fight this thing together!"

She laughed. "I have been sick every *morning* for the last three weeks. You are a doctor. Shouldn't that tell you something?"

He paused for a moment as though to absorb the full impact of what she implied.

"You mean ... you're ... oh! Are you?"

She nodded. "I'm expecting."

His face grew pale while scanning the room. "You must sit down and put up your feet—and you shouldn't be dancing—not in your condition."

She couldn't keep herself from breaking out into laughter. "Richard, I'm fine. I'm just thirsty and need something to drink."

He led her to the punch bowl. "When are you due? He whispered.

"Next summer—in early June."

Richard's eyes brightened. "We shall immediately begin our search for a nanny. I intend to make good on my promise that you continue your career and use all of the gifts God has given to you."

Anna agreed that a nanny was important, but she added, "I'd like to have an office in our home. I don't want to miss any precious moments with our baby. What do you think? A nanny would be present at all times, but I'd still be there to nurse and hold our child between patients."

He kissed her on the tip of the nose. "That's a fine idea. You know that I will support whatever you wish. I'll arrange my own schedule to be there for both of you. After all, babies need their father as well as their mother!"

Anna could hardly believe her good fortune. She was so thankful for Richard's willingness to accommodate her desire for continuing her medical practice. It was nothing short of a miracle, and she was amazed by how God had worked things out for them.

"Did I hear you say something about a nanny?" Claudette interrupted their conversation. "I was just telling Mrs. Vanderbilt how much I would love having grandchildren before I'm too old to enjoy them." She lowered her voice to a whisper. "Are you expecting?"

Anna nodded. "Next June."

"Oh, how wonderful. At last, I shall be a grandmother." Her voice caught the attention of Mrs. Vanderbilt who joined them, followed by George, Daphne, and Edward.

"Am I about to lose my doctor?" George had a crooked grin on his face.

"Not if you don't mind her practicing from our home," Richard replied.

George shook his head. "No, not at all. Your home isn't so far from here, but wait a second. I can have a special cottage with an office, built on my estate if you like." He grinned and slapped Richard on the back. "I'll talk to my architect about drawing something up. We can get started on it after the holidays and have you moved in by spring. What do you say?"

Richard smiled. "Perhaps we can talk about it tomorrow after Anna and I have had a chance to think it over. We always discuss things before making major decisions."

"Of course." George motioned for the band leader to stop the music and everyone gathered closer. "I'd like to propose a toast to my two best friends who—" he paused and cleared his throat, "who will be welcoming their own little stranger into the world, next June. To Richard and Anna!" He raised his glass. The crowd applauded, and congratulations were exchanged while the band struck up another cheerful Christmas tune.

Daphne gave Anna a hug. "I'm so happy for you."

"Thank you, dear." Anna replied. "I can think of none better than you and Edward to be our baby's godparents."

Daphne gasped with delight. "We'd be honored, wouldn't we, Edward?"

Edward smiled, drawing Daphne closer. "We most certainly would!"

Richard tugged Anna away from Daphne and the merry makers. "How about some fresh air, Mrs. Wellington?"

Slipping out of the ballroom, they walked onto the balcony where he pulled her into his arms and traced a finger along her cheek, causing a little thrill of pleasure to race down her spine. "Thank you for making my dream of becoming a husband and father come true," he said, holding her face between his hands.

She sighed. "And thank you for making my dream of being a wife, mother, *and* doctor become a reality."

He replied with a long kiss, causing a flood of warmth to fill her chest, making jelly of her knees.

"How I wanted to do that on this same balcony last year, but if you recall, we were interrupted by Mrs. Wharton. Listening to Mrs. Vanderbilt read *The Night before Christmas* totally spoiled our romantic moment." His voice dropped to an intimate whisper. "And when she read the part about sugar plums dancing through the children's heads, I wanted to kiss you right there in the nursery. I was certain your lips would taste far better than any old sugar plum, and I was right."

"You are such a darling!" She snuggled closer into his arms.

"There you are." Claudette stepped out on the balcony. "Mrs. Vanderbilt is ready to read to the grandchildren and thought you might want to join us."

"Not this year." Anna feigned a yawn. "I'm tired from all the excitement and we plan to retire early this evening."

Richard nodded his support. "Yes, I'm afraid I've already told George we would be leaving before midnight. Anna needs her rest and we've had a busy week."

Claudette raised a brow. "In Anna's condition, no one will give it a second thought. But we *will* see you tomorrow for Christmas dinner, won't we?"

"You shall." Richard placed a reassuring arm around his mother-in-law's shoulder.

Claudette smiled. "Oh, I'm so happy for you! I do hope we sail to London after the baby is born. I'd love to spend time with your family, and I'm quite certain Mrs. Astor will want to host a party for your parents when they come to America."

Richard nodded. "I'm certain mother and father will cross the pond for a visit after our baby is born. And of course, we shall all sail abroad just as soon as Anna and the baby are able to travel.

Claudette seemed pleased by his answer and bade the two of them good night.

As some of the other guests headed to the nursery, Anna took Richard's arm, and they hurried away from the glitter and laughter, out into the crisp night air with a full moon illuminating their path to the carriage. "Ever since the Pinkerton helped settle that business with the estate, it has been so much easier to make my stepmother happy. Honestly, Richard, she's like a new person!"

"Perhaps having a grandchild on the way has brought out her maternal instincts." He placed a protective arm around her shoulder while the footman closed the door behind them.

"Was it rude of us to leave early?"

His deep, baritone laugh caused her heart to dip.

"No, my love. Of course not." He dropped a string of kisses across her brow. "Next year, and for many holidays to come, we'll be reading stories to our own beloved child. But this Christmas Eve I want you all to myself."

She gazed up into the warm brown eyes and cuddled closer into her husband's arms while the hastening hooves of horses carried them home.

END

Author's Note

Lady Doctor at Biltmore House is a work of fiction grounded on facts concerning late nineteenth century women doctors and Asheville, North Carolina.

My main character, Dr. Anna St. James, lived in a time during which female doctors endured oppressive discrimination. One might think after Elizabeth Blackwell graduated Geneva Medical College in 1849 that the doors would have opened wide for more women to follow. Unfortunately, this was not the case. At Blackwell's graduation, Charles Lee, Dean of the college, publicly declared his admiration for the first female doctor who graduated at the top of her class, then added that he would oppose the future admittance of women, due to the inconveniences of allowing them to attend all the lectures. His statement stemmed from the explosive issue of women students collaborating with men at the anatomy table. Charles Lee's statement, along with the theories of Harvard Professor, Edward H. Clark who proclaimed that women seeking advanced education would develop monstrous brains, puny bodies, and abnormally weak digestion, closed the doors even tighter to women in their effort to enter a coeducational medical school. (Harvard Medical School did not admit women until 1940.)

Thankfully, Dr. Blackwell and her colleagues opened female medical colleges, thus allowing women to attain an MD. Prior to her stint in medical school, Dr. Blackwell taught music at an Asheville girls academy owned by Reverend John Dickson, who was a physician before he became a clergyman. Dickson approved of Blackwell's career aspirations and allowed her to use the medical books in his library for study.

Historic discrimination against women plays a central part in my fiction. It is true that during Anna's lifetime it was an absolute for the few career-minded middle-class women, to forego marriage. And it was considered shameful for a husband if his wife continued to work after matrimony. Churches supported this middle-class stereotype, believing the woman made the home a sanctuary for her husband and children—a haven from the world of commerce, politics, and competition. Immigrants and women of the lower classes were more accepted in the labor force, as were servants in middle-class homes and in factories.

Anna's dream of relocating to Denver, Colorado, was a typical aspiration for women doctors in the late 1800's. Doctors of both genders were welcome on the western frontier. In 1893, Colorado gave women full voting rights, (following Wyoming). While the Old West is usually thought of as a wild land that was 'no place for a woman', westerners proved far more willing than other Americans to promote women's rights and welcome them as full and equal citizens.

In the late 1800's, Asheville was nicknamed 'Paris of the South' and was the first city in the country (alongside Richmond, Virginia) to establish an electric streetcar system, a full four years before San Francisco ran electric streetcars on its famous lines. At that time, Asheville also quickly emerged as one of the premier locations for tuberculosis sanitariums. While the TB Sanitarium in my story is fictitious, it certainly could have existed, alongside many others scattered across the region. What many do not know is that Vanderbilt was visiting Asheville with his mother when he decided to settle in the mountains. His mother was often ill with chronic malaria, and George himself had a 'weak chest' and faced the fear of tuberculosis throughout his entire life. He decided that Asheville would be the perfect climate for his mother and himself. He began building his home in 1893, and on Christmas Eve of 1895, George Washington Vanderbilt opened Biltmore House with a grand party for his family and friends.

As a child growing up in Asheville, I remember hearing my grandparents tell stories they heard from their parents about the luxe festivities of that first party. He was also a very generous employer, paying his staff New York wages—which was unheard of in the mountains at that time.

George Vanderbilt openly expressed his faith, and built a church in his community, (Now the Cathedral of All Souls). George's niece, Consuelo was forced into a loveless marriage to the 7th Duke of Marlboro by her mother, Alva. It was all the rage in those days for wealthy Americans to buy their daughters a title, but George never approved and did not attend the wedding.

Daphne Vanderbilt is a made-up character, and Bosworth, the butler is also fictitious, along with the names of the servants. While American households generally employed a head housekeeper instead of a butler, the Vanderbilts had both.

Finally, as for the many local mountaineers in Asheville who spoke in the Elizabethan dialect and descended from Scottish royalty—I am one of them. My own ancestors were part of the Jacobite uprising, and I still have my "native Elizabethan tongue" but do not use it other than for the purpose of writing!

About the Author

Patricia Riddle-Gaddis is a native of Asheville, North Carolina. She grew up near the Biltmore Estate, hearing delightful stories from her grandparents about the Vanderbilt family. She is a published author, essayist, and poet, with a variety of writing and editing experience. She is the fiction editor for *Woman's World Magazine* (America's Bestselling Woman's Weekly). Visit her online at www.carriage-n-castle.com.

If you enjoyed Lady Doctor at the Biltmore, try these other Hartline titles

Donna Smith's *Meghan's Choice*: Meghan Gallagher complies with her father's demand that she work on her own for a year by choosing to tutor eight children in a wild Kansas railroad town. But she had no idea just how wild it was until she was hit by a stray bullet and rescued by a local dance hall girl. In short order, she meets a dark, handsome cowboy and a wholesome, attractive doctor who both vie for her heart. As things heat up around town, Meghan's love life catches fire as well. Is she scandalous to allow both men to court her at the same time? And—how close a relationship with God does Meghan want? Will she draw near?

Kacy Barnett-Gramckow's *The Blessing*: May Somerville has suffered a year worthy of the Bible's Job, and the man who unknowingly prompted all her troubles has fallen in love with her. Isolated in Colorado's rugged mountains, her beloved family shattered by tragedy and loss, May Somerville questions her Creator amid her struggles to survive. Beset by unexpected storms, both physical and spiritual, May seeks blessings—reasons for hope as she works to restore her family. Separated from May by unforeseen circumstances and the expectations of others, Alex Whittier is determined to reverse injustices suffered by the Somervilles. But is it too late to redeem himself for the sake of the courageous young woman he's been unable to forget?

Lena Nelson Dooley's *A Heart's Gift*: Because of an earlier betrayal, Franklin vows never to open his heart to another woman. But he desires an heir. When Lorinda is finally out from under the control of men who made all the decisions in her life, she promises herself she will never allow a man to control her again. But how can she provide for her infant son? Marriage seems like the perfect arrangement until two people from Franklin's past endanger Lorinda. How can he save her? And how will this affect the way they feel about each other?

Kay Moser's *Christine's Promise*: Christine Boyd is the envy of all the ladies in Riverford, Texas, in 1885. She is, after all, the daughter of a revered Confederate general and the wife of a wealthy banker, Richard Boyd. Beautiful, accomplished, elegant—she exhibits the exquisite manners she was taught in antebellum Charleston. She is the perfect southern lady. Or is she? The truth is that Christine's genteel outward demeanor hides a revolutionary spirit. When she was ten years old and fleeing Union-invaded Charleston, she made a radical promise to God. She plans to keep that promise. Tradition-bound Riverford, Texas, may never be the same.

Marlene Banks's *Son of a Preacherman*: A historical romance novel set in the 1920s in Tulsa, Oklahoma, *Son of a Preacherman* depicts the highly segregated life of African Americans in the Greenwood District, in Northern Tulsa and the tensions leading up to the Tulsa

Race Riots. Billy Ray Matthias is the handsome younger son of the church's new pastor. Benny is the daughter of an oil rich family. Billy Ray is convinced that Benny is the woman God would have him settle down with. Benny, on the other hand, recently had her heart broken. She is not the least bit interested in getting involved anytime soon. As Billy's pursuit of Benny intensifies, so does the political and social climate in the prosperous African American neighborhood known as the Greenwood District. Racial tensions in Tulsa escalate when Dick Rowland, a black man, is accused by a local newspaper of raping Sarah Page, a white woman, on an elevator. Benny's brother Ethan and a radical white attorney by the name of Maynard Vaughn despite continuous threats put their weight and energy behind helping Dick. Meanwhile, the White Glove Society, a racist group seeks to destroy not only Dick but all the African Americans in this successful black owned community. As tensions come to a head and violence breaks out, Billy and Benny are caught up in the heat of chaos. He vows to keep her safe, but will Benny let him? And will faith in God be enough to sustain the people of the community as their lives are being changed forever by deadly acts of hatred?

CPSIA information can be obtained
at www.ICGtesting.com
Printed in the USA
LVHW041700191218
601074LV00002B/326/P

9 781722 948887